# A CHRISTMAS BABY AT GOODWILL HOUSE

FENELLA J. MILLER

Boldwood

First published in Great Britain in 2023 by Boldwood Books Ltd.



Cover Design by Colin Thomas

Cover Photography: Colin Thomas and Unsplash



A CIP catalogue record for this book is available from the British Library.

Paperback ISBN 978-1-80162-885-3

Large Print ISBN 978-1-80162-884-6

Hardback ISBN 978-1-80162-883-9

Ebook ISBN 978-1-80162-886-0

Kindle ISBN 978-1-80162-887-7

Audio CD ISBN 978-1-80162-878-5

MP3 CD ISBN 978-1-80162-879-2

Digital audio download ISBN 978-1-80162-881-5

Boldwood Books Ltd
23 Bowerdean Street
London SW6 3TN
www.boldwoodbooks.com

*For Emma Bevan and Sean Douchay.*

# 1

## JULY 1941

Joanna, Lady Harcourt, was in London and this time she wasn't alone. Jean, her dearest friend and housekeeper at Goodwill House, was with her, as was her mother-in-law, Lady Elizabeth Harcourt, and her adopted daughter and son, Liza and Joe. They would be meeting her older daughter Sarah and her new husband Angus at Hornchurch. There had already been two weddings at Goodwill House this year and she wished there could have been a third – her own.

'Look at the roof! It's smashed to bits,' Liza said, pointing up. 'That must have been when the bomb dropped on here in May.'

They all stopped and gazed up at the roof of St Pancras Station. 'They won't be able to repair it until after the war. Glass is almost impossible to locate,' Joanna said. 'I'm still trying to get the drawing room windows at Goodwill House reglazed after the explosion last year when the crashed bomber blew them in.'

Jean was holding Elizabeth's arm just in case she tripped, but her mother-in-law seemed remarkably sprightly for someone of seventy-nine years of age. There'd only been one further bout of confusion since the two episodes last year and the local doctor was confident these had been caused by something else and weren't the beginnings of senile dementia.

'I think it's remarkable that they got the station repaired and open again within a week,' Jean said as they moved towards the exit.

Joe had wandered ahead carrying three overnight bags – Elizabeth's, Joanna's and his own. His sister was carrying her own small suitcase as well as Jean's. The station was noisy with trains letting off steam, porters and guards shouting and the general hubbub of the passengers alighting, arriving and departing.

'Thank goodness, my dear, that it isn't too hot today,' Elizabeth said as they trooped out of St Pancras Station and headed for the taxi stand. They had to get a taxi across town to Liverpool Street Station, then had to travel to Romford where Angus had arranged for them to be collected and taken to the base.

'It was over ninety degrees two weeks ago, Grandma,' Joe said cheerfully.

'It's not quite as warm today,' Joanna said, 'as it would be most unpleasant in Town if it was.'

She glanced across at the press of passengers emerging into the warm morning sunshine. Since the bombing had lessened, no longer a daily occurrence, London was a safer place to visit.

'Over there, everyone, isn't that Sarah waving at us?'

Her daughter looked well; married life was suiting her. Joanna smiled and waved and her daughter responded. It had been too long since she'd seen her beloved daughter and her heart was full.

'Mummy, look what Angus has managed to organise for you all,' Sarah called out from beside two smart RAF staff cars that were parked in the street outside the station.

Joanna ran forward and embraced her daughter. 'Good heavens, are we to be taken all the way?'

'You are, much better than having to catch another train. How are you feeling, Mummy? You look very well.'

'I am, but I must admit that I'm a bit nervous.'

'Not nearly as nervous as John, I expect.'

'I was married before and it wasn't a happy experience. We hardly know each other and wouldn't be marrying if it wasn't for the baby.'

It was a long drive to Hornchurch and the constant swerving, stopping and starting to avoid the potholes and bomb damage was making Joanna nauseous. This was no doubt caused by her unexpected pregnancy – although she'd not suffered from any form of morning sickness when she'd been carrying Sarah. No doubt being so much older this time was the reason. She was delighted to be having this unforseen baby but having one in the middle of a war, when the baby's father could well be killed at any moment, wasn't ideal.

Of course, it could just be nerves and excitement at the prospect of marrying the love of her life, Warrant Officer John Sergeant. He was now an experienced and highly valued fighter pilot and based at Hornchurch – the same base as her son-in-law.

Angus was no longer flying but had some administrative, very senior, role about which she knew very little. The only thing that mattered to the family was that his life was no longer in danger every time he took to the sky. She tried not to think about her beloved John risking his life on a daily basis.

It had been a revelation when she'd had her affair with John last year – she'd never experienced emotional or physical love before. After having Sarah, she had been told she was infertile, and so from that point on, her husband David had not come into her bedroom again. She'd always wondered if he'd had a mistress somewhere but if he had, he was very discreet. It had just been an enormous relief not to have to endure his attentions, which had been far from pleasant.

And now, because of the surprise, but very welcome, baby due in December, Joanna and John had no option but to marry and to do it quietly. Hence the family trip to London.

'You look a bit pale, my dear. If you're going to vomit, do please put your head out of the window,' Elizabeth said.

'I'm fine, thank you, but will be glad to get out of this car.'

She closed her eyes and her stomach settled when she wasn't watching the road flash past the window. Dr Willoughby was overseeing her pregnancy and had assured her that despite her age, thirty-seven, the pregnancy was progressing well and he saw no problems ahead for when the baby would be born at the end of December.

Joanna smiled wryly to herself. So far she'd been able to disguise her small bulge beneath her clothes but when the baby quickened, anytime soon, she would get bigger faster. God knows what the WI and WVS would say when she announced she was now Mrs Joanna Sergeant, no longer Lady Harcourt.

The Manse, the house they would all be moving to in January next year, would make things a bit easier, but she expected to be asked to step down as chairperson of the WVS and probably to leave both organisations.

Losing her title hadn't been a consideration when she'd sent John away last year – in fact, she'd not even considered it as at that time she'd no intention of remarrying, not because it would mean losing her title, but because it would mean losing some of her independence.

If it wasn't for the unexpected pregnancy, they wouldn't be getting married so soon. John wasn't concerned that the marriage would end in disaster. He was convinced that the depth of their love would be enough to overcome any problems. But Joanna was ten years older than him and inevitably, she'd believed, he would look to a younger woman at some point and she hadn't wanted to tie him down.

Having a baby out of wedlock was untenable and that was something they'd both agreed on. The padre at the RAF base where John was currently based would marry them later this morning.

There would be no honeymoon – John's squadron was at readiness; she just had to pray the bell didn't ring before they'd exchanged their vows. Angus had arranged for John to have an hour to complete the ceremony, then he'd have to race back on his motorbike and join the others on his squadron.

Surreptitiously Joanna brushed away an unwanted tear before her eagle-eyed mother-in-law could see it. John was her life; if anything happened to him, she doubted that she'd ever recover. However, being his wife had never been something she'd considered. Being anybody's wife again was something she'd not contemplated if she was being honest.

She put her hands protectively over her stomach. She'd always wanted a big family and this baby was a blessing. Indeed, her entire family, her children and Elizabeth, were delighted – so why was it that she was the only one with regrets? Being the lady of the manor, chair of the WVS, was an important part of her life but this wasn't why she was less than ecstatic about being a wife and mother again.

In fact, she didn't know why she was having lingering doubts. John was thrilled at the thought of being a father and had insisted over and over again that it was his dearest wish that they married, that the age difference had never been a barrier as far as he was concerned.

She must have dozed off as the car slowed almost to a halt and she opened her eyes.

'You look a little better now, Mummy,' Sarah said from the front seat. 'We've arrived and are in a queue waiting to be checked by the guards.'

'I hope that won't take long because I'm desperate for the loo.'

'Please don't mention such things, Joanna, it's not seemly to discuss one's bodily functions.'

The driver, a pretty blonde-haired WAAF, glanced over her shoulder. 'There's a ladies' room in the main building where I'm taking you right now. You'll be there in a tick, my lady.'

The driver pulled up smoothly next to the main building and Angus was waiting outside to greet them. The guard at the gate must have rung through the information that they were on their way.

Sarah was out of the car in seconds and ran to his side. She didn't throw herself into his arms, that would be unacceptable when he was on duty, but the smiles they exchanged showed just how much they loved each other. Joanna knew that her daughter didn't want to start a family until she finished her training and had qualified as a doctor. She'd just started her third year so had at least two more years to do before she even thought about having a baby.

'Welcome, Joanna, everything's ready,' Angus said. 'The padre is waiting in my office. Not very glamorous but needs must. The main difficulty is that John's not here...'

Joanna laughed nervously. 'I think it might be better if you'd started with that fact. John's an essential part of the wedding.' She regained her composure and managed a genuine smile. 'Unless you intend to be his stand-in as happened in mediaeval times when the groom was elsewhere doing something violent on a horse.'

Angus grinned. 'I'd be happy to act as proxy, but it won't be necessary.

He's on his way and will be here in ten minutes. I'm afraid he'll have to vanish immediately after the service. I promise you that he'll get some leave as soon as things are less hectic here.'

'I do understand. His duty must come first.'

A friendly WAAF directed her to the appropriate place not a moment too soon. It occurred to her, as she checked her appearance in the mirror above the wash basin, that it was quite possible this baby would be an uncle or aunt to a niece or nephew only a year or two younger than them.

Thank goodness Sarah wasn't already pregnant as that would have been really odd for all of them. No doubt there were dozens of families with nieces and nephews older than their uncles or aunts, but Joanna felt relieved it wasn't going to happen to them.

She emerged from the ladies' room to be lifted from her feet by her future husband. 'Darling Joanna, I'm so sorry our wedding has to be such a shambles. I've only got twenty minutes.'

John kissed her fiercely. He tasted of oil, but she was used to that. 'It doesn't matter, my love, as long as we're married. We've got the rest of our lives to celebrate.'

They remained in the embrace for a few moments longer then separated. He kept his arm firmly around her waist and she pressed against him, knowing that as soon as the vows were exchanged, he'd be gone and she might never see him again. She pushed this unhappy thought away and tried to be happy he was here to marry her today.

Angus was waiting at an open door further down the passageway. They hurried to join him. The padre kept the service brief. John slipped a plain gold band over her knuckle and it was done. From now on, she was Mrs Joanna Sergeant and there would be only one Lady Harcourt residing at Goodwill House.

Angus and Elizabeth signed the certificate as witnesses, and it was handed to her. She barely had time to exchange a kiss with her new husband before he had to go.

'I love you, my darling wife, and I'll come and see you as soon as I get any leave.'

'Don't worry about that, just fly safe.'

Then he was gone and she was left alone, blinking back tears, surrounded by her family.

'I've arranged for some sandwiches and tea and coffee to be served in my office. I'm sure you don't want to stay here any longer than necessary but after the drive Lady Harcourt needs an hour to recuperate,' Angus said.

Joanna swallowed the lump in her throat and nodded. 'Thank you, you've thought of everything. John looks so tired – how many more sorties is he obliged to do before he gets any respite?'

'He's already flown more than he should without a break, but he's one of the best fighter pilots on the squadron, he's a flight leader, and he just can't be spared at the moment.'

'I daren't ask how many of your brave young men have been lost this year. I just pray that my new husband lives to see his son or daughter in December.'

Sarah threw her arms around Joanna. 'You mustn't think like that, Mummy, it's not good for you or the baby. Remember that Angus told you that it's the new pilots who suffer the most fatalities. John knows how to take care of himself.'

'I hope that you're right, my dear, as losing him would be quite unbearable.'

Somehow, Joanna endured the interminable, well-meaning chitchat without breaking down. Dr Willoughby had told her being tearful was a natural part of being pregnant. She loved all of them but wanted to be on her own, which just wasn't possible right now.

She flinched every time she heard a squadron taking off or landing. Eventually the others were ready to depart and the cars were waiting for them. This time, Sarah didn't accompany them as she was remaining at Hornchurch to spend an extra precious hour with Angus. He would be on duty soon and then wouldn't be able to spare any more time for his lovely young wife.

Joanna had promised the twins they could go to the cinema and had no intention of disappointing them. Therefore, the cars took them to the Savoy, where rooms had been reserved.

* * *

Jean and the twins headed off down the Strand towards Trafalgar Square as there were more than a dozen cinemas in that neighbourhood. There were six in Coventry Street, four in Regent Street and another two or three near Leicester Square. They had no idea what they wanted to see and had told her they would look at all the cinema programmes before deciding.

They were going to a matinee so would be back in time for dinner. Jean had kindly settled Elizabeth in the smaller bedroom of the suite that Joanna had reserved. Jean and the twins were sharing another suite on the same floor.

The last time Joanna had been at the Savoy was with Peter Harcourt on that ill-fated weekend when he'd invited her to become his mistress. Naturally, she'd cut off the connection immediately after his appalling error of judgement.

Carefully she removed her wedding dress, not a white silk or satin floor-length gown as she'd worn the first time, but a simple blue cotton frock with a small floral pattern, scooped neck and elbow-length sleeves. She had a more formal ensemble to dine in tonight as it wouldn't do to appear in the evening in anything less.

She unpinned her matching hat and carefully placed it on the dressing table. Weddings should be celebratory, the bride and groom staring joyously into the camera for the wedding photographs, but no one had even taken one snap of her and John. She had nothing to remind her of this day except the gold band on her finger.

Was she being maudlin? Making herself miserable for nothing? No one else seemed to think there was anything wrong with such a hurried and unusual ceremony. She smiled sadly as she stretched out on top of the bed. It was far too warm to get under the covers.

If she wasn't carrying John's child, then they wouldn't be married at all. Indeed, they should have been married weeks ago when her monthly courses had first stopped.

* * *

It hadn't occurred to her that she was pregnant as the doctors who had attended to her when she'd had Sarah in a smart London clinic had assured her that there would be no further children.

Only after her third course had failed to arrive did the truth finally dawn. Dr Willoughby had confirmed the pregnancy and the plans had been made for this hurried wedding. Elizabeth had laughed when she'd been told. Joanna recalled the conversation exactly.

'David will be turning in his grave, my dear. I am delighted that you are going to have another child and that now you have to marry your delightful young pilot.'

'I thought you would be shocked. The ladies of the village certainly will be.'

'There's no need for them to know your marriage was rather later than it should have been. Marry in London and then when your pregnancy begins to show you can let them assume you've been married for months.'

'I haven't been wearing a ring.'

'Fiddlesticks to that! If anyone has the temerity to ask, you can say it was a secret wedding.'

'If that was the case then I've been falsely living as Lady Harcourt and that would be even worse than knowing this baby was conceived out of wedlock.'

When she next went into the village, if she had the courage, her ring would be seen and soon after that her bulge would be also. Did she care that she would lose her good name, bring scandal to Goodwill House? Would she have resumed her affair with John if she'd thought for one moment a baby would be the result?

Her lips curved. Nothing could have kept her away from the man she loved and having his child was a miracle, one they were both delighted with. Things would be very different if she wasn't impossibly rich, if she didn't own most of Stodham, but she did. This baby would be loved by all the family, would have devoted parents, and by the time he or she was old enough to hear any unpleasant gossip, it wouldn't matter.

She pushed aside any doubts about how her husband would fit into his role as the much younger husband of a wealthy wife. It wasn't important that she was alone on her wedding night as she'd already experienced everything a honeymoon should be without the benefit of clergy. She fell asleep dreaming of the day when they could be together, when her beloved John was no longer risking his life a dozen times a day in his dangerous fighter plane.

# 2

Joanna fell asleep and dreamed she was searching for John, but every time she was close enough to call to him, he vanished and she had to begin looking again.

'Joanna, I think you are having a nightmare – or to be more accurate an afternoon mare,' Elizabeth said from beside the bed.

'Sorry, did I wake you up? Thank you for coming in as I wasn't enjoying my dream.' She sat up and was about to swing her feet to the expensive Persian rug when a wave of dizziness stopped her. She sat for a few moments with her eyes closed, waiting for her head to clear.

'Shall I fetch you a glass of water, my dear?'

'No, this has happened a few times. I must remember not to sit up too quickly.'

After a few moments, she was ready to stand. Her mother-in-law was watching anxiously. 'Too much excitement isn't good for an expectant mother. Perhaps you shouldn't get up at all but have room service bring you your supper on a tray.'

'Absolutely not. I promised the twins an outing to Town months ago and this is the first opportunity we've had. If it hadn't been for the wedding, we wouldn't have come today either – it's still far too dangerous. There was a massive raid here only a few days ago.'

'Well, my dear, we are perfectly safe at the Savoy as I'm sure they have converted a basement or two into a luxurious shelter. Claire Rickmansworth told me that at the Ritz they transfer everything underground and then the dancing, drinking and general jollity continues during a raid.'

'I'm going to freshen up, do you want me to assist you with your evening gown or will you wait for Jean?'

Elizabeth snorted inelegantly. 'Good heavens, I'm perfectly capable of putting on my own gown if necessary. I might be almost an octogenarian, but I'm as fit as a fiddle – a lot fitter than you are at the moment.'

'I'm not unwell, Elizabeth, I'm expecting a baby. But if you're quite sure you don't need my help then I'll leave you to get on with your toilette.'

There was a handsome ormolu carriage clock on the bureau and she saw it was almost six-thirty. A flicker of unease ran through her. Surely Joe, Liza and Jean should have been back by now?

'I'm concerned the others aren't back from the cinema.'

'Oh, didn't I say? Jean came in half an hour ago – that's why I was up, not because you woke me.'

'That's a relief. The table's reserved for seven o'clock so we don't have long.'

She'd been resting in her chemise and petticoat, had only removed her frock, girdle and stockings. The sink in the palatial bathroom was big enough to bathe a baby in and she smiled. Would she ever be bringing this infant to stay here? As she didn't intend to employ a nanny, if she wished to come to Town, the baby would have to come with her.

John had had a week's leave in March which was when they'd reconnected and when this baby had been conceived. They'd written regularly, she more than he, and spoken on the telephone but until today she'd not seen him in person.

She leaned against the basin, feeling the cold beneath her fingers. She'd probably spent no more than three weeks with John and now they were married. How could such a rushed affair be successful?

Pushing these worrying doubts aside, Joanna quickly rinsed her face and hands and returned to her bedroom. All she'd packed in her suitcase was an evening gown, matching kitten-heeled court shoes, plus a washbag and clean underwear for the morning.

The weather was so warm there'd been no necessity to bring even a cardigan. Ignoring the silk stockings she should have been wearing, she pushed her bare feet into her evening slippers. These were more comfortable without hosiery.

Stockings were no longer available to purchase as all the silk was being used to make parachutes. Jean and Liza were quite happy to apply the liquid stocking product that coloured their legs to look as if they were wearing stockings. As the seams ran down the back of the calf, a line had to be drawn in order to complete the deception. But if she didn't have the real thing then she would go without.

Her teal-blue gown had cap sleeves, a V-neck and was fortunately loose fitting around the waist and hips. The material was satin, the underskirt lawn, and it was the only one she owned that she could wear without her pregnancy showing.

Her hair needed re-pinning as she'd let it down in order to have her afternoon rest. This didn't take long as it was a task she did every day.

* * *

'My word, you look quite lovely, my dear,' Elizabeth said. 'I'm so sorry that John couldn't be here with you. It's not right that a bride should spend her wedding night alone.'

'I'm just fortunate that I am a bride and not having our child without a ring on my finger. I'm sure you realise that the only reason John and I got married today was because of this baby. I do love him but there are so many things against this being a successful union.'

'Loving each other is all that matters, my dear. Not many women get a second chance at happiness and I'm so glad that you have found your soulmate.'

Joanna was just about to thank her mother-in-law for being so supportive when Elizabeth continued.

'Just imagine how bad it would have been for you and the baby if John had been killed before you had tied the knot. At least now the child won't be illegitimate.'

This wasn't an encouraging remark, but Joanna could hardly criticise the sentiment behind it as this was the only reason that the wedding had taken place so quickly.

'We must go down to the dining room immediately as the others will be waiting for us. I'm surprised Jean didn't look in to see if you needed any help.'

'I told her I could manage when she called in earlier. I think we both look very smart. That shade of blue complements your colouring. It's obvious why David was so taken with you – your cornflower-blue eyes and golden hair are a stunning combination.'

'Thank you, Elizabeth. What colour was your hair when you were my age?'

'I was a blonde, blue-eyed young lady, but never as lovely as you. David's father married me for my money and never forgave me for the fact that he could only access a small portion of it as the rest was held in trust for me.'

They reached the upstairs hallway where the lifts were situated. 'Do you want to go in the lift or take the stairs?' Joanna asked.

'The lift, I find stairs tedious nowadays.'

The attendant was a boy so small that his uniform jacket swamped him. There was no need for him to ask which floor they wanted as everybody would be heading for the ground floor.

Joanna slipped a silver threepenny bit into his hand as they exited, not necessary, but he looked as if he could do with the tip.

Jean and the twins were hovering by the lift and smiled in relief when they emerged.

'We've been receiving funny looks, Ma,' Liza said. 'We don't belong here.'

'That's nonsense. All three of you look absolutely splendid. I can assure you that the only reason other guests are looking at you is because you look so smart and they don't recognise you and are puzzled as to who you might be.'

Jean nodded. 'I think that several young gentlemen would definitely like an introduction to you, Liza. You look so much older than your years dressed in an evening gown.'

'Do I? I certainly feel very grown-up. Does that mean I can have Champagne with my dinner?'

Joanna was about to say no but reconsidered. 'Absolutely – today's a family celebration, albeit without the groom.'

They were ushered by a bellboy to the dining room where the maître d' took them to one of the best tables. He addressed her as Lady Harcourt and she thought now wasn't the time or the place to disabuse him.

* * *

Once they were seated, the menus perused and their choices made, she glanced surreptitiously around the room to see if there was anyone she recognised or anyone who might recognise her. The Champagne was poured and Joe made a toast.

'To Ma and John, may they live happily together for decades.'

They all took a sip and Liza pulled a face. 'I'm sorry, I don't like it. Can I have a shandy?'

Joanna laughed. 'You can have anything you want, my love, but asking for that might well cause consternation. I doubt anyone has ever drunk shandy here.'

Their waiter smiled at Liza and vanished to return with commendable speed, carrying her drink. Sarah had promised to join them later if she could.

'Thank goodness Tony's taking care of things at Goodwill House. Your son has been an absolute godsend, Jean, and our home's running more smoothly than it has ever done.'

'It's wonderful to have him with me after being so long apart. I can't believe his foster mother kept my letters from him.'

'Of course she did, Jean,' Elizabeth said. 'She wanted to keep him to herself. Mind you, if he'd come to you then he would never have inherited their money and the house.'

'Quite right, my lady, but money isn't everything.'

'No, but it certainly helps.'

The meal was delicious as was only to be expected at somewhere as prestigious as the Savoy. Rationing and shortages were scarcely noticeable if you had the money to pay for luxury items.

Joanna smiled and laughed, chatted gaily, but it was a struggle to keep up the pretence of being completely happy. She knew if she retired then her children wouldn't stay and they were so enjoying themselves.

'That dance is unseemly, Joanna, whatever is the world coming to?' Elizabeth said sourly as she watched the twins and other couples gyrating madly to some American music.

'It's called the Jitterbug, I think. It looks a lot of fun.'

'Jean, would you be kind enough to escort me to my rooms? I'm fatigued.'

'I'd be happy to, my lady. I'll come straight back, Joanna, so don't go anywhere. I'd love another pot of coffee and a brandy if that's possible.'

'Goodnight, Elizabeth, we'll meet down here for breakfast unless you intend to eat in our suite.'

'The toast is always cold when one eats upstairs. We'll eat together down here.' Elizabeth nodded and smiled fondly. 'You did the right thing, my dear, and I'm certain given time you'll come to see that marrying your handsome young pilot was exactly the right thing to do. Shrugging off your title and the Harcourt name means you can make a fresh start.'

As Joanna watched the dancers, she had time to mull over what had been said. The implications of her marriage were only now becoming apparent. How strange it was that a year ago the twins had taken the name Harcourt and now she had abandoned it.

Her oldest daughter was now a Trent, she was a Sergeant, and Liza and Joe were Harcourts. If it hadn't been for the war, none of this would have happened. David would still be alive, Elizabeth would still be in France, and the twins would be living in the East End with their feckless mother.

She was thankful that her life was now so full of promise, that she and her family had so much to look forward to despite the world being ravaged by war.

She was smiling when Jean returned and her friend commented on this. 'You look better, Joanna. I was worried you were regretting what's happened.'

'I'm fine, Jean. Whatever happens, I'll never regret meeting John. How could I when I'm expecting his child in December?'

'A Christmas baby at Goodwill House – that's perfect. We've had a wedding so a baby will round things off nicely. Did you ask for the coffee?'

'I'm sorry, I'd forgotten all about it. Look, there's a waiter hovering over there. If you wave, he'll come over.'

The twins returned and wanted more shandy, so this was added to the order. Eventually Joanna toppled into bed at midnight and, as she fell asleep, she sent her love to her husband and prayed he'd stay safe and be able to spend time with her soon.

* * *

Joanna slept surprisingly well considering the situation. She decided to take a shower, not something she was familiar with, and after this novel experience she vowed that she would have several installed at the house she was having restored for them to move into at the end of the year.

She did enjoy a soak in lemon-scented water but only being allowed five inches of water made it a less enjoyable experience. She felt cleaner when she stepped out of the tiled shower cubicle than she did after her twice-weekly bath.

They'd agreed to meet for breakfast at eight o'clock and it was only a little after six-thirty. She was fortunate not to be suffering from the quite common early-morning nausea associated with pregnancy. Bouts of dizziness and fatigue were all she'd had to worry about so far as she only felt unwell in the motion of a car.

Once dressed, she went to see if Elizabeth needed her help but her mother-in-law was still soundly asleep and it didn't seem right to wake her. She'd give her another hour and then do it.

She quietly closed the door to the bedroom and was considering whether to send for some tea when someone knocked gently. Frowning at the unexpected interruption, she hurried across to open the door.

'Darling, does this still count as our wedding night?'

Astonished and overjoyed to see him, she tumbled into John's waiting arms and he kissed her. Next she was being carried across the sitting room and into the bedroom she'd just vacated. He kicked the door shut and headed for the bed. He dropped her none too gently in the middle and was about to join her when she finally got her breath back.

'My love, how are you here? Are you AWOL?'

'Angus wangled me a twenty-four-hour pass. I don't have a kite at the moment anyway.'

Joanna stared up at him in horror. There were only two reasons that she knew of for him to be without a plane to fly. He'd crashed it or had been shot down. She sat up and held up a hand, making it clear he wasn't to move. 'Did you get shot down? Crash?'

He shook his head and laughed. 'No, sweetheart, some silly sod crashed into it after I was down. Wrote both Spits off. He's not a popular bloke with the skipper at the moment.' His smile made her knees weak. 'He's my best friend from now on. If he hadn't pranged my kite, I'd not be here with you.'

As he was speaking, he was ripping off his clothes. His chest was bare and her pulse raced. Just looking at his broad, well-muscled shoulders made her forget everything but how much she loved him and how much she wanted to make love with him.

He was magnificent and he was her husband. She knelt on the bed and pulled her dress over her head, leaving just her underwear on. No stockings or girdle this morning and her shoes had fallen off when he'd snatched her up.

'I'll do the rest, darling, I've been dreaming about this moment since March.' He knelt in front of her and slipped the ribbon straps of her chemise from her shoulders.

'Be careful, my love, I don't have anything else to wear.'

His smile was fierce, compelling, demanding and she forgot about everything but the joy of being with him. A considerable time later, they lay in each other's arms, deliriously happy and oblivious to their surroundings.

He was stroking her tummy lovingly. 'I never thought to have children of my own. Just having you was enough for me but now that I am going to be a father, I'm so pleased.'

Joanna didn't want to answer, she just wanted to revel in these unexpected and wonderful moments of intimacy she'd never thought to experience today. Then she happened to glance at the overmantel clock.

'It's almost eight. We have to get up. Someone will barge in—'

'No, they won't, darling, I left my shoes outside the door. They'll know I'm here.'

She wriggled from his embrace. 'And so will everyone else in this hotel. How could you?'

He wasn't at all abashed and smiled lazily whilst threading his fingers through her hair. 'I'm your new husband. I'm not only entitled to be here, but it's also where all your family expect me to be.'

'I said I'd be having breakfast with them.'

'We have twenty-four hours and I'm not letting you out of this bed until I have to leave tomorrow at dawn.'

She slithered down. 'You are under a serious misapprehension, my love, if you think I am a woman who takes orders from anyone.'

He propped himself up on one elbow, keeping her mesmerised by his intent gaze, and continued to run his fingers through her hair. Maybe if she closed her eyes she could break the spell. She couldn't.

An hour later, she escaped to the loo and turned on the shower. She sniffed her arm. What was that strange smell? Then she smiled. It was engine oil – her husband's particular scent and she loved it.

She was enjoying the luxury of a long, refreshing, hot shower when John joined her. They were both half-drowned when they eventually stumbled out.

'That was an experience I've no wish to repeat, my darling,' he said as he snatched up a giant bath towel and enveloped her in it. 'Making love under water isn't safe.'

'I'd not even used one until yesterday.' She shook her head as he moved to assist her. 'No, I need to eat. All this exercise has made me ravenous.'

# 3

John had never been happier. Joanna had no idea just what being married meant to him. He'd never expected to be her husband, to have her give up her title and her name and take his. He'd just accepted he would always be slightly outside her family circle, not really a part of them.

Angus was a good bloke, had given him the pass when he could have insisted he remained at readiness in case any of the other flyers were unable to go on the next sortie. He hoped his being absent didn't mean that Angus took his place. Were they now related somehow in law or did the familial link only apply to Sarah?

'Bloody hell!' He jack-knifed upright, waking his bride.

'What's wrong, darling?'

'I've not told my parents that we're married or that they're going to have a grandchild.'

'You can write to them. There's headed paper provided by the hotel.'

'Later. First I'm going to ring for something to eat. We never got around to it earlier.'

'What's the time?'

'Midday.'

'Then we could have breakfast or lunch.' She yawned and stretched and he almost decided to ignore his rumbling guts and jump back into bed.

'Champagne, sandwiches and cake. Followed by coffee and chocolate.'

'Sounds perfect. I need to arrange for us all to stay another night. We should have checked out by now.'

'I'll do it.'

She sat up, not bothering to hold the sheet over her breasts. 'I suppose we should tell them I'm not Lady Harcourt any more. They might be a bit shocked to be asked to send up room service otherwise.'

'Do you mind very much having been forced to give up all that?'

'Not at all. In fact, I'm thrilled to no longer have the weight of being a Harcourt on my shoulders.'

'I can't do what a husband should, which is provide for you financially,' John said. 'You've already got more money than Croesus. What I will do is be the best husband and father that I can be. I'm going to do my damnedest to stay alive through this bloody awful war now I've got a family of my own.'

'I couldn't ask for anything else. Believe me, once the scandal has settled, I'm going to be the envy of the neighbourhood, married to such a handsome young man when most of my peers are tied to boring middle-aged gentlemen.'

He smiled, more than happy with her answer. He picked up the receiver and waited for the telephonist to answer.

'Warrant Officer Sergeant, I would like sandwiches, a jug of coffee, Champagne and whatever cakes, pastries and chocolate you've got available sent up for my wife and me. I've been given one day's leave for our honeymoon. Also, we'll be staying the night, as will my wife's family.'

'Yes, sir, your order will be with you shortly. Congratulations on your nuptials.'

'That was well done, my love, all the necessary information and none of the awkwardness. Much as I enjoy watching you wandering about in your birthday suit, I think you'd better put something on before the waiter arrives,' Joanna said.

He grinned. 'Anything for you, my darling.' He found his discarded underpants under a chair and pulled them on. 'Do I really have to put my trousers on as well?'

She raised an eyebrow. 'You certainly do, but I'll not insist that you have your vest and shirt on as well.'

He was barely decent when the food arrived. He strode across and opened the door. He blocked the waiter's view of Joanna by standing in the doorway.

'Thank you, there's no need for you to bring it in.' He had half a crown ready and tossed it to the gawping old bloke, grabbed the end of the trolley, whisked it into the room and slammed the door.

His beautiful wife sprang out of bed and collected her flimsy underwear from where he'd flung it over the end of the bed earlier that morning. He was forced to look away, otherwise he would have tossed her back between the sheets.

He was the luckiest bloke in the world to be married to this woman. He'd do anything for her but could think of only one thing that would really make her happy. With his back firmly towards her, he made the suggestion.

'I was offered a commission months ago but turned it down. Angus said the offer's still on the table and I think I'll accept it when I go back.'

She drifted up beside him and he caught his breath. He thought even when he was ancient she'd still have that effect on him. 'You don't have to if it's against your principles.'

'I might end up a squadron leader like Angus.'

'If, like him, you can then take a desk job after you've flown sufficient sorties that would be wonderful.'

His voice was gruff as he answered. 'I love you; you and our baby are my world. I told you, I'll do anything for you and becoming an officer is the first of those things.'

Joanna kissed his bare shoulder as she stretched past and picked up an empty plate and began to fill it with a selection of sandwiches. 'You don't have to do anything that you don't want to, my love, just for me. However, I think you might prefer the Officers' Mess.'

He copied her lead, placed his overfull plate on a nearby table and then popped open the Champagne. 'Why's that?'

'You've got a first-class degree from Oxford. I don't suppose anybody in the NCOs' Mess has one of those.'

'You'd be surprised, darling. There are two sergeant pilots that I know of who like me have refused a commission but also like me attended university.'

He poured them both a glass of the insipid fizzy drink that females seemed to adore. He'd much rather have a pint of beer, but Champagne seemed appropriate in the circumstances.

'Are you going to put a shirt on to eat? Somehow it doesn't seem quite right for you to be sitting in such a grand chair half-naked.'

She tilted her head to one side, pursed her lips and then nodded. 'I'm finding you as you are most distracting, and I really want to enjoy my lunch. Curled, dry sandwiches are something I dislike.'

He grinned and couldn't stop the flash of desire that roared through him and her eyes widened. He gulped down his drink and then hastily poured himself a cup of coffee to drown the taste.

'I didn't realise how much you disliked bubbles. I suppose you prefer beer.'

His flicker of irritation at her words must have showed on his face. Her alluding to his working-class background mustn't become a problem between them.

'John, there's no need to look so cross. Most RAF men that I've had dealings with prefer beer to Champagne. It's got nothing to do with your background.'

He relaxed and smiled. 'I expect we're going to rub each other up the wrong way a lot until we get to know each other better. I was working it out and I don't think we've spent more than twenty-four hours in total in each other's company. We can't expect to be entirely comfortable together.'

'I thought exactly the same thing. I fell in love with you the first time I saw you but didn't realise it was more than physical attraction until the second or third time we were together. Do you think our baby will have different coloured eyes like you?'

'Good God, I've no idea. I'd love a daughter who looks exactly like you.'

Her smile was radiant. 'And I'd like a son who looks the image of his father.'

'Maybe you're expecting twins and we'll have one of each.' Her look of absolute horror made him laugh out loud.

'I'm going to have enough to do with just one baby, let alone two.' She looked down at her bump. 'I'm about four months and don't think I'm particularly big, do you?'

'I haven't the foggiest – you've had a baby, you're a woman, you should know these things.'

'It's years since I had a baby and be honest I was so fussed over by the very expensive team of doctors and nurses at the London clinic that I really don't remember anything about the pregnancy apart from being bored and feeling trapped.'

This was the first time she'd told him anything about her first marriage and he poured himself another coffee, refilled his plate and hers and then they curled up together on the comfortable sofa in front of the log fire. The more they knew about each other, the easier it would be going forward. Now wasn't a time for further lovemaking but for meaningful conversation.

* * *

Joanna told John everything about her marriage, her parents and her life since Dunkirk. He reciprocated with anecdotes about his family and by the end of the afternoon it was as if she'd actually met his mother and father, his uncles, aunts and his two older sisters.

'I'm going to have a long relaxing bath and fill it up way past the five-inch limit. Very unpatriotic of me, but if you share it then I won't feel so guilty.'

'We nearly drowned making love in the shower. Are you suggesting we give it another go in the bath?'

'Good heavens, absolutely not. Much as I enjoy what we do together, I prefer to be in a bed to do it.'

His smile was wicked. He picked her up and strode across the bedroom. Some considerable time later, they did share a bath and she insisted that they dressed for the first time that day.

'I need to know how my mother-in-law and my children are coping without me. There's more than enough room for all of us to sit around the table. I would love to dine with them up here – but if you don't want to then I'll understand.'

Although he'd told her more than once that he'd do anything for her, she still wanted to ask him, she'd no intention of taking advantage of his willingness to please his new bride.

'I think we need to get housekeeping in as well. I'll let you order the dinner as you know what your family likes to eat.'

'They're your family now as well, my love. You need to shave as you look like a pirate and your beard is unpleasantly scratchy.'

John ran a hand around his chin and grinned. 'I'll do that now. It'll give you a few minutes to speak to your – our – family. It's quite possible that they've gone out for the day. Which reminds me, we've been bloody lucky not to have had an air-raid.'

'Would you have gone down to the shelter in the basement if there had been one?'

'Not a chance.' He was still chuckling to himself as he vanished into the luxurious bathroom.

Joanna hesitated with her hand on the bedroom door, a little embarrassed to emerge and face the others when they would know exactly what had been going on behind the closed door. Honeymoons weren't supposed to be conducted under the full view of one's family.

As she walked into the spacious sitting room of the suite, she was greeted by Elizabeth, who was stretched out on a chaise longue, happily reading a newspaper.

'They've gone to the cinema for a second time, my dear, but will be back shortly. There is no need for you to worry about us.'

Joanna rushed across and embraced her mother-in-law. 'I can't tell you how happy I am that John was able to come even though it's only for twenty-four hours. I've learned so much about him this afternoon.'

'So there was some talking going on behind that door then?'

'Elizabeth, I'm shocked by your indelicacy. I'm going to order dinner to be served up here for all of us but first I'm going to see if I can get in touch with Sarah...'

'There is no need to do that, Joanna, as she telephoned the suite an hour ago to say she is on her way.'

'That will make this day absolutely perfect. Do you need me to have anything sent up, as I'm not ordering dinner to be served until seven?'

'No, thank you, I went down for afternoon tea an hour ago. I felt rather underdressed as there were silly women in mink coats and dripping with diamonds. Some were even in formal attire,' Elizabeth said.

'I expect they're staying on for dinner and to dance later. Excuse me, I must make this telephone call.'

* * *

Housekeeping sent along two chambermaids immediately and by the time they'd cleaned and dusted everywhere and changed the sheets in both bedrooms, Jean and the twins were back from their excursion and Sarah arrived at the same time. John had spent the last hour regaling Elizabeth with risqué stories from his exploits and from the amount of laughter coming from them both they were clearly now firm friends.

Joanna really wanted a few minutes alone with her daughter. She was hoping Sarah could examine her and would know if there was even the remotest possibility there would be more than one baby arriving in December.

John was on his feet and shook hands with Joe but embraced everybody else. Joanna drew her oldest daughter aside.

'Come into the bedroom for a moment, darling, there's something I need to ask you.'

'I have to be back on duty at first light but will stay here until after dinner,' Sarah said. 'I've never seen you look happier – being married to John obviously suits you.'

'Jokingly John suggested I might be having twins. Do you think that's possible?' Joanna half-expected her daughter to say that she'd not done obstetrics so far in her training but instead she nodded.

'Actually, Mummy, I've just been reading about exactly this. It does seem that women in their thirties are slightly more likely to have twins than other age groups. Shall I have a quick look?'

'Please do. I've not felt any movement yet and Dr Willoughby said the baby will quicken during the fourth month. If there were two, then surely I'd have felt that fluttering sensation already?'

She clambered onto the bed and pulled up the front of her frock. As her bra and knickers were a single unit, she couldn't do much about that.

Sarah examined the bump through the silk of her cami-knickers. 'Your dates are accurate, so you are quite a lot bigger than I'd expect you to be.'

'Really? I hardly show much at the front.'

'But you've got no waist at all now. You're expanding sideways rather than in front. I'm not an expert, of course, but I think it could be a slight possibility. You might have to wait until delivery before you know for sure because quite often it's impossible to hear both heartbeats.'

This wasn't the news Joanna had expected or wanted. 'I'll take comfort from you saying it's only a slight possibility. I really don't think I could cope with two babies at the same time, especially as we expect to be moving immediately after Christmas.'

'Don't be silly, Mummy. You're the most efficient and well-organised woman I know. You'll have plenty of help. Anyway, it's only a very slim chance that you're carrying twins so I shouldn't worry about it at the moment.'

'Thank you, my darling, I'm so happy you think so highly of me. I must say, I'm somewhat relieved that the likelihood of having twins is slim. One baby at my age is more than enough.'

Joanna had just rearranged her clothes when there was a tap on the door and John came in. 'I guessed what was going on here but didn't like to intrude. Is everything all right?'

'Absolutely splendid, my love. Sarah says here's a slight possibility that I'm carrying twins but if I am, I'll deal with it when it happens.' Joanna noticed he was carrying a beautifully wrapped parcel. 'Is that for me?'

'It's from Elizabeth – I gather it's the necessities that you don't have because you're staying an extra night.'

Sarah had left them alone. 'How kind everyone's being. This feels like my wedding day now that all the family, apart from Angus, are here.'

She walked into his arms and he kissed her, not passionately this time, but tenderly, lovingly, and she reciprocated.

'I do wish your parents and sisters had been able to come. I really want to meet your family. Do you think they would be prepared to travel to Goodwill House if I invite them?'

'I'm sure they'd be delighted. They know all about you and your huge house.' He laughed at her horrified expression. 'No, sweetheart, I didn't tell them we were involved. I love my family but my mother's very straitlaced.'

'Oh dear, that means she'll be scandalised by the pregnancy. Perhaps it would be better not to invite them until the baby's here and we're safely settled at The Manse.'

'Yes, I think you're right. I haven't written to them yet about today and won't do so now. I'm sure if we present them with a *fait accompli*, a new grandchild and a new wife, then they won't mention the slight irregularity of when the baby was conceived.'

'I'm not entirely comfortable about keeping them in the dark. I know how I'd feel if Joe got married and didn't tell me until months later, but you know your family and you must do what you think is right for them and you.'

'Today is about us, my darling, so let's not worry about things that might not even happen.'

'Then I'll say no more. You know your parents and if you're happy keeping them in the dark then so be it.'

# 4

John didn't drink any more Champagne or wine with his meal as he had to leave in the small hours in order to report back to base no later than dawn the next day. His squadron had another week before there was any possibility of them being moved away from the action. They'd been at permanent readiness for the past three weeks and during that time five kites had been lost and three flyers had gone for a Burton.

You had to be ready for action, waiting for the bell to ring and the order to scramble to come over the telephone. The Luftwaffe attacked cities at night nowadays, but his squadron was kept busy during the light hours being sent on seek and destroy missions – called rodeos – over Northern France, Belgium and Holland. Patrolling the Channel, protecting the convoys of shipping, was not their job any more. He wasn't going to get any sleep tonight – at least he hoped he wasn't.

'John, how many Germans have you shot down?' Joe's question jerked him back to the present.

'Three definite, three probable and two damaged.'

'Does that make you an ace?'

Joanna's fingers clenched. The last thing they needed was to talk about dogfights and death. She was well aware that every time he went up, there was a 50 per cent chance he wouldn't come back in one piece or come back at all.

Lady Harcourt expertly changed the subject. For an old lady, she was remarkably astute. He'd expected her to treat him coldly, like an outsider, someone beneath her notice, but the reverse was true.

'I want to go down and listen to the music and I'm sure you and Liza want to dance again. Jean, would you be kind enough to escort me?'

Sarah was on her feet immediately. 'I need to get going as well as I'm on duty in a few hours and it can take that long to get across London sometimes.'

Nobody argued with the redoubtable old lady and minutes later, John and Joanna were alone – God knows how long it would be before this happened again.

'Do you want to go down? It seems a shame that only the family have seen you in your stunning gown.'

'I want to spend these final few hours with you. If you let reception know that the debris from dinner can be cleared, I'll be waiting next door.'

* * *

John slipped out of bed just after two. Joanna was sleeping and they'd agreed they didn't want a tearful goodbye. His bag was packed and it only took a few minutes to take a quick shower and dress.

He paused at the bedroom door to take one last look at the woman he loved with every fibre of his being. He barely paid lip service to religion, didn't believe, but this morning he sent up a heartfelt prayer that he wouldn't be shot down and would be here to meet his son or daughter.

The hotel was quiet, just minimal lighting, but more than enough for him to make his way rapidly down the sweeping staircase. His motorbike had been parked at the rear of the building but the concierge had promised to have it waiting for him at the front when he left.

It was remarkable that there'd been no air-raids on either night. Hitler had turned his attention to the Russian front, which probably accounted for the lessening in attacks on Britain.

John kicked his bike into life and rode away, trying not to think about how much he had to lose now. The one consolation was that if he died, Joanna would have his baby, and wouldn't be entirely alone.

Five minutes after leaving the Savoy, his mind was clear, focused on the job in hand. He wouldn't survive if he allowed his personal feeling inside the cockpit of his Spit. The kite he'd lost would hopefully have been replaced by one of the new Mk Vs. These were faster and more manoeuvrable than the earlier models.

Hornchurch was a busy base so even this early in the morning there were vehicles waiting to be checked by the guards at the gate. The sky was clear, the sun would be up in half an hour, he'd arrived in time to grab some scoff in the mess before heading out to dispersal in the back of a lorry. He dumped his bag by the door, hoping it would remain there until he had time to take it to his room. He much preferred using the canvas duffel bag but as an officer he'd be expected to use a suitcase for his belongings.

Angus was waiting to speak to him. Having a squadron leader lurking in the NCOs' Mess was probably making the blokes uncomfortable.

'Good show, I wondered if you'd make it in time. You'll be relieved to know we had a quiet day yesterday. Two scrambles, everybody tickety-boo.'

'I'll never be able to thank you enough for stepping in and taking my place. If anything had happened to you—'

'It didn't and Sarah was all right with it, Joanna doesn't have to know. To be honest, I'd like to be a squadron leader flying again and not stuck behind a desk.'

'You've done your bit and with your dodgy ears flying isn't good for you,' John said. 'The bigwigs would have you leading a squadron somewhere if the medics would allow it.'

'You're right. To be honest, I've got a filthy headache after flying yesterday. I'll let you get your scoff.'

John touched Angus's arm. 'There's something else you could do for me. I'd like to accept a commission if that's still on the table.'

'It bloody well is. About time you saw sense. I'll get the paperwork done. We'll skip pilot officer and jump you straight to flying officer. Welcome aboard, Flying Officer Sergeant.'

'Just like that? I thought I'd have to jump through a few hoops.'

'You've been top of the list ever since you arrived in March. I know we've got dozens of senior NCOs who are pilots but not many of them have your calibre or your education.'

John couldn't quite take it in. 'Does that mean I move my billet today?'

'Of course it does.' Angus gestured towards the cylindrical canvas bag leaning like a drunken sailor against the wall by the door. 'I take it that's yours?'

'It is. I thought eating was more important.'

'Absolutely. Don't worry, I'll take care of everything. I'll get your batman to attach the new stripes to your spare jacket.' Angus slapped him on the back. 'Of course, you'll have to get the correct uniform, but you get the funds to do that.'

'This will do until I've got time to do that.'

'Next time you get a few hours free, I'll buy you your first drink in the Officers' Mess.'

John gobbled down his breakfast – not much sign of rationing today as he'd got two rashers of bacon and a decent sausage to go with his fried bread and fried egg. He wondered if the food would be better in the Officers' Mess than it was here. More importantly, would the drinks be more expensive in the bar?

He vaulted into the rear of the lorry and waited for the inevitable comments about his absence but then remembered he'd told no one why he was having a day off. So as far as they were concerned it could have been because of compassionate leave due to the death or critical illness of a close family member. He wasn't going to disabuse them. He liked to keep his personal life separate from his professional one.

There were twenty-four pilots heading for dispersal, the majority officers but three others were senior NCOs like himself. They piled in together, nobody called anyone sir, and there was certainly no saluting.

At the dispersal, they clambered into their flight suits, collected their Mae Wests and parachutes and headed for their own kites. They would lounge about on the grass, talking, reading the newspapers, having a smoke or in his case catching up with much-needed sleep.

He was glad to be back but already missing his darling wife. He had his duty to King and Country and must put his personal feelings to one side until the war was won.

* * *

John's squadron was only scrambled twice during his long shift, both were false alarms and they returned to base without engaging with the enemy. It was too hot with his gear on sitting in direct sunlight, so like most of the other bods he found himself a patch of shade behind his kite.

The NAAFI van had been around twice but there was no substitute for a hot meal and he was as eager as everyone else to find one. His squadron was on duty from dawn until ten o'clock.

He'd told no one about his promotion. They'd got eyes and would see for themselves when he got his stripes that he was an officer. That evening he smiled as they bounced across the turf and headed for the admin block. Joanna had given up her title for him, become a commoner – well, for the baby really – and he'd just gone up in the world.

This was something he'd definitely tell his parents. His mother would be cock-a-hoop to have her only son an officer. Maybe when he wrote the letter, he'd also tell his parents that he was married, but he wouldn't tell them about the baby just yet. Joanna had assured him the pregnancy was going well, that she was as fit as a woman ten years younger, but he couldn't help worrying something might go wrong.

The lorry jolted to a halt and as he'd got on last, he'd be first off. It was barely light enough to see but a vigilant corporal spotted him and hurried over.

'Squadron Leader Trent has asked me to take you to your new billet, sir.'

'Good show, lead on, Macduff.' John, having enjoyed studying Shakespeare for his higher certificate, knew this was a misquote from Macbeth but used it anyway.

Becoming an officer was something he'd vowed never to do, but now he was one of the Brylcreem boys himself. How his life had changed. A year ago, he'd been ground crew in charge of the fire tenders at Manston and here he was married to an incredibly wealthy woman ten years older than himself, about to be a father, and an officer to boot. He beamed as he followed the corporal. He'd never been happier and life could only get better – as long as he didn't go for a Burton.

* * *

Joanna was returning to Goodwill House literally a new woman. She'd departed as Lady Harcourt and returned as Mrs Sergeant. Hopefully there'd been no disasters in her absence and the cat, dog and miscellaneous poultry were all intact. Tony, Jean's long-lost son who now lived with them, would have taken care of everything splendidly, she was sure.

The remaining land girls would be relocating to The Old Rectory three miles away next week and they were as eager to go as she would be to have the house free of boarders and have just family residing there. Two had left to get married, which left ten still there. Charlie was now Mrs Willoughby, the wife of the local doctor, and Daphne was married to an RAF sergeant based at Manston.

Joanna's next project was to persuade someone at the War Office that the Harcourt ancestral home would make an ideal small hospital and convalescent home for RAF men. She knew that there were already such places in other parts of the country and as her home was conveniently situated just a few miles from Manston, it would be a good location.

The Manse, a substantial Georgian house that she'd purchased just outside Stodham, wouldn't be ready for occupation until the end of the year. The builders were there but with so much to do, and the scarcity of materials, it was going to take months, not weeks, to complete the refurbishment and modernisation of the house.

Lazzy, her huge wolfhound, was ecstatic to have them all home. 'Silly dog, I'm pleased to see you too. Get down now, you're going to knock me over.'

Joe grabbed the dog's collar and pulled him away. 'Bad boy. No jumping. Go on your bed.'

Lazzy slunk off and she heard him flop onto his blanket under the kitchen table with a loud sigh. 'Thank you, I really must be firmer with him.'

'Too late for that, Ma, he knows you're going to let him get away with it. He listens to me and Tony but not to anyone else.'

'To a female, you mean?' Jean said, laughing. 'You're right, we're too soft on him.'

They heard the dog's tail thumping but he remained where he was.

'I find travelling tiresome, Joanna. I don't think I shall go to Town again,' Elizabeth announced as she headed for the terrace. 'I am going to sit outside. My lungs are clogged with fumes from the train.'

'I'll join you shortly,' Joanna said. 'I'll bring us some tea and sandwiches. It seems a long time since breakfast.'

Jean was already upstairs changing, and she and the twins followed. As she hung her frock in the closet, Joanna wondered how long it would be before she was able to wear it again. She glanced down at her stomach. Was she imagining it, or had it grown an inch or two since she'd last looked?

After trying and rejecting several frocks that no longer fitted, she settled on a pair of slacks that she could hold together at her waist with a safety pin. Fortunately, she had several loose-fitting blouses that would do for the moment. Jean was in the process of altering some garments to accommodate the pregnancy and hopefully these would be ready soon.

Now the idea was in her head, she would be constantly looking for signs that she might be having twins. If John hadn't made a joke about it, she wouldn't have even considered such a thing. Thirty-seven would be considered dangerously old to be having a first baby but thankfully as this was her second Dr Willoughby was confident there would be a happy outcome. She certainly felt well and was more active than she'd been with Sarah. David had kept her in cotton wool and she'd been too young and obedient to complain.

She heard Liza hurry down the passageway, no doubt eager to get back to her job looking after the vicar's small children. Tony had acquired a motorbike from somewhere and had managed to repair it, so it now worked perfectly. She heard the distinctive throaty roar and moved to the window to see it heading down the drive with her daughter in the side car.

Tony and Liza had been spending a lot of time together – inevitable as they lived under the same roof. But her daughter was not quite sixteen, far too young to be having a boyfriend. Tony was in his mid-twenties – surely he wouldn't be romantically interested in someone so young?

She dismissed her thoughts as nonsense caused by her condition and hurried downstairs to collect the small pile of letters neatly stacked on the silver salver on the telephone table.

Jean rushed past. 'Miss Biggins has done sterling work as a substitute housekeeper, Joanna, but has now resumed her duties looking after Lady Harcourt.'

'Good for her. To think that you were doing exactly that last year and are now my closest friend as well as running the house so expertly.'

'We make a good team, Joanna, and with my son here as well, there's nothing we can't do for ourselves.' Jean smiled and nodded at the pinned-together slacks. 'I'll finish altering those things for you later. I'm wondering how the ladies of the village will take it when they know what's happened.'

'I really don't care what anyone thinks. I believe, on balance, they'll be less shocked that I married John than if I'd continued the affair. That was bound to come out eventually.'

Jean smiled and nodded. 'I'll take some sandwiches and tea out to the terrace. I'll not be long.'

'Thank you, Jean. I've just these to read, and possibly to answer, and then I'll join you. Please invite Miss Biggins to come as well.'

* * *

Joanna had only been away two nights but nothing seemed the same. The house remained as it always had been through the centuries, but she was the one who'd changed. She'd been the custodian of this magnificent edifice for many years, but now it was time to hand it over to someone else. Sarah and Angus didn't want the responsibility and neither did the twins. The baby she was carrying had no claim on Goodwill House. This child would grow up at The Manse and have a quite different life.

She was smiling as she glanced through the letters until she reached the third one. She recognised the bold black scrawl. It was from Lord Peter Harcourt. Why would he be writing a personal letter to her? Joanna had a nasty feeling whatever was enclosed within the envelope wouldn't be good news.

They had met since the disastrous car journey back from Town when he'd suggested she became his mistress and had been civil but were no longer friends. Had he heard about her marriage, about the baby, and felt as the titular head of the household it was his business to comment on both?

This was something she wanted to read in private so she headed for the study, confident nobody would disturb her there. She put the letter from Lord Harcourt to one side on the desk and, picking up the letter opener, quickly examined the other three.

They were just business letters about the running of the estate, financial matters that could be dealt with later. She couldn't put off opening the last one any longer.

*Dear Lady Harcourt,*

*I'm not sure a letter is the best way to give you this news but as we are no longer on good terms, I have no alternative but to write to you.*

*I have not been at all well recently and finally found the time to visit my doctor in Harley Street. It was the worst possible news – I have a malignant tumour and was told the unpalatable news that I had only a few months to live.*

*That was in March and it is quite possible when you receive this letter I will already have died. I don't expect you to mourn my passing or attend my funeral – there will be more than enough making an unnecessary fuss, none of them will be related to me.*

*I am leaving everything to you. I have nobody else I wish to inherit my substantial fortune. I know you don't need it but I'm sure you'll think of something worthy and responsible to do with it.*

*I wish we could have been better friends. I enjoyed your company and that of your children and am sorry that I ruined it for both of us by my stupidity.*

*I wish you well in the future.*

*My best regards,*

*Peter Harcourt*

For a moment, Joanna couldn't take it in – the words blurred as she absorbed the dreadful news. He was right, they were related even if only in the most tenuous fashion and had until two days ago shared the same name.

She was glad he hadn't known about her marriage as it would have upset him to know that the only Harcourts left did not have that name by birth or marriage but by adoption.

She dropped the letter and ran to the telephone and asked the operator to connect her to his office at Horse Guards.

'I just received a letter from Lord Harcourt telling me that he might well have died from an incurable illness before I received this news. Has that happened?'

'Unfortunately, Lord Harcourt passed away yesterday. His funeral with full military honours will be held next week. Am I speaking to Lady Harcourt?'

'My family and I would like to attend the funeral if that's possible. But I am no longer Lady Harcourt. I got married three days ago so no longer hold that title.'

She blinked back tears. Peter was so very young to have died from such a cruel disease. They could have been friends, perhaps more than that if she'd not met John, and now he was gone.

# 5

John was too knackered to go to the mess as he'd intended, and his orderly offered to fetch him something to eat. 'Thank you, Benson, that's kind of you.'

'It's my job to look after you, sir, I'll just be a tick. Pilot Officer Brown, the bloke you share this room with, is in the bar but will be back soon.'

'Right, I hope he's not drunk and keeps me awake.'

He was stripped to the waist washing in the sink when Angus appeared at the open door. 'Good show, I hoped to catch you before you turned in. Joanna has been trying to get in touch.'

John's stomach plummeted. 'What's wrong?'

'Nothing, at least nothing with her. I don't know if you ever met Lord Harcourt, but he died from cancer yesterday, poor sod. He was a good soldier, he didn't deserve to go that way.'

'I'm not sure what this has to do with me.'

'Joanna wants us all to go to Harcourt's funeral. It's next week and your squadron will have completed its rota and will get a few days' leave before starting the next round.'

John yawned, making his jaw crack loudly. 'Sorry. I was hoping to get down to Goodwill House, not spend it paying my respects to a bloke I never met.'

'All the family will be there – you can go back with Joanna afterwards. Best blues will be worn.'

John grinned and saluted. 'Yes, sir. Thanks for bringing the message. How's your headache?'

Angus grimaced. 'Not too bad, but I don't think I'll be going up again any time soon. When the medic heard he wasn't impressed and neither was our commanding officer.'

Benson arrived at the door with a tray. 'Got your scoff here, sir, I'll put it on top of the chest of drawers. I'll bring you both tea at five.'

'I'll leave you to eat,' Angus said. 'Be outside the admin block at eight o'clock next Tuesday. I've arranged for a car and driver. We're collecting Sarah on the way through London.'

John devoured everything on the tray and drank the large mug of stewed tea then crashed out on the bed, not bothering to put on his pyjamas.

* * *

The next few days passed without any major incidents. Two kites had been shot up, the flyers had escaped unscathed and the holes in the fuselage of both Spits had been repaired by the ground crew. He'd also now acquired his officer's smart uniform.

He'd written to his parents with his good news and promised to send them some snaps of him with his officer's stripes, and of Joanna, when he could get some done.

She had written to him apologising for dragging him to the funeral when he had so little time off.

*My darling John,*

*I am so sorry you have to waste your precious free time to attend Lord Harcourt's funeral. The poor man has no family apart from us. I'll explain everything when we see each other.*

*They've delayed the start on the renovations for our new home again as after the air-raid the other night the builders are needed to do emergency repairs on the houses that were damaged in Ramsgate.*

*Our baby will be born here – I know he or she won't be a Harcourt but I've no intention of having it anywhere else. Dr Willoughby will be on hand if necessary, but the local midwife will be in attendance. She has an excellent reputation.*

*The land girls will be leaving at the end of the month and it will be quiet here without them.*

*We are travelling to the funeral in our Bentley, Tony will act as chauffeur. That means the four of us – the twins, obviously, don't want to come – won't have to endure the inconvenience of travelling on the train and the Underground. I love you and can't wait to see you again.*

*Be careful, take care of yourself,*

*All my love now and for ever, your wife,*

*Joanna*

He'd read the letter several times as he could almost hear her speaking to him through the words. There wasn't much point replying as they'd be seeing each other tomorrow. The funeral with full military honours would take place at the church where Harcourt's wife and baby were interred, a small village close to St Albans.

So far, he'd not been able to visit the Officers' Mess as by the time he returned from dispersal all he wanted to do was eat and sleep. How Browny found the energy to drink every night he didn't know.

On the Tuesday morning he should have been on his way his home but instead he was in his best blues heading for the funeral of a man he hadn't known and hadn't liked the sound of.

'Good morning, old boy,' Angus said with a smile. 'Congratulations on your latest hit. How many is that confirmed now?'

'Been so many I've lost count.' John made light of the question. This wasn't true but he was uncomfortable celebrating the death of anyone, even an enemy. 'Shall we get off?'

He feigned sleep to prevent his companion from talking to him and it worked rather too well as he actually dozed off. He was jerked awake when the WAAF driver suddenly stamped on the brakes, catapulting Angus and himself forwards.

He cracked his knees on the rear of the front passenger seat painfully. 'Bloody hell, that hurt.'

Angus was jammed behind the driver's seat but was unhurt. 'Bugger me, that was exciting. Are you okay, John?'

'I'm fine.' He leaned forward and tapped the girl behind the wheel on the shoulder. 'Are you all right?'

'I think so, sir. I think I've just killed a cat. It ran out and I couldn't stop.'

'Not your fault, we'll have a dekko. You stay where you are,' Angus said as he shouldered the door open.

John pushed open his door, dropped to his knees and peered under the car. Two baleful yellow eyes stared back. Then with a yowl the wretched animal launched itself at him, sending him backwards onto his arse in the road.

Angus hauled him up. 'That feline has only eight lives now. How the hell it wasn't killed we'll never know.'

The incident lightened the mood. They shared stories of their respective exploits and when they picked up Sarah in London, John was in a better frame of mind. He jumped out and hugged his stepdaughter.

'Good to see you. Not an ideal way to spend a rare day off.'

'This is a "compassionate" day so even going to a funeral is a bonus as now I can spend the time with Angus.'

'Fair enough. I'll sit in the front.' He was in the seat beside the driver before she could argue. He'd not really looked at the WAAF when he'd got in but now saw her face was almost grey, her gloved fingers clenched on the wheel. Surely the near demise of a cat hadn't upset her so badly?

Sarah was being thoroughly kissed by her husband and not yet in the car. He beckoned her over and gestured towards the girl, who hadn't looked around even with all the activity.

He nodded at Angus. 'There's something wrong with your driver. She's not fit to drive us anywhere.'

They watched as Sarah spoke to the girl, examined her for a few moments, and then slid out. 'She only started today, and this is her first job...'

'Good God, that shouldn't make any difference. They're well-trained and have to be able to drive any vehicle anywhere before they're passed fit for duty.'

Sarah glared at her husband. 'If you'd allowed me to finish, Squadron Leader Trent, then you'd know what's wrong.' Angus nodded his apology and Sarah continued. 'When she had to brake so suddenly she hit her head on the steering wheel. She's concussed. I'm amazed she got you here without crashing off the road.'

'Bloody hell. Can she be admitted to the Royal Free as we're outside right now?' John asked.

'Of course. If you two can get her out and carry her in it will be quicker than waiting for a stretcher.'

Half an hour later, the WAAF had been admitted and they were ready to continue their journey. 'I'll drive, I used to drive a fire tender so am perfectly competent.'

'Good, but do you know the route to the church?'

Angus had a good point. 'Hopefully you do and can navigate.'

'Not from the rear seat I can't.' He turned to Sarah. 'Sorry, darling, I'll have to sit in the front.'

'I've been on duty all night so will welcome the chance to sleep. Wake me when we get there.'

* * *

Joanna travelled in style in the back of the Bentley with the only remaining Lady Harcourt sitting next to her. She'd not ventured into the village so far herself but had made sure that word would spread via the twins and Jean.

'Elizabeth, what sort of reaction have you heard from your friends to my recent marriage?'

'Not what you would expect, my dear. All of them were obviously shocked by the reason you married so hastily but all said that in your position they would have done the same.'

'Of course they would have – nobody wants an illegitimate child if they can avoid it. Am I to be sent to Coventry, no longer invited to functions, and thrown out of the WI and WVS?'

Her mother-in-law laughed gaily. 'Good heavens, why would you think that? My son wasn't a popular figure in the community and nobody censures you for wanting to be happy.' The old lady reached out and patted her hand. 'Anyway, as you don't accept invitations or go anywhere apart from to the village hall then I don't see it makes any difference if you are removed from anybody's list.'

Joanna laughed too. 'You're right, I hated David's friends and didn't really know anyone else. I'm not so sure Mrs Thomas will be quite so kind.'

'You might be surprised, my dear, as since you have donated so much to several of her favourite causes, as well as making sure her daughter and son-in-law got two land girls to help on their market garden, you can do no wrong in her eyes.'

'Then I'll attend the next meetings and maybe not resign. I was definitely thinking of doing so as I've no intention of being in a position where I have to justify my decision.'

The car lapsed into friendly silence and she thought her companion was asleep but then Elizabeth spoke from the other corner of the car.

'Isn't life strange? Our family is now made up of six people, none of whom are related by blood, and yet we are close, don't you think? I was never fond of my son and definitely disliked my husband, which is why I left when I did. However, I think of you as my dearest daughter and love the twins as if they were my actual grandchildren.'

'They are – in fact they are now the only members of our family who share a name with you.'

'Jean and Tony are not even connected by marriage, but I would be bereft if either of them left. I fear that Miss Biggins will never fit in in with us in the same way that they do.'

'She's efficient, kind and does the job we employed her to do. The fact that she lives in doesn't make her a member of the family.'

The sliding glass panels that separated the passengers from the driver were closed so there was no danger Tony had been listening – not that it would matter if he had.

'I hope this is the last time I have to wear black and attend a funeral. I look like an emaciated crow but even in this dreary colour you look quite beautiful.'

'Thank you, Elizabeth, that was a kind thing to say. And I rather think that you're fishing for compliments as we both know you look a grand lady in your floaty black garments. The hat with a thick veil is a nice touch as it makes you look very mysterious.'

'I thought so too. You know that I like to make a lasting impression on anyone I meet for the first time. Do you think that the other Harcourt family, the one that tried to steal the title, will be present at the funeral?'

'I should think not. It's sad to think that there won't be another Lord Harcourt, that the title will vanish now.'

'The aristocracy have had things their own way for far too long,' Elizabeth said. 'Hopefully this second war will do something about that. I have found that mixing with ordinary people has broadened my appreciation of society. I never thought that one day I would have friends not from my background. I now make my decisions on acquaintances based on who they are, not where they come from.'

'As do I – I imagine David's spinning in his grave at the thought that his wife is now married to a man from the working classes and a socialist as well.'

'Your husband has a better education than most of the so-called upper classes, he's now an officer and a brave fighter pilot.'

'I'm so glad that you approve of him as I know he thinks highly of you.'

'Look, my dear, I think that is the cathedral on the left. This must be St Albans and we are nearing our destination.'

'Not before time as I'm desperate for the loo. I don't suppose there'll be one available at the church so I'd better get Tony to stop.' Joanna leaned forward and slid the glass open. 'We're in good time, so will you stop at the next place where I might be able to use the facilities and we can stretch our legs for a while.'

'Yes, I know this area. There's a decent hotel a mile from here.'

Fortunately, even with the stop for refreshments they arrived in good time. It wouldn't have been acceptable to arrive after the coffin. John, looking every inch an officer in his best uniform, was waiting with Sarah and Angus outside the church.

If Tony had been an actual chauffeur, both she and Elizabeth would have waited for him to come round and open the doors for them, but he wasn't, so Joanna was out of the car and almost running across the churchyard and into John's arms.

'I love you; I'm so pleased to see you.'

'Not as pleased as I am to see you, my darling. Let's hope this funeral doesn't take too long. Do we have to go to the wake, or can we slope off?'

'I haven't thought that far ahead, my love, can we wait and see how things go?'

She tilted her face and he kissed her – not the way they would both prefer as passion wasn't appropriate at a funeral.

Her daughter was waiting to embrace her. 'Mummy, we've spent more time together this month than we have in the past year.'

Joanna's reply was drowned out by a squadron of Hurricanes roaring overhead. The sirens didn't go off so hopefully the fighters were heading to the Channel for escort duty protecting a convoy of merchant ships, not to the air to drive off the Luftwaffe.

She'd forgotten about Elizabeth and smiled in relief when she saw the old lady approaching on Tony's arm. Without his peaked cap, he looked like any other civilian mourner.

'Shall we go in, my dear? I really don't want to be standing out here when the hearse arrives,' Elizabeth said.

The church was full. The majority of the men in the congregation were in khaki, but there was a sprinkling of civilians. As far as Joanna could see, Angus and John were the only RAF present.

A smart young officer asked Elizabeth for her name. 'Lady Elizabeth Harcourt,' she announced loudly and several heads turned. The young man jumped to attention and led them to the front of the church where they were ushered into the left-hand pew. A row of bemedaled, gold-braided, high-ranking army officers occupied the pew on the right.

There was appropriate music being played on the organ, but the hum of conversation almost drowned this out. Joanna blinked back unwanted tears. How sad that no one here thought enough of Peter Harcourt to sit quietly and mourn him. She was so glad that she'd decided to come. She bowed her head and was pleased her family did the same.

The organ music stopped and there was a stir around the church as everybody stood. The vicar walked ahead of the coffin reciting the appropriate words and six officers marched solemnly behind carrying the coffin on their shoulders. It was draped with the Union flag.

The last funeral she'd attended had been for her dear friend Betty when there'd been no eulogy, no hymns and no sermon, but this was different. Four officers stepped up and praised the deceased and she learnt more about Peter – the man she'd initially enjoyed the company of but ended up disliking – in that brief time then she had in the year that she'd known him.

He might not have had any family, but he was respected and well-liked by his peers. Such a dreadful shame to have died from a disease and not in combat when still in his forties. They followed the coffin around to the churchyard where an open grave stood waiting to receive the remains.

A six-gun salute was fired and then it was over. She'd not decided if she would attend the wake – in fact, didn't even know where it was being held – when Elizabeth touched her arm.

'Very sad, a handsome young man, he had so much more to live for. I'd like to go home now if you don't mind.'

'Then that's what we'll do. I'll just say goodbye to Sarah and Angus.'

'Tony can take me to the car. Perhaps we could stop at the same hotel for some luncheon?'

'That's an excellent idea, Elizabeth. We could all do with cheering up after this.'

Joanna embraced her daughter and son-in-law and then walked to the car with her husband's arm around her waist.

'Good gracious, Elizabeth's sitting in the front with Tony. I wondered why she was in such a hurry to return to the car.'

John laughed. 'She knows we want to spend every minute we can together and is allowing us to do that. I think she'll prefer talking to Tony rather than listening to us.'

'It's strange that she's no longer my mother-in-law, has no actual connection to me at all now...'

'Of course she has, darling, she's your children's grandmother, that doesn't change.'

# 6

John settled into the corner of the rear seat and Joanna snuggled up against him. Even dressed in black she was stunning. He ran his palm over her burgeoning bump.

'This has grown since I saw you last week. Is the baby moving now?'

'I'm not quite sure but I think so. I've felt a faint fluttering at night but I'm not aware of it during the day.'

'Pregnancy suits you. You've always been beautiful but now there's a glow to your skin that's quite remarkable.'

'I do feel wonderful but I think that's more because I'm married to you. I spoke to the doctor about the possibility that we might have another baby despite my advancing years.'

'Bloody hell – I hadn't thought of that. I never expected to be a father to even one.'

'Dr Willoughby said he'd known of mothers in their forties who'd had successful pregnancies. He also said that he wouldn't recommend having another one immediately as it takes longer for someone my age to fully recover.'

'Do you want more children with me?'

She laughed. 'I certainly don't want any with someone else. The only reason I ask is that I know Sarah was lonely being an only child and it would be good for this baby to have a sibling closer to them in age than nineteen years.'

John closed his eyes, loving the weight of her against his chest, inhaling her exotic perfume, and for a few blissful moments he was able to forget about the war, that it was perfectly possible he wouldn't be alive when this baby came so the prospect of any more children seemed pretty damned remote.

Unlike other women he'd been involved with, Joanna didn't demand that he reply but accepted sometimes he needed to be quiet. She pulled his hands closer around her waist and with a small sigh relaxed and closed her eyes.

'Don't go to sleep, sweetheart, we'll be stopping for lunch shortly. Save your rest for the long haul to Kent.'

'I'm not asleep, I'm resting my eyes, as Elizabeth would say. I found the funeral rather sad and awkward but I'm glad that we went.'

'I hope I have more friends and family at my funeral...'

'Don't say things like that, I can't bear it.'

'I'm sorry, that was clumsy of me,' John said. 'My squadron has three more weeks after this short R and R then we'll be posted inland for a month.'

Both her feet were now on the floor and he straightened also. 'I thought that after you'd flown a certain number of sorties you were moved somewhere safe, a desk job or something like that.'

'That might have been the case, but it certainly isn't now. Experienced fighters like me are in short supply. If the Luftwaffe stopped coming in such numbers then I might get posted to train the new bods.'

'You don't have to tell me that would mean being somewhere we couldn't see each other, but I'd rather not see you at all and know you're safe than have you risking your life several times a day as you do now.'

He changed the subject. 'I wrote to my parents and there should be a reply when I go back on duty the day after tomorrow. I'll let you know what they say.'

Joanna had discarded her hat and it had slipped to the floor. Casually he put his foot on it and it collapsed beneath the weight.

'Oh, sod it, I've just crushed your hat.'

Her delightful laughter filled the rear of the car. 'Thank you for doing that, my love, now I don't have to put it on again.' She looked around at him. 'I suspect its demise was deliberate, but I forgive you.'

The car slowed and Tony wound down his window and stuck his arm out to indicate he was turning right into the forecourt of the hotel. The car had indicators, little illuminated arms, but they were unreliable, so hand signals were safer.

'I didn't want the loo until I knew we were stopping, now my need's desperate.' Her smile, as always, made him want to kiss her. 'This is the only thing I'm not enjoying about my pregnancy.'

There were no other cars outside the imposing entrance – John thought the shortage of fuel accounted for this. When the stash of stored petrol cans behind one of the barns at Goodwill House ran out there wouldn't be any more. He wouldn't be able to refuel his motorbike on the base which would mean having to use public transport to come home. Only essential vehicles would have access to it, which was only right.

He kicked the ruined hat to one side, leaned over and opened the rear door. Joanna, graceful and elegant as always, slid out. It didn't matter if she wasn't Lady Harcourt, anyone seeing her would know at once that she was a member of the upper classes.

Thinking about the differences in their beliefs and upbringing wasn't helpful and must wait until the end of the war. With any luck, things would have changed in post-war Britain and it would be run by the working people, not the chinless wonders born with a silver spoon in their mouths.

'I'm going ahead, John, could you please make sure Elizabeth comes in safely and that Tony knows he's part of our group, not actually our chauffeur?'

His assistance was unnecessary as Lady Harcourt was already on Tony's arm and marching briskly towards the entrance. As the man of the house, so to speak, it should really be him that went in first and organised the table for lunch. He'd no intention of offending the old lady so left her to it.

John found the men's room and when he returned to the foyer only

Joanna was there waiting for him and they joined the others in the dining room.

The food was well cooked, plentiful but dull. They cleared their plates and made no complaints. There was no coffee – hardly surprising – so they settled for a pot of tea between them. An hour after arriving, they were on their way.

Joanna had kicked off her shoes and put her feet on the seat as soon as they'd got into the car. Lady Harcourt insisted she was very comfortable in the front passenger position so for a second time they had the spacious rear of the limousine to themselves.

Like most flyers, John had learned to sleep whenever he got the opportunity and after stretching out his legs, he relaxed into the corner, hoping that he wasn't woken up so abruptly as he had been on the way there.

* * *

The Bentley arrived home late in the afternoon and John whispered to Joanna as the car was rolling to a standstill at the rear of the house. It would be driven into the barn where it lived as soon as everybody was out.

'Pretend to be asleep, then I can carry you upstairs without anyone commenting.' She didn't answer with words but squeezed his hand. Joe was waiting to open the door.

'Thanks, I'll take her up. Good to see you, Joe. We'll talk tomorrow.'

'I'll get Jean to leave something in the pantry for you both later. Ma was so pleased that she was going to spend a couple of days with you.'

John nodded, ducked his head, and shuffled sideways, emerging safely into the sunlight with his precious burden in his arms.

A few hours later, more or less dressed, they wandered downstairs long after everybody else had retired. Jean had as promised left them a cold collation in the pantry.

'It's a perfect summer's evening, my love, shall we eat this on the terrace? Jean has found a bottle of decent claret to go with our supper. It's already open which makes things simpler.'

'I prefer a beer.'

'Tony buys a crate of light ale from the local hostelry when they have any to spare. There might well be few in the pantry somewhere.'

He found the bottles easily enough and had no qualms about taking one. Tony would understand. John insisted on carrying the laden tray and she brought the bottle of wine and the beer. No need to worry about the blackout as they'd not put any lights on in the grand hall.

He put the tray on the enormous walnut bureau whilst he unbolted the front door. It was still impossible to go out through the drawing room as the glass hadn't been replaced and everywhere was boarded up.

'It's a bomber's moon tonight, sweetheart, let's hope we get to eat this before we have to make a dash for the summerhouse.'

'Let's pre-empt the air-raid siren and go to the summerhouse now,' she suggested.

'Will everybody else go down there or do they go into the shelter in the basement?'

'The basement – Elizabeth can't manage the walk safely in the dark. Mind you, it's almost as light as day tonight. I know exactly what you mean by a bomber's moon.'

There were rugs, tables, chairs, and cushions stored at the back of the small wooden building. Together they set out what they needed inside which would mean if there was a raid they wouldn't have to move.

'I've just thought, someone will bang on our door expecting us to go down with them.'

'They won't because I left it open just in case. Anyone will be able to see that our room's unoccupied. I'm sure they'll realise where we are, and nobody will be worried.'

* * *

Joanna was just eating the last delicious mouthful of strawberries picked from the kitchen garden when the siren at Manston began its hideous wail. Moments later, the one in the village joined in.

Then the scream of two squadrons of Hurricanes taking off drowned out the noise and made conversation impossible. 'It must be a bad one.

The search lights are already scouring the sky over Dover, and you can hear the ack-ack guns firing.'

John wasn't listening. He was standing out in the open watching the trails of fire streak across the sky behind the fighters. Even in the moonlight they couldn't be seen if there were any lurking fighter bombers heading in underneath the radar.

After the Manston fighters had gone, she saw dozens more from other bases, probably including Hornchurch. It took hours by car to cover the distance but only minutes in a plane. She joined him in front of the summerhouse.

'I'm so glad you aren't up there tonight but safe here with me.'

He looked down and she didn't recognise him as the man she loved, the man she'd just married. He was a stranger.

'For God's sake, Joanna. There's a war on, I should be up there doing my bit, not here avoiding the battle.'

His tone was harsh. She should have kept quiet but ignored the warning signs and continued. 'It's not up to you to win this war on your own, John. You've already done more than most. Be happy...'

'Happy? How can I be happy when I should be protecting you and our baby? We could lose this war. Only the RAF are keeping the Nazis from winning. Do you want to hear jackboots marching though London?'

Her instinct was to retreat, to be upset at his anger, but she understood why he'd spoken so fiercely. 'I'm sorry, my love. It's hard for me too. Go back to your base in the morning if that's what you need to do.'

'Sodding hell. I'm talking bollocks...'

'John! Please don't use language like that.'

He laughed, an unexpected reaction. 'I apologise, my darling. Every time I scramble I do it for you and the baby. The other blokes are the same. This war's personal to us. We couldn't do what we do without being emotionally involved.'

He pulled her almost roughly into his arms and they kissed; she forgot about the war and just lived for that moment. She knew there might not be many more of them.

The search lights were criss-crossing the sky, the big guns being fired by the army on the coast were clearly audible. The bombers must be close. The lights and guns didn't fire until the Luftwaffe were within range.

'Can you hear the Germans, John?'

He tilted his head, stared into the distance and nodded. 'They're heading for London but will be flying overhead in a minute. We're safe here, sweetheart, they'll not be looking for individual targets.'

'Safe unless one of them gets shot down as happened last year. If it hadn't, we'd never have met.'

'Never thought I'd be grateful to a Jerry. Let's get inside.'

'The house?'

'No, we'll stay out here until the all-clear sounds.'

She stood on tiptoes and said softly into his ear, '*Al fresco* is something we've not tried so far.'

He snatched her from her feet and they were inside the summerhouse seconds later. They didn't hear the all-clear and didn't return to the house until dawn.

* * *

The next morning, the three girls who worked on the dairy farm were just finishing their breakfast when Joanna greeted them politely but didn't initiate a conversation. The land girls would be leaving soon and moving into the newly converted hostel a couple of miles away.

There was a slight awkwardness when she was in the room as apart from Sal and the two girls she was sharing with, nobody else had cleared the debt they'd run up last winter. They'd not been able to work during the freezing cold and hadn't been paid by the farmers, but she'd continued as their landlady and they'd lived without paying for their board and lodging for several weeks.

John was waiting on the terrace and was engaged in a meaningful conversation with the dog when she came out carrying their breakfast on a tray. Lazzy was sitting in front of him, sweeping the ground with his long tail, staring intently at John and almost seemed to be nodding whilst he was being spoken to.

'What are the two of you talking about so earnestly, my love?'

Lazzy bounced to his feet and almost sent the tray flying with his enthusiastic welcome. John's smile made her warm all over.

'I was just explaining to him where we've been all night...'

'As long as you didn't tell him what we'd been doing – he's only a young dog and would be horribly shocked.'

'We're still improperly dressed, darling, I bet that raised a few eyebrows in the kitchen.'

'It's my house and I can do what I like in it,' Joanna said. 'I've enjoyed having the girls living here but things are different now. I don't want to share with anyone but you and the other members of my family.'

'I wish I'd come on my motorbike, then I could stay longer. It's going to be a bugger getting back and I've got to leave on the last train this evening as I'm sure I won't be back in time otherwise.'

'As long as you're not going now. You've not seen The Manse and as it's such a lovely day I thought we could cycle there. The builders have started to clear out what I don't want but haven't started to put in what I do. There's still time for you to have some input...'

'Don't forget I come from a two up, two down terraced cottage – I know nothing about grand houses and am quite happy to leave it to you. That said, I would like to see where we're going to be living when this bloody war's over.'

She shook her head in mock reproach. 'Your language has deteriorated since we married, Flying Officer Sergeant, and as an officer I would have thought it would have improved.'

'I'm a rough working man, my darling, and I'm not going to change.'

She didn't rise to the bait. 'You already have and so have I and that's a good thing. I think we'd better go up and get ourselves sorted out before Elizabeth comes down. I find it a bit disconcerting she's taking such an avid interest in our love life.'

'She's a game old bird – she even made me blush with some of her stories of her antics in the south of France when she was younger.'

Joanna laughed. 'I must admit I was shocked when she told me she'd had several lovers. She also said it had been much easier for her to behave disgracefully as nobody knew who she was.'

John snorted. 'That's not true. Can you imagine her living anywhere without making sure everybody called her Lady Harcourt?'

'I hadn't considered that. If she was publicly galivanting all over the continent misbehaving, then small wonder David never mentioned her name.'

'I'll leave the tray here and take it through to the kitchen later. Shall we go upstairs and get properly dressed?' His smile was wicked and she blushed.

Laughing, they returned to the house and fortunately made the sanctuary of their own bedroom without bumping into anybody. An hour or so later, she was lying naked in his arms, loving every moment of this intimacy. 'I didn't think to ask Dr Willoughby if it's harmful to the baby to make love so often.' He didn't answer immediately and she glanced up to see a glitter in his eyes.

'God knows how long it might be before I see you again, certainly weeks, but it might be months. Even I know that it wouldn't be good for you or the baby to make love when you're in your final months.'

'I don't care how long it is as long as I do see you again. Now, I refuse to be maudlin on such a lovely day. I'm getting up – don't argue or look at me like that – I'm taking a quick bath and no, you're not joining me.'

'Leave the water in, we can share,' he called out as she left the room in her peignoir a few minutes later. She deliberately took her underwear with her as she didn't trust either herself or John not to tumble back into bed.

As always, she locked the door as she didn't want one of the family to burst in on her. As she relaxed in the few inches of water they were allowed, she was astonished at how much the baby had grown in the last few days. She put her hands over her distended belly and for the first time was certain she felt movement beneath her fingers.

She scrambled out of the bath, pulled on her robe and without stopping to put on her underwear raced back to the bedroom.

'John, quickly, I think you'll be able to feel the baby moving.' She flung herself onto the bed, exposing her belly. He'd been lounging against the pillows with his eyes shut but was instantly alert. He put his hand on the mound and the baby kicked again.

'My God, that was quite amazing. I definitely felt something. What's it like for you?'

'Astonishing and wonderful. I don't care if it's one baby or two. I just know this pregnancy is going to be successful and sometime in December you're going to become a father for the first time.'

# 7

John took a deep breath and with remarkable restraint, he thought, kissed her gently on the lips and then rolled out of bed and headed for the bathroom. Joanna squealed and he froze, for a second terrified there was something wrong.

'You can't go out like that. What are you thinking? Imagine their shock if Liza, Elizabeth, or even worse Miss Biggins, saw you completely unclothed.'

'Sorry, it's all blokes on the base – at least in the ablutions blocks – nobody bothers about nudity. Seems a waste of time to put on clothes only to take them off again minutes later.'

'There's a dressing gown in my closet Jean made especially for you. I should have told you it was there.'

He pulled open the door of the walk-in wardrobe and smiled to himself. He thought it was almost the same size as the bedroom he'd had at home. He paused for a moment, inhaling the delicious aroma of her clothes. Then with some reluctance he snatched up the garment and shrugged into it.

'This is all right, far better than I'd expected. I must thank Jean for her expertise. Is it silk? Where on earth did you get this?' He ran his fingers down the sleeve in appreciation and looked at her.

'We found several trunks of material in the Victorian wing that must've been there since one of David's ancestors returned from a visit to India. The trunks were lined with copper which kept out the moths and the damp. There's sufficient cotton and silk to keep us well clothed until the end of this wretched war.'

'Then our baby will have a layette second to none. Are you knitting matinee jackets?'

She smiled and shook her head. 'Sadly, that's not one of my skills. I can knit a scarf, maybe even a balaclava, but intricate patterns are beyond me. I still have Sarah's baby clothes and no doubt will be given other items when the baby arrives. Now go away and get yourself clean.'

John met Liza in the corridor and was grateful for the dressing gown. 'Good morning, did you stay in the cellar all night?'

'No, Grandma refused to remain there for more than two hours. It's really crowded with all the land girls as well crammed into such a small space. We went back to bed when Grandma did.'

The girl hurried off and he wondered why she was in such a rush and then remembered that she worked at the vicarage as a nanny to three small children.

He'd no intention of wasting a second he didn't have to on his ablutions and was washed, dried and in his underwear in minutes. Another useful skill he'd picked up since he'd been in the RAF.

The £40 available to purchase his uniform had been more than enough to get him everything he needed and some of the £20 left over had gone towards a smart suitcase. He'd bought it all second-hand. Wearing a dead man's clothes didn't bother him but it might be better not to tell Joanna. The cloth was superior to that of an NCO and the cut better. The greatcoat, which he wouldn't need for months, had a belt whereas his previous one hadn't. Everything about being an officer was an improvement on being a senior NCO.

Like all flyers, he'd been issued with goggles, helmet, Mae West, boots and an Irvin suit but he only wore the sheepskin jacket of that as the trousers were too bulky in the small cockpit of a Spit. He reckoned the bomber boys would be glad to have the whole thing as it was bloody cold flying in a Wellington.

When he returned to their bedroom, Joanna was dressed, looking radiant and beautiful as always, and for some reason her bump looked even bigger today. Perhaps this was because he or she was now more mobile.

'You're so lovely, darling, I can't understand how an ordinary bloke like me is married to someone like you.'

'Because I'm carrying your baby and we had no choice.'

'Are you saying we wouldn't have married otherwise?' He couldn't keep the hurt from his voice.

She came over and put her arms around his neck, immediately sensing his upset. 'If you'd asked me that six months ago, my love, I'd have said that was the case, but not now. We belong together and I'm the lucky one. I'm married to an intelligent, kind, handsome officer who's also a lot younger than me.'

'And I'm married to the most beautiful woman in Kent, and probably the wealthiest too.'

'Then we're both more than satisfied with how things are. There's something I don't know about you. What do you want to do when the war's over?'

'Not fly, that's certain. I have a good maths degree so would like to do something useful with that.'

She knew him well enough to realise he wouldn't be content sitting around twiddling his thumbs.

'Good, I thought maybe you could take over running the estate. We have a factor, accountants and so on, but after what happened I'd rather someone I trusted was in charge.'

'It seems odd your husband wasn't aware he was being comprehensively swindled by the accountant and the bank. Your offer sounds interesting. I would consider it if I had carte blanche to change things, modernise and so on.'

'I know very little about agriculture and not much about finance, therefore, I'm quite happy to hand the management of the estate over to you. We have six farms, all occupied by excellent tenants, and a substantial amount invested in war bonds and other things.'

He wanted to point out that the use of the word *we* was incorrect as everything belonging to the Harcourt family was hers alone.

'Are you happy with your present estate manager, accountant and banker?'

'I don't know how efficient they are, but I do know that they're honest, unlike the previous regime. I'm hoping that if you get more than two days' leave you could meet with them yourself.'

'Aircrew are supposed to have sixty-one days a year but that isn't happening nowadays. When things calm down a bit I ought to be allowed a block of seven or fourteen days but I'm not holding my breath.'

'What about the short passes that you get? Do these count towards your allocation?'

'I'm certain that they do but as I've only had about two weeks so far this year and it's already almost the end of July, I've got plenty of days owing. I've already told them I'm taking two weeks when the baby comes.'

Joanna raised her eyebrows, making him laugh. 'You told them? I doubt that went down very well with the Group Captain in charge of fighters at Hornchurch.'

'I'd better rephrase that – what I actually did was put in a written request but so far have had no response.'

'That sounds more accurate, my love. Shall we go down? I know we had toast and tea earlier but I seem to be permanently hungry at the moment.'

The house was quiet as the land girls had left for work and only Joe, Tony and Jean were in the kitchen. Lady Harcourt had her breakfast taken up to her on a tray by her maid.

'I'll make you both some scrambled eggs, tea and toast. Do you want to eat in here or in the breakfast parlour? The girls have gone, and Doris is here this morning. She'll already have cleared the room.'

'Then that's where we'll go. Joe, can John borrow your bicycle this morning?'

Her son nodded, his mouth too full of toast to answer politely. He swallowed noisily and then grinned. 'Course you can, you're one of the family now.'

Tony looked up from reading the paper. 'Why don't you use my motorbike?' He saw Joanna's look of horror and chuckled. 'It's got a sidecar; you won't have to sit on the pillion. Mum loves it and we do all the shopping in it.'

'What do you think, John? Is it safe?'

He nodded. 'It's the safest form of transport on the roads. After breakfast, shall we have a look and if you don't feel comfortable travelling in it then we'll cycle?'

'I don't think you should be cycling in your condition, Joanna, what if you fell off?' Jean said firmly.

'It's too far to walk and I'm certainly not using the Bentley for such a trivial reason so, Tony, it's either your motorbike and sidecar or not going at all.'

* * *

Whilst Joanna put on the obligatory hat, John remained in the kitchen.

'I'll take you to the station later, John, that means you can stay a bit longer with Joanna.'

'Thank you, Tony, I appreciate the offer. I'm sure Joanna will too.'

John enjoyed the excursion to what would be his home one day and after having the full tour of the house, the grounds and the outbuildings, Joanna looked at him enquiringly.

'What do you think? Is it somewhere you think you'll be happy?'

Ignoring the two builders who were bringing wheelbarrows of debris out of the front door, he gathered her close. 'I'd be happy anywhere at all as long as I've got you with me. But, contrary to my expectations, I think this place will be perfect. It's a substantial property but not too grand. Six bedrooms is perfect.'

She gestured at the pretty dower house a hundred yards away from the main building. 'That's where Jean and Tony will be living.' She turned and pointed to the French doors that opened, as those at Goodwill House did, onto a raised terrace. 'Elizabeth will have her own apartment with all the necessary facilities as well as accommodation for Miss Biggins at that end of the house. That means when she's less able to get about she can come out onto the terrace and enjoy the fresh air.'

'You've thought of everything. I can't believe I'm going to be living here with my family for the rest of my life.'

Joanna relaxed into John's arms and he hugged her before they wandered back to the strange vehicle that he'd borrowed from Tony.

'I didn't know Tony had this contraption. I'm losing my grip on the household. It has to be because I'm pregnant.'

'I think your family are overprotective. They don't want you to be burdened with trivial things and Tony acquiring this bike's one of them.'

She scrambled into the sidecar, shaking her head when he offered his assistance. 'I can manage, thank you. What time do you have to leave?'

'Tony's giving me a lift in this. The last train I can catch and still get to Hornchurch tonight is at six. I can get the Underground to Liverpool Street and the last train from there is at ten-thirty.' He squeezed her shoulder as he straddled the bike and kicked it into life. 'I have to be on duty at dawn, sweetheart, or believe me I'd stay longer.'

She didn't complain, there was no point and it wouldn't be fair on him. He was the one risking his life for his country; all she had to do was stay safe in her luxurious home and carry his baby to term.

'Don't worry about telephoning or writing when you come off duty. It's more important that you get some sleep.'

'Please continue to write to me, darling, your letters are what keep me sane.'

'I'll do so every other day. Did you know that Tony's a keen amateur photographer and is going to take photos of me and the family and then develop them himself?'

'That man's a revelation. What can't he do?'

The bike roared into life. She rather enjoyed travelling in this sidecar, whereas she'd hated being on the pillion. On the return journey, she thought about John's last remark. Tony was indeed a talented young man. Not surprising really, having Jean for his mother.

Despite the fact that her hat had been pinned on securely, it worked its way free and flew from her head halfway home. She reached up and poked his thigh. He glanced round and grinned, seeing at once that her headgear had vanished. He coasted to a stop and stood up.

'Stay where you are, sweetheart, I can see it lodged in the hedge. It'll be quicker to fetch it on foot than turn around twice.'

'If you don't mind fetching it for me, it is one of my favourites.'

He left the engine ticking over, swung his leg over the pillion and took off like a sprinter. It was impossible to turn her body in the confined space of the sidecar but she managed to swivel her shoulders and saw him remove the hat from the hedge. She wasn't entirely comfortable having the engine running, thinking that it might move off under its own volition.

Then he was back. 'Here you are, it seems to be intact. I should have told you not to bother. Next time wear my spare helmet and goggles.'

'I'll do that as the Perspex windshield only protects my face. Oh dear, I think I can hear a bus approaching behind us. I doubt it can get past safely.'

'It won't have to, we'll be turned into the drive long before it catches us up.'

He was right and they were safely out of the way before she heard it rumble past. They were slowly coasting down the drive when something moving in the trees on the left-hand side of the drive caught her attention. There was no time to warn John as Lazzy burst through the undergrowth and launched himself at the sidecar.

John didn't swerve, which was what she would have done, but slammed on the brakes, pitching her forwards. Her knees cracked painfully on the curved metal in front of her. She'd had a split-second to brace herself so her head didn't smash against the windshield.

The enormous dog was half in the contraption with her. 'Lazzy, are you all right? Silly animal, what were you thinking?'

Her head was spinning, her knees were bleeding, but all she was worried about was whether her precious dog had been injured. John was beside them and he leaned in and carefully lifted the dog.

'There you are, stupid mutt, you could have killed all of us.' He was fussing Lazzy and she could see the dog's tail was wagging furiously. 'He's absolutely fine, darling, just his rear paws have been scraped.'

'Thank God – it could have been so much worse than it was.'

Only then did John notice that she was injured. His face paled as he looked down at her frock. It was liberally stained with blood and she guessed what he feared.

'No, it's not the baby. It's my knees. Can you drive us the rest of the way? Lazzy can sit on my lap as he obviously can't walk.'

'He bloody can. He's a dog. He'll be fine.' The bike hadn't even stalled and seconds later they were on their way and he parked directly outside the boot room door – the one everyone used to go in and out as it faced the barns where the bicycles and other things were stored.

Joanna twisted round to see if the dog was following but he was lying on the drive, his head between his front paws, looking miserable and abandoned. As soon as they were stationary, she was out of the sidecar and punched John on the shoulder.

'Now go back and get my dog. That's an order, Flying Officer Sergeant.' She'd deliberately phrased her command in a semi-humorous way, knowing he'd be less likely to refuse than if she'd really yelled at him.

He ignored her and with slow deliberation switched off the engine, clambered off and stood facing her. 'He's a dog. Humans first. Up you come, Mrs Sergeant.'

She was picked up and he strolled into the house as if he was carrying a bag of feathers and not a large pregnant woman. There were gasps of horror as she arrived in this undignified way from Jean, Joe and Tony.

'I'm perfectly well, just my knees are cut. However, Lazzy can't walk as he damaged his paws trying to jump into the sidecar just now.'

'We'll fetch him, Ma,' Joe said and by the time her annoying husband had put her down on the nearest chair, Joe and Tony had gone.

Jean fetched the first-aid tin and John was on his knees examining the injuries. He still had on his flying helmet and the goggles were pushed back so the lenses were staring up at her. Her irritation changed to overwhelming love for this wonderful man who put her first and loved her unconditionally. She rested one hand on top of his head.

'Thank you, darling, for taking care of me.'

He glanced up and his eyes blazed. 'If anything happened to you, I'd not want to carry on,' he whispered, echoing her own words to him a few weeks ago.

Jean coughed, letting them know she was there. 'Shall I deal with the knees, John, or will you?'

He held out his hand and she placed the tin on it. 'I'll do it, thanks. I need warm boiled water and a clean cloth. I'm pretty sure the bloody dog will need more attention than you do, darling.'

'You love him really – if you don't then it'll be a very short marriage.'

Ignoring Jean, he rose smoothly to his feet, leaned forward, placing one hand on each side of her head resting them on the back of the chair, and then kissed her thoroughly.

She was breathless when he raised his head. 'I'll see to your knees first.' Her breath caught in her throat. He was making it quite clear from his wicked smile what he intended to see to afterwards.

He was gentle as he bathed the scrapes and when the blood was gone there were two quite deep gashes, one on each knee.

'Jean, could you see if you can get hold of the doctor? Joanna is going to need a couple of stitches in each of these.'

'I'm on my way, John. If the dog's badly hurt them perhaps Dr Willoughby can sew him up too.'

'Do I really need stitches?'

'Sorry, you do. The bleeding has only stopped because I'm applying pressure to each knee. I also want him to give the baby a once-over just to be sure.'

'I'm sure he or she is fine, darling.' She sounded confident but like him she was a little concerned. One couldn't be too careful when as old as she was.

Two hours later, her knees were painful but no longer bleeding. Lazzy's paws had been bandaged but he'd needed no actual veterinary attention. The dog was now stretched out under the kitchen table feeling sorry for himself and he wasn't the only one.

'What a kerfuffle and it's quite ruined our afternoon. At least you can leave knowing the baby and I are perfectly fine.'

They were in the small sitting room where she could put her feet up on the chaise longue. Her legs were more comfortable that way. She pushed back the cuff of his blue shirt and stared in dismay at the face of his very smart RAF-issue Movado wristwatch.

Her eyes filled – he'd have to leave in an hour and they both understood that there was always the chance that they might never see each other again.

# 8

John just had time for a couple of hours' kip before he had to report for duty. It was too hot for his Irvin jacket so like others in his squadron he'd taken to wearing a Prestige navy-blue cotton overall suit, again purchased when the belongings of a deceased flyer were auctioned and the proceeds sent to his widow or family.

These overalls were made privately, not RAF issue, and consequently no RAF badges of rank or anything else were allowed to be attached. At least the Air Ministry hadn't been silly enough to ban the wearing of them altogether.

He always wore his knee-high flying boots, however hot the weather – poor old Tommy had insisted on flying in his Oxfords and when his kite had caught fire his ankles had been horribly burned. Better to have hot feet than burnt legs.

He wolfed down a substantial breakfast followed by two mugs of tea. The food for officers was no better or worse than that he'd eaten in the NCOs' Mess. So far he'd not dined in the mess as by the time he was off duty it was too late. The NAAFI remained open until after midnight so he went there most nights. Replete and ready for action, he headed for the lorry that was waiting to take them to dispersal.

He was A-Flight leader but today the squadron was taking the fight to the enemy – not lounging about at readiness waiting to be scrambled. They were to fly a sweep across France called a Rhubarb. This meant pairs of Spits would fly over the Channel at roof height and then attack anything military that they saw.

These Rhubarbs only took place when there was low cloud as it was believed the kites would be concealed by the clouds and be able to attack a German airfield without being seen. This made no sense to him as everybody knew how well defended a German base was. There'd been a horrendous loss of life for very little gain and all the flyers prayed these excursions would be abandoned.

To John's relief, this morning's operation was cancelled just before the first pair were about to take off as the clouds had cleared to show a bright sunny day. His flight was sent on a routine patrol down the coast instead, but they saw no bandits and returned unscathed. The low clouds returned and he was worried they would be sent to France to complete the operation that had been abandoned that morning.

He was called into the dispersal hut to sign a couple of papers relating to his recent promotion. There were a dozen bods in there sitting at the battered wooden tables playing cards, chatting or reading. He wandered over to join the group nearest the door as they were members of his flight.

'Skip told me we're being posted to Catterick for a couple of months when we finish this rotation but he's not sure exactly when we'll be going,' he told them.

'About bloody time – I've flown over a hundred sorties without a break. What about you, John?'

'Double that, but I've no real idea. I'd have to check my logbooks to be sure.'

Suddenly there was the ominous snarl of an approaching bomber. No sirens had gone off, the bell hadn't rung. Why the hell hadn't they been scrambled? The kites and his men were sitting ducks. There were no underground shelters within reach but there were slit-trenches behind the dispersal huts they could dive into.

He was on his feet, as were the other blokes, when the telephone rang. By then they were heading for the door. The hut vibrated.

'Get down, under the tables, too late to get out.'

He threw himself flat. Everything on the tables shot onto the floor. Glass flew in every direction. The bastards were dropping bombs on them! Now the sirens went off – too bloody late. He hoped his precious Spit wasn't smashed to bits.

The chairs and tables overturned on top of him and through the clouds of dust and broken furniture he could see the legs and arms of his fellow flyers poking out. Despite the racket, he heard a squadron taking off and hoped they would destroy the Nazi bomber before it could do any further damage.

Then the remaining walls of the dispersal hut disintegrated as a shock wave from another stick of bombs finished it off.

For a second he was deafened, unable to hear anything. Then his ears cleared, his head stopped spinning and he was able to take stock of his injuries and the damage done to any of his fellow flyers.

He sat up, shaking his head like a dog coming out of the sea, and looked around. 'Anybody hurt? Anyone need a medic?' His voice sounded odd, hoarse, and deeper than usual. Must be the quantity of dust he'd swallowed.

Slowly the others emerged from the broken furniture, smashed windows, the other detritus from the tables and thank God nobody was seriously damaged. A few cuts and bruises were inevitable but when they all staggered away from the wreck of the dispersal hut, they were pretty much as good as new.

'Bloody hell – that was a close one. Someone needs a rocket up their arse for the lack of warning,' someone said loudly, and the others agreed.

'More importantly, by some miracle, none of the kites are damaged and there are just a couple of holes in the runway.' John shook off the worst of the splinters as he didn't want to use his hands; he was pretty sure there was glass embedded in his overalls. He had something lodged in his neck as well, but that could wait.

The ambulance screamed to a halt beside them, and two nurses and the medic piled out, anxious to see if their able assistance was in fact required.

'All tickety-boo here, thanks, Doc, one or two of the blokes might need a plaster. I'm going to check on the ground crew.'

'You're not going anywhere, young man, until I've removed the piece of wood from the back of your neck. Surely you can feel it?'

'I knew there was something sticking in me, but I thought it was trivial.'

John refused to go back to the medical centre and insisted the object was removed where he was. One squadron was still airborne, the other two were grounded. As the kites were dispersed around the edge of the airfield for just this sort of eventuality, he and his bods had got the worst of it. They were all bloody lucky to be alive and more importantly that none of the kites had been hit. As far as he could see they were okay but without closer inspection and a talk with the ground crew he couldn't be certain.

'Here's a chair, young man, sit on it. That's an order,' the doctor, who held the rank of squadron leader, said firmly.

John's legs were feeling a bit wobbly so he was only too happy to obey. 'Will I need sutures?'

'I've no idea until I examine you more closely. You really should come back to the hospital where I have the proper instruments and sterile surroundings.'

The medic used his scissors to cut away the collar of John's overalls and even the slightest tug on the material sent shafts of pain radiating up his neck and down his spine.

There was an ominous silence then the doctor whistled through his teeth. That didn't sound good. It wasn't.

'I'm going to pack gauze around the wood and tape it in place and then, very carefully, you're going to walk over to the ambulance and get in. Don't move your head and for God's sake don't fall over. It could be fatal.'

This time he didn't argue. The adrenaline coursing through his veins must have made him unaware, until now, of the severity of his injury. Cautiously, and with the doctor holding firmly to his elbow, he regained his feet and was escorted to the open doors of the ambulance.

'Carefully up the step, my boy, don't jiggle it whatever you do.'

John didn't bother to reply and was about to do as instructed. If he sat on the bench – obviously he couldn't sit back – he'd have to remain perilously perched on the edge of the slippery seat.

'That won't do. You'll be better off in the passenger seat. You'll be able to brace yourself sitting there.'

The nurses were abandoned to their ministrations, as were the stretcher bearers. To John's astonishment, the doctor jumped into the front seat, released the brake and set off smoothly. He'd obviously done this before.

John's heart was thudding, swallowing was difficult, and he wasn't sure if this was because of the dagger of wood in his neck or sheer terror. Flying a Spit was a piece of cake, even though you could die at any moment, compared to the short journey across the base to the hospital.

* * *

Joanna slept fitfully as the baby seemed to be turning cartwheels inside her. It seemed extraordinary to her that a week ago she hadn't felt any movement and now this was happening. Slowly she completed her morning toilette and thought of her beloved John. What was he doing right now? It was a misty morning, low cloud rolling in from the sea and this could mean there wouldn't be any aerial activity today.

The sun might be hidden but the temperature was unpleasantly hot and the thought of doing anything energetic didn't appeal. Her ankles were a little puffy, not something that had happened last time – but that was a long time ago. Dr Willoughby had said swollen ankles meant more rest and this made her come to a decision she'd been considering for a while.

She was going to resign from her position as chair of the WVS and went at once to the telephone to ring the area organiser who resided in Ramsgate.

'Good morning, Mrs Thorrington, I just want to tell you that I'm stepping down from my position in the service. I'm sure there are several able women who can take over the role.'

'Lady Harcourt...'

'No, I am Mrs Sergeant now. I married Flying Officer Sergeant some time ago and am now in an interesting condition so have been advised, because of my advanced age, to rest as much as possible and have no outside activities.'

Most of this was untrue but she could think of no other way of explaining this without causing this elderly lady to be scandalised by the news. She had indeed been married 'some time ago' and she was in an 'interesting condition' but the rest were basically white lies.

'Well, I must say I'm surprised by your news. It would appear that double congratulations are in order. I hope that after the happy event you will continue to attend the meetings in the village?'

'I'm moving to Stodham immediately after Christmas so I'm certain I'll be able to attend the meetings and help with whatever projects the new chair has in store.'

'Thank you for letting me know, Lady... er... Mrs Sergeant.'

Mrs Thorrington disconnected and Joanna was certain that this unexpected news would be all over the neighbourhood by this evening and that she could expect a flurry of telephone calls.

Joe, Tony and Jean must answer the telephone in future as she had no wish to have to lie again to women she liked and had known for years. Time enough for them to discover the truth next year.

When she made the request, Jean nodded vigorously.

'If I was you, I'd not go to church either. I'm sure in the circumstances Mr Evans will be happy to call in and take a short service here once a month for us.'

'Liza has to go as she's in the choir. Won't it seem odd if everybody absents themselves from morning service when it's supposed to be only me that's required to remain out of the public eye?'

'It wasn't very long ago, Joanna, that women were expected to stay out of sight if they were pregnant. They'll just think it's Lady Harcourt who's insisted that you do the same and that if you can't go we are remaining to keep you company.'

'Joe and Tony don't go every week, in fact, my son has strangely found something else urgent to do on Sunday mornings for the past few weeks,' Joanna said.

'There you are then. Miss Biggins will go whatever we do but she's loyal and won't say anything.'

'Obviously I can't go to the WI meetings either. I really don't want to put you in the position of having to lie to your friends. If anybody asks you directly when I got married or when the baby's due, you have my permission to tell the truth.'

It must be her condition that was causing her to vacillate from one opinion on this matter to another.

'I certainly won't,' Jean said. 'None of their business. I think I'll stop going to the meetings as well. To be honest, I don't enjoy them and would much rather just be told what was wanted rather than sit around and talk about it for two hours and then drink tea and eat stale biscuits when I could be doing something more useful at home.'

Joanna smiled. 'If you're going to have a free afternoon twice a month, perhaps I could ask you to make maternity clothes for me? I seem to be ballooning and have absolutely nothing that fits.'

'You've no need to ask me, I'm already working on that. I'll also have all the necessary items for the layette ready long before the baby comes.' Her friend smiled. 'I'll have most of the day free once the girls have gone. The ladies from the village are disappointed they'll no longer have regular work here.'

'I'm going to keep them on for a few weeks so they can spring clean those rooms, launder and iron all the bedlinen and so on. As soon as the house is ours again then I'm going to start making enquiries about who might like to have it for the duration of the war. I'm hoping the RAF will want to use it as a hospital and convalescent home for injured airmen and aircrew.'

Jean didn't look convinced. 'It'll cost a small fortune to convert this house into a working hospital and convalescent home. Let alone the time it'll take. The war might be over before it's done.'

'I'm going to offer to pay for the works and get the architect who did the plans for The Manse to draw up something for here. Even when the war's over, it could continue as a cottage hospital and convalescent home. Sarah might agree to transfer here once she's qualified and Liza could actually train to be a nurse under this roof.'

'In which case I think they might bite your hand off. Don't forget we've got Dr Willoughby in the village and he's already a qualified general surgeon. I'm sure he'd be happy to work here.'

Joanna beamed. She was so lucky to have this wonderful woman and her son as part of the extended family. 'I don't know what I'd do without you, Jean. Tony's a blessing too.'

'Best thing I ever did was answer the advertisement in *The Lady* to be Lady Harcourt's personal maid. To think that my son and I will have our very own home when we move next year. It's so kind of you.'

'Nonsense, I love you both and don't want to lose you. My motives were entirely selfish. I'm going to ignore the telephone if it rings again – feel free to do the same.'

* * *

That afternoon, Elizabeth was resting in her bedroom with the windows open and the curtains drawn and Joanna thought she'd follow suit.

The girls would be leaving next week and she'd thought they might ask to hold a farewell party in the ballroom to mark the occasion but nothing had been said so far. This group didn't feel a part of the household as the previous girls had. Whenever she overheard a conversation, it was about how much they were looking forward to living in a hostel with twenty other girls.

The telephone had rung several times whilst she was upstairs but as Jean had the afternoon off and had gone into Ramsgate with Tony, Joe was somewhere about the estate shooting game for the larder and the ladies from the village had gone home, no one answered it. Aggie would be back at six o'clock to help prepare and serve the supper for the ten remaining girls.

As it didn't get dark until almost eleven o'clock, only the girls that worked at the dairy farm would be there to eat at a sensible time. Therefore, it would be a cold meal for the others as they came back any time between eight and ten. The land girls had only worked for a few hours a day during the winter so didn't resent having such long hours in the summer.

Later that evening, Joanna and Elizabeth were relaxing on the terrace after supper listening to the nightingales singing in the woods that ran along the edge of the drive when she saw the doctor's car turn into the drive.

'I wonder what he wants, Elizabeth, it has to be a social call as there's nobody unwell here.'

'It's far too late for that, my dear. No respectable gentleman arrives uninvited and unannounced after seven o'clock. I fear it might be bad news of some sort. I think it might have something to do with the many telephone calls that you ignored.'

Joanna was about to deny this but a sick dread settled in her stomach. She was on her feet, rushing along the terrace and down the stone steps at the far end so she could be there to speak to Dr Willoughby when he arrived.

One look at his face as he pulled up convinced her Elizabeth had been right. Was she a widow so soon? Would this little baby never meet his father? Her head spun. She heard someone calling her name – then everything went black.

# 9

John gripped the dashboard of the ambulance, leaning forward so there was no danger of the protruding wood coming into contact with the back of the cab. The doctor glanced at him several times through narrowed eyes and drove at a snail's pace.

'Don't try and get out unassisted. I'll send two orderlies with a wheelchair. I'm going to get things organised inside.'

'How bad is it?'

'Bad enough. However, once it's out you'll be fine and back on duty fairly quickly. Constantly turning your head, the way you flyers do, isn't on for a couple of days at least – might be longer if you need a lot of stitches.'

By this time John was wary of even speaking in case he caused irreparable damage. He had basic first-aid knowledge as he'd been obliged to take a course or two when he had been in charge of the fire tenders on Manston. One thing he was certain of was that if his spinal column was damaged, he might well be paralysed. Remaining totally still was the sensible thing to do.

When the orderly opened the door he was smiling, didn't look apprehensive or as if he was treating a patient who might be about to suffer catastrophic spinal damage.

'Right you are, sir, anyone for the skylark? Hop out and into the chair and you'll travel in style.'

John was reluctant to move at any speed after what the doctor had said – after all, these orderlies weren't medical experts any more than he was. He ignored the obvious impatience of the LACs and with infinite care eased his body from the seat and lowered himself into the wheelchair.

'You will wheel me very slowly and carefully. No sodding around. That's an order, Leading Aircraft Man. Do I make myself clear?'

'Crystal, sir. I never realised you had a bleeding great bit of wood sticking out of your neck. We'll be ever so careful – piece of cake.'

The young man was true to his word and pushed him delicately through every door, over every lintel and into the operating room. There the doctor was gowned and masked, two theatre nurses and another orderly similarly attired.

'Good show. You shouldn't be in here in your uniform but needs must. Help Flying Officer Sergeant very, very carefully onto the table so that he's lying face down.'

The orderly who'd pushed the wheelchair took one of John's arms and the second one, who hadn't been needed up until this point, took the other. Somehow, they manoeuvred him face down without disturbing the object sticking out of his neck.

'Right, young man, I'm not giving you a general – just a shot of morphine. We'll give it a few minutes to take effect.'

'Are you going to cut it out or just pull?' His head was beginning to swim and he was becoming rather relaxed about things.

'I'm just going to remove the packing and the bandages. Try not to move.'

'Too bloody tired to go anywhere, sir,' John said sleepily.

Gentle hands turned his head to one side and checked his tongue wasn't anywhere near his teeth. There was a bit of tugging and pulling and then something cold was rubbed on his neck. He didn't care what was going on. He let the drug do its work.

He felt a scalpel slice into his neck but that didn't really hurt. There was a sudden searing pain and for a moment he lost consciousness. Then it was over. A sticky wetness was trickling down his neck and he guessed it was blood.

'Good, that's the worst over. I'm pretty certain you've suffered no permanent damage as fortunately the spike was shorter than I'd feared and appears to have missed anything important. After I've inserted a few stitches, we'll get you into bed and keep an eye on you for a day just to be sure.'

Someone jabbed a needle into his backside. Vaguely he was aware of the quack sewing him up but the morphine and whatever other drug had been shoved into him made it all seem far away. As he drifted off to sleep he remembered he had a wife who needed to know about this accident.

'Make sure someone telephones my wife,' he mumbled, and the doctor understood his slurred words.

'It will be done, young man. Don't fight the sedative. I need to finish stitching you up and you need to rest.'

* * *

John didn't know where he was. He attempted to turn his head, but his neck was so securely bandaged this was impossible. There was an unpleasant taste in his mouth and his head was a bit woolly.

He blinked a few times and then swivelled his eyes from side to side. No wonder he didn't recognise his surroundings – when he'd been injured last year he'd been based at Manston and taken to a hospital in Ramsgate. RAF Hornchurch had its own small hospital and the fact that he was still on base meant he wasn't in a serious condition.

It must be early because the small ward was quiet, the blackouts still drawn and he couldn't hear the voices of patients or nurses. His hearing was excellent – he slowed his breathing, a trick he'd learned from a fellow student from India when he was at university.

He couldn't confirm his deductions as he couldn't look either to the right or to the left but he was pretty sure he was the only one in this ward unless the other occupants were dead – which was unlikely. He could do with a cup of tea and something to eat but unless they loosened the bandages he doubted he'd be able to swallow anything, even water.

Breathing was becoming increasingly difficult. His hands still worked perfectly well so he was going to loosen the constriction that was causing his panic.

With frantic fingers, he scrabbled at the strips of cotton gauze and found an end. It would be stupid to try to rip the bandages apart. He closed his eyes and concentrated on slowing his pulse until he was back in control. Methodically he reached around the back of his neck with one hand and passed the end of the strip from one to the other, then back again to the front. He repeated the process. It took longer than he wanted but eventually he could breathe freely and swallow normally.

He vaguely recalled asking the doctor to ring Joanna. He needed to reassure her himself by calling in person. He sat up slowly – good – he wasn't dizzy and his head had cleared. It was probably the morphine that had made him unsteady as he knew it took a while to get this drug out of your system.

Carefully he rewound the bandage, ensuring that this time it didn't constrict his throat but would still offer some protection to what seemed like a far bigger wound than he'd expected. Of course, he'd not seen it, but his fingers had explored the sutures and there seemed to be seven or eight at least.

He was wearing RAF-issue pyjamas. God knows where his uniform was and he needed to get dressed. He looked in the locker, but it was empty. They hadn't removed his watch, he checked the time and smiled. It wouldn't be sensible to call his wife at three o'clock in the morning.

Then he remembered that the dairy girls would be up and about at Goodwill House and would answer the telephone – at least he hoped they would as he'd no wish to disturb the rest of the house. He padded through the silent building until he found an office with a telephone.

He'd made so many calls to Joanna over the past few months from the base that he knew how to get an outside line. The operator connected him and to his surprise Joe picked up the receiver.

'Joe, what the hell are you doing out of bed at this time?'

'Ma said I was to sleep down here in case there was any more news about you. As you're up and speaking to me, I assume you're tickety-boo.'

'I've got a lot of stitches in my neck which means I won't be able to fly until they come out. As soon as the doctor's back on duty, I'll get him to sign me off. Then I'll come home for a few days.'

'That's good. Ma fainted when Dr Willoughby came to tell her you'd been injured.'

John interrupted. 'Why didn't you tell me that first? Is she all right?'

'She twisted her ankle and will have to stay off her feet for a week at least. She was lucky. The baby's suffered no harm either.'

'Thank God. Go to bed, Joe, and tell Joanna I'm hoping to be home later today.'

It took him a few moments to gather his thoughts. He had a nasty suspicion that he might be told if he was well enough to ride his motorbike to Kent then he was well enough to fly. He might well be labelled as lacking in moral fibre if he insisted on leaving the base.

'Good heavens, Flying Officer Sergeant, what are you doing out of bed?'

John turned to face the senior nurse who'd spoken to him so sharply. 'I needed to speak to my wife and tell her that I'm fine. I've also adjusted the bandage. I was being throttled by it and couldn't breathe.'

'Come with me and I'll have a look. You look as if you could do with a nice cup of tea, so I'll put the kettle on to boil whilst I examine you.'

* * *

Joanna hadn't been asleep and had heard the strident ring of the telephone downstairs through her open bedroom door. She was tense, straining to catch a word or two that would give her the good news she was praying for. Dr Willoughby had told her John was in the base hospital and undergoing surgery. He didn't know more than that but insisted if it had been serious they would have transferred him to a bigger hospital.

Joe raced down the passageway and slid to a halt outside her door. The wooden floors were highly polished and Joe liked to walk about in his socks. 'I've just spoken to him, Ma, he's fine. He'll be home later today with any luck and can recuperate here.'

'Thank you, darling boy, for waiting up for the call. Go to bed now and get some well-deserved sleep.'

'I forgot to ask him what happened. Something to do with his neck.'

'I don't need to know the details now. He can tell us when he gets back. Goodnight, Joe.'

Despite the throbbing in her injured ankle, she fell asleep immediately. It wasn't good for the baby to be anxious; a happy mother produced a happy baby was what everyone said.

Joanna woke refreshed and excited the next morning to find her daughter opening the blackout curtains. Liza was taking a few days off from the vicarage in order to take care of her.

'Good morning, my dear, I'm going to have to hop to the bathroom. Could you help me, please?'

This essential start to the day was accomplished and then Liza helped Joanna dress.

'You can't come downstairs. The doctor said so.'

'I've no intention of doing so, I'm going to stay in my boudoir and recline on the chaise longue.'

'That's the ticket. When you're settled, I'll fetch up your breakfast. We're all relieved John's not badly hurt.'

'I think that I'm in a worse case than him.' She hesitated, feeling awkward about asking her young daughter to wait on her. 'I'd like boiled eggs and toast if that's possible, my love.'

'Coming right up.' Her youngest daughter put her hands on her hips and pretended to scowl. 'I'll be very cross if you move from here.'

Joanna laughed. 'Bossy boots, I promise I'll remain where I am.' Liza grinned and turned to go. 'You have become a very lovely young woman, my dear. Why don't you start putting your hair up every day? Pigtails are for young girls.'

Liza touched one of the long, glossy light-brown braids. 'Really? I'd rather have it cut short. Would you mind if I got one of the modern styles we were looking at in the *Woman's Journal* the other day?'

'I'd be sad to see all that glorious hair shorn but it's your decision. Maybe have it cut to shoulder length first and if you like that then have it shorter next time?'

'I'll do that. I love you, Ma, you're the best ma in the world.'

'And I love you, too, my darling girl. You and Joe have made me so happy.'

Joanna heard the girl laughing as she dashed off down the corridor. Her daughter might be legally a child, but she had the maturity of a young woman. Perhaps it was growing up in the East End that had made her adopted children so independent for their ages.

She'd belatedly realised what a bad idea it had been to ignore the telephone so from now on it would be answered. It was fortuitous that she was unable to get to the phone because of her sprained ankle as she had no wish to speak to anybody about anything to do with her personal life.

Liza returned with breakfast and Joanna could hear her singing something that was definitely not a hymn. It was a lively tune and it could be something by the American bandleader Glenn Miller, but she wasn't sure.

It would have been nice to have had the sitting room wireless brought upstairs for her to listen to. But it wouldn't be fair to deprive Elizabeth of the programmes she liked to listen to. Surprisingly, her mother-in-law had become obsessed with *Music While You Work*, which was aimed at the men and women working in the factories. It was half an hour of live, jolly band music on the Home Service between ten-thirty and eleven o'clock every weekday. No doubt the intention behind it was to keep those in the factories alert and producing the maximum amount of goods.

The telephone jangled insistently twice and both times it was answered by somebody downstairs – either Joe, Tony or Jean would be doing that for her. Liza had just helped her back from the bathroom for a second time when Joe appeared.

'That was John, Ma, he's got six days' sick leave and is just about to leave the base. He can get the stitches removed here if they're ready to come out before then. He'll be back on active duty at the end of the month.'

'Thank you for coming up to tell me. I so wish he'd broken his arm...'

The twins both laughed. 'Blimey, Ma, that's a bit harsh,' Joe said with a grin.

'You know exactly what I meant so please don't tease me. With a broken arm he could have come home and stayed here for six weeks – been safe – without being seriously incapacitated.'

'I read somewhere that in the first war the poor sods shot themselves in the foot just to get out of the trenches,' Joe said.

Joanna didn't reprimand him for his bad language as it seemed appropriate in the circumstances. How much longer would she be able to intervene in their lives and be listened to? Joe was determined to volunteer for the RAF and become a fighter pilot like John. He could do that when he was eighteen, or possibly a bit younger. He would be seventeen next September which was frighteningly close.

Liza intended to leave home to become a nurse – they had to live on the premises whilst they were training – so she would be gone slightly earlier than Joe. The fact that there would be a nine-month-old baby in the family by then would make things a little bit easier to bear. If John was home then she wouldn't miss the twins as much, but that was very unlikely.

The wretched war wouldn't be over by then as Britain was fighting it alone. The Commonwealth countries were a massive support but that just wasn't enough to tip things in Britain's favour. The talk over the kitchen table was that America needed to join the war as without them victory was remote.

'Ma, are you all right?'

'Sorry, Joe, my mind keeps wandering, I blame it on my condition. I don't want to talk about the last war or this one. John will be here until the end of the month and then on 1 August, our land girls will depart for their new accommodation.'

'The house will seem too big and too empty when they've gone. I wish we could move to The Manse before it's done. Tony and I are working on the dower house where he and Jean are going to be living. I think he might move into it when it's habitable so he can crack on with things.'

'I do hope not – Jean likes to have him under the same roof as her,' Joanna said. 'Having missed most of his life whilst he was being fostered, she's determined not to miss a second more.'

'He's got his bike and there's still enough petrol to keep it going for years so he could come back every day to see her.'

'I'm being selfish, aren't I? When the girls go, Jean will have most of the day free so she can help with the redecoration of her new home if she wants to.'

Joe grinned. 'Tony suggested that, but she was clear she didn't like the smell of paint and had every confidence that the two of us can get it looking nice. She said she's going to start dressmaking not just for the family but for others – I think she'll earn a good bit of extra doing that. I'd better get on, we're going to the new house soon unless there's something you want me to do here?'

'No, you're still working for the family over there. I'm not moving until after Christmas even if the house is ready. I want to have the baby here and it's not due until 21 December.'

Joanna was talking to an empty space as her son had sloped off. Hardly surprising as not many men wanted to discuss such things. They considered anything domestic, and particularly to do with babies, women's business and nothing to do with them.

John was different to the majority of his gender because he appeared to be as interested in her pregnancy as she was. Having John home even for a short time would be wonderful. He understood her and he made her feel loved and safe.

# 10

John turned into the drive of what was now his home, on the lookout for the daft dog that had launched itself into the sidecar last time he'd come down here on a motorbike. In the last letter Joanna had written she'd said the mutt was enjoying the extra attention and that his pads had now fully recovered.

Lady Harcourt was standing at the end of the terrace looking over the balustrade, obviously watching for him. He glided to a halt, pushed his goggles up and saluted.

'Good afternoon, my lady, how are you today?'

'A lot better than either you or your wife, I should think. Please call me Elizabeth – I think of you as my son-in-law, although I don't believe that is actually correct.'

He wasn't too sure about the informality but smiled and nodded. 'I'm yours to command.' He grinned and continued. 'I say that to Joanna and she usually responds by saying that she's the Queen of Sheba.'

The old lady laughed, which was his intention. 'You are a very charming young man and I can see why Joanna is besotted with you. I have a favour to ask.'

'I'll do it if I can.'

'I want an excursion on your motorbike.'

'Absolutely not. Far too dangerous for someone of your age but I'd be happy to take you for a spin in the sidecar if Tony will allow me to borrow his motorbike again.'

'Very well. Joanna is resting and I am sure you don't want to wake her up. Please park your bike and I will go and speak to Tony as I know he came back for lunch today.'

She vanished, moving far more speedily than he'd expected for someone of her advanced years. The last thing he wanted was to traipse all over the country with her sitting beside him when he could be upstairs with his beloved wife in his arms.

Was this deliberate? He thought not, but perhaps she resented the attention Joanna was getting from him and wished to keep them apart.

He had a spare helmet in one of the panniers and would insist that she wore it. He was eager to see her face when he did so. Tony was waiting for him by the back door.

'You can take my bike, John, good luck with your passenger. I warn you, she's got some ulterior motive. It won't just be a ride to the village and back.'

'I thought as much. I don't care what she has planned, I'm not going to be out more than half an hour. I want to spend every minute available with my wife.'

The motorbike and sidecar were facing in the correct direction, the engine ticking over, when the old lady reappeared. She looked no different from when she'd gone in and had had the good sense not to put on a hat.

'You'll need to wear this, Elizabeth. It'll keep your hair from blowing all over the place.' He waited expectantly for the argument but there was none.

'Thank you, an excellent solution. I think I might need your assistance to clamber into this.'

She was small slender lady and instead of offering her his hand he put his hands around her tiny waist, lifted her easily, and placed her into the sidecar as if she was a child. 'There you go. I can give you exactly thirty minutes. Fifteen there and fifteen back.'

'It will only take a couple of minutes to reach my desired destination.'

He pulled down his goggles, swung astride the bike and waited for directions. 'To the village hall – there's a jumble sale I particularly wish to attend.'

If she'd said she was eager to swim the English Channel, he couldn't have been more surprised. The very last person he'd expect to enjoy the wrestling match that most jumble sales descended into was Lady Harcourt.

'Right, but it'll have to be a brief visit and don't expect me to come in with you.'

She smiled in a way that he didn't quite trust – the old biddy was up to something.

'Go as fast as you can, make the engine roar, I want to cause a stir.'

Now he understood – she wanted to introduce him to her cronies in the loudest and most unusual way possible. He'd no objection to that and loved her for it.

John revved the engine and glanced sideways to see her laughing. Lazzy, the dog that had caused all the problems before, was nowhere in sight so he thought it safe to open the throttle a little and they tore down the drive, scattering flocks of pigeons from the treetops.

They turned onto the main road – such as it was – at the correct speed and once he was sure there were no horse-drawn vehicles, pedestrians or cyclists on the open stretch ahead of him, he gave his passenger what she'd asked for.

Although he slowed to a safe speed as they'd entered the village, he opened the throttle a few times to make the engine roar and turn as many heads as possible. There was a scrum of eager housewives waiting to be let into the hall. Every single one of them stopped talking to their companions and turned to stare.

'Well done, young man, exactly the entrance I wished to make with you. Please reverse the earlier procedure and put me on the ground so I can join the queue.'

They both knew she'd no intention of going into the hall to look for second-hand clothing, bric-a-brac or anything else. The object of this exercise was to show him off and he was happy to oblige. He pushed up his goggles and did as she asked.

She actually winked at him as she sailed through the air, and he grinned. 'We'll show them. Joanna will love you for this.'

'She already does, my boy, she's the daughter I never had. I didn't like my son – horrible man, just like his father.'

His shout of laughter made the nearest ladies smile. Where were the posh biddies? These were the ones they'd come to impress. Then he saw a row of behatted ladies gathering in the open doors. He was slightly surprised they weren't mowed down by a rush of eager bargain hunters.

He offered his arm and Elizabeth took it. 'Bloody hell, I've still got my helmet and goggles on.'

'They make you look very dashing. I thought they had been left on deliberately.'

The ladies smiled and nodded and he returned the gestures. They moved apart as if for royalty and he supposed Elizabeth was the nearest they had in Stodham.

'Will your friends come out to be introduced?'

'Mohammed must go to the mountain.'

'Your wish is my command, my lady,' he said with a straight face. This time she laughed, making anyone watching see that they were the best of friends.

The three formidable ladies at the door stepped forward. One was smiling, the other two were not.

'Ladies, allow me to introduce my son-in-law, Flying Officer Sergeant. He is on sick leave as he was almost blown up two days ago and has a myriad of sutures in his neck.' She didn't bother to tell him their names. The object of the exercise was to let them see him and make it clear he was part of the family.

He thought it wise not to offer to shake hands. A refusal would be embarrassing for Elizabeth and he didn't want that. He'd struck up a rapport with her when he and his corporal had been invited to convalesce at Goodwill House last year. Had she known about his affair with Joanna back then? If she had, then she'd not taken umbrage about it.

One of the disapproving matrons dressed in a hideous puce frock, with an alarming hat, stared at him. 'I cannot imagine why anyone would give up her title in order to marry a junior officer in the RAF. I certainly wouldn't.'

The smiling woman spoke next. 'You can be very sure, Mildred, that no handsome young fighter pilot would look twice in your direction so you've nothing to worry about on that score.'

Elizabeth sniggered, which made the disagreeable one turn the shade of her frock. 'Mrs Forsythe, have you nothing to add?'

'If your daughter-in-law was prepared to give up so much to be with this officer then good for her. I never liked Lord Harcourt and she deserves to be happy.'

Mission accomplished. John felt his companion squeeze his arm. Time to go. 'A pleasure to have met you all, ladies, but I have to curtail the visit as I've yet to see my wife.' He nodded and smiled down at the old lady. 'I'm afraid, Lady Harcourt, you will have to miss the delights of the jumble sale. I apologise.'

'Ladies, I shall leave you to your jumble.'

He lifted her into the sidecar again and he belatedly noticed that she also hadn't removed her borrowed helmet. Good for her – she should be everything he most despised but was in fact a woman he respected, admired and was inordinately fond of.

'You will be back in less than half an hour and I doubt that Joanna is even aware that you've returned.'

He grinned, pulled down his goggles and kicked the bike into life. This time there was no need to make a show, so he travelled at a more sensible speed, giving him a few minutes to think about the encounter with the ladies of the village. It made no difference to him if those women didn't like him but he wanted Joanna and his new family to be happy with their neighbours.

His diction was as good, if not better, than those who were turning up their noses at him, which had obviously surprised them, so his three years at Oxford hadn't been a complete waste of time. He'd not stayed in touch with any of his so-called friends – God knows where they were or what they were doing in this bloody war. They'd be officers in one of the services, but more likely army than RAF.

As he cruised up the drive, he was forced to admit that if he hadn't got a fully paid scholarship to Oxford, he wouldn't be here now.

Joe must've seen them as he was there waiting to assist his grandma from the sidecar. 'Liza is just making you and Ma some lunch.'

'Excellent, I'll take it up. Does Joanna know I'm back?'

The lad shook his head. 'Nope, we thought that you'd like to wake her up. By the way, I took your case up and put it outside the bedroom.'

'Thank you.' He paused at the door and nodded at Elizabeth. 'And thank you too. I really appreciate what you did. I don't think we won over Mildred but the other two seemed all right.'

'Take no notice of Mildred, she's the village grouch. Her fiancé died at the Somme and nobody else has been silly enough to offer for her. It's made her very sour.'

'That explains it. Excuse me, I need to visit the ablutions before I collect lunch.'

* * *

Joanna sensed that her beloved husband was on the premises even though there was no firm evidence to confirm this. 'Liza, would you help me to freshen up, please? John's here and I want to look my best for him – not bedraggled and puffy eyed.'

'I didn't hear his bike. Are you sure?'

'I'm certain. Do I need to change my frock?'

'It won't be on for long so I shouldn't bother.'

'Liza, that's not something I expected to hear you say.' Joanna was shocked that her young daughter was so worldly.

Unabashed, Liza grinned as she offered her arm. 'Everybody knows that there's very little *resting* going on in here. I'm from the East End, Ma, I know what's what and have done since I was a little one.'

'I don't doubt it, my love, but I would prefer it if you pretended that you didn't.'

'I hope when I fall in love that I feel the same way about my man that you and John do about each other.'

They'd reached the bathroom and Joanna smiled. 'I can manage from here, thank you. Could you come back for me in ten minutes?'

Liza and Joe now spoke beautifully, were being well educated but sometimes when they were excited or upset they reverted to their roots. Joanna didn't mind this, coming from such a difficult neighbourhood had made them the fine young adults that they were. Children from wealthy families went to boarding schools and although this made them able to live independently from their parents, it didn't equip them for real life in the way that struggling to survive in the East End did.

She was sitting by the window enjoying the sun on her face when John walked in carrying a tray. His eyes blazed and his smile made her pulse race. He strode across the room and dumped the tray unceremoniously on the table. She was in his arms where she belonged in seconds. A highly satisfactory few minutes later, he gently returned her to the chair.

'Darling, I thought you'd be asleep. Did someone tell you I was here?'

'No, I just knew.' He was still holding her hand and she raised it to her lips and pressed a kiss on his knuckles. They were ingrained with black residue, and she inhaled the familiar smell of soap and oil. 'I'm not going to worry about you any more.'

He raised an eyebrow and his mouth quirked but he didn't speak.

'I'm certain now that I'll know if anything happens to you, so as long as I don't get that feeling, I don't have to worry.'

He ruffled her hair affectionately, ruining her carefully arranged chignon and sending hairpins flying in all directions. 'I like the idea that we're somehow connected telepathically, sweetheart, but I'm not sure it works like that.'

'At least you're not dismissing it as total bunkum. I don't want you to worry about me as I'm obviously well – apart from my sprained ankle.'

He carefully removed all the items on the tray and then leant it against the wall when it was empty. 'There is a selection of sandwiches made with freshly baked bread followed by raspberries and strawberries from the garden. We also got a jug of cream.'

'Scrumptious, and exactly what I want to eat right now.'

He put neatly cut triangles on her plate and she looked inside a couple hopefully. 'What I'd really like is cheese and tomato, but the girls don't seem to be bringing us anything back lately. As they're working on farms that belong to us, I honestly think we should get the occasional treat without having to ask.'

'We'll go in search of some cheese tomorrow. Tony's going to use my bike whilst I'm here if he's not ferrying his mother around. I've an amusing story to tell you. You want to hear it now or after lunch?'

They were both laughing when he finished his tale. 'Elizabeth's an absolute dear. I'm so glad that she's welcomed you into our family so enthusiastically.'

'I think she's a remarkable woman and not like her class at all. I can't see anyone else from her strata of society welcoming Joe and Liza first and then me into her inner circle so lovingly.'

'She was actually born into the aristocracy. Her father was a lord, incredibly wealthy as well as titled, and that's why my father-in-law married her. I don't think there was ever any affection between them, which is why she took her money and ran away as soon as she could.'

'I'm surprised that she had access to it – why hadn't her husband taken control of her finances? Isn't that what happens in this sort of family?'

Joanna didn't think this was a genuine question. 'Does that mean you're not happy with how things are arranged in our marriage?'

For a second he thought her serious, then he grinned. 'Too right I am. I was expecting to have complete control of everything, be the cock of the roost and for my wife to follow my every order without question.'

'Oh dear, disappointed on every front. Never mind, I'll make you a generous allowance if you like?' This too was meant to be humorous but at her light-hearted words the atmosphere changed. His smile vanished and he sat back in his chair as if wishing to distance himself from her.

She was about to apologise, tell him that she'd been joking, but something stopped her. He'd married her knowing how things were and it was far too late for him to be objecting to the arrangement, such as it was.

She picked up a sandwich and began to eat as if there wasn't a chill between them. He was the one who'd overreacted, taken offence when none was given, so it was for him to break the silence.

It was hard to swallow the fresh bread and after chewing for some time she put her napkin to her mouth and spat it out. The alternative was choking or vomiting, and either was unpleasant.

John appeared oblivious to her distress and was tucking into the food with obvious enjoyment. There was freshly made lemonade in a jug, so she poured herself a glass. A few of the citrus trees kept in the orangery had survived despite the appalling winters recently and the lemons would be from there. This was a real treat, but he didn't seem to appreciate that either.

'As you're obviously enjoying your lunch and I'm not, I shall leave you to it. No, please don't disturb yourself, I'm perfectly capable of hopping to my bed where I'm going to take another rest. I expect I'll see you this evening.'

She was up and balancing on her good foot before he reacted. He stood up so violently his chair flew back, crashing against the wall.

'For Christ's sake, Joanna, let me carry you.'

She flinched at his anger, didn't understand why they were fighting. How could things have turned from happy to this in the space of a few minutes?

Somehow she kept back her tears and nodded. 'Thank you, that would be kind. You can come back and finish your lunch.'

He picked her up and carried her silently to their bedroom. She'd expected him to toss her on the bed but he put her down gently and instead of retreating sat beside her. She risked a glance.

'Oh, my darling, don't cry. I love you so much and it's inevitable that occasionally we're going to have an argument.' She sat up and cupped his tear-streaked face between her hands. 'I forget what a terrible strain you're under and I promise I'll be more—'

'Don't apologise. You're my world and I don't care how much money you've got, how much you give to me or to anybody else. All I need to be happy is for you to love me as much as I love you.'

'I am so lucky to have married you. I love you so much and there's absolutely nothing that will change my mind.' She was deeply moved by his tears. She vowed not to make him so upset again.

# 11

John couldn't recall the last time he'd shed tears for anyone or anything but his unwarranted anger towards his beloved wife had unmanned him. Being in love was an amazing, life-affirming thing, but it was also bloody horrible at times.

'I don't care about your money; I knew the score when I married you. I was a total arse to react as I did. I'm so sorry, my love.'

'Let's forget about it. I'm sorry to be a nuisance, my darling, I find my appetite's returned. I'm also worried that you'll injure your back carrying me about the place.'

'You don't weigh very much even now. I think our baby's growing fast – it has to be a boy.' He put a hand on her stomach and immediately there was movement beneath it. He'd never cease to be amazed by feeling a half-formed baby, their son or daughter, wriggling about inside her.

'I am alarmingly large when you consider I'm not quite five months and I'm still not completely convinced that we're not having twins. The midwife has yet to call but I believe she'll visit in a week or two. I'm sure someone with her expertise and years of experience should be able to give me an accurate answer.'

He ran his fingers through her glorious golden hair and his thoughts turned to other things. She shook her head.

'No, not now. I'm hungry and I need to eat first.'

'If you insist. Having twins might be a good idea, then you won't have to go through this a second time if you want a sibling for our child.'

She punched him none too gently on the arm. 'You'll not be the one having to look after two screaming babies so I can see why you might think that two is better than one.'

'I'm a battered husband...'

'You will be a decapitated one if you don't take me into the other room so I can eat.'

Every morsel was devoured and every drop of the delicious lemonade drunk. 'I know I'm not supposed to put any weight on my injured ankle but I really want to get some fresh air. I think I heard a rumble of thunder a few moments ago. We've not had any significant rain for some time and farmers are crying out for it.'

John sighed theatrically. 'I suppose I have to carry you downstairs now. I'm not sure I can do that as I'm so full.'

'Oh dear, disappointment after disappointment for both of us. I was under the impression I had married a fighting fit young pilot, now I find I've been sadly mistaken. You told me a while ago that I'm light as a feather – I'm sure a few sandwiches and strawberries can't have added much.'

He kissed her. 'Ridiculous woman – I'm not only battered but henpecked. I'd never live it down in the mess if they discovered how badly you treat me.'

Her delightful laughter filled the room. 'I'm quite sure any one of them would volunteer to change places with you. Not only am I stunningly beautiful, incredibly intelligent but I'm also extraordinarily wealthy. Definitely the catch of the season, I should say.'

'I think you're being a little hard on yourself, sweetheart, you don't look anything like a large trout.'

They spent the remainder of the afternoon on the terrace. None of the family came to join them apart from Lazzy, the big hairy dog, and he was always welcome.

Liza appeared at the French doors. 'Jean said she's just about to serve supper, Ma.'

'I was going to suggest that we ate out here but I felt the first drops of rain just now. Are Joe and Tony back from Stodham?'

'Not yet but I'm sure they'll be here in a minute or two. Did you sit at this end of the terrace so you can't be seen, or hear any arrivals?'

'Got it in one, Liza, every moment I can spend with Joanna without interruption's precious.'

The girl nodded and returned to her duties in the kitchen. He wouldn't dream of saying so to Joanna, but it seemed to him that although the twins were now Harcourts, they still acted as if they were employees most of the time. Surely, wealthy families like this one usually sent their children away to expensive boarding schools?

Joanna somehow sensed his thoughts. 'Liza likes to be useful, Joe also, and I admire that in them. I have to tell you what she said to me this morning.'

When he'd heard, he wasn't shocked or even surprised. 'We're newly-weds, of course we're going to spend as much time as possible making love. I hesitate to ask this as you might think I'm being insensitive, but at what point in your pregnancy will we have to stop?'

'I did ask Dr Willoughby and he said as long as I'm comfortable it's fine, but not in the last month.'

Dinner was now called supper as nobody changed and the family ate before the land girls returned as most of them didn't get back until dusk.

Joe and Tony had been busy all day at The Manse and the pair of them said the small house Tony and Jean would be living in would be ready for occupation in a few weeks.

'As long as you come most days, Tony, I won't mind too much that you'll be living somewhere else,' Jean said.

'I can oversee the builders far easier if I'm living there, Mum. Everything that had to be removed from the main house has gone, Joanna, and the new wiring and plumbing is the next task.'

'How exciting. John you will come and see the progress before you leave, won't you?'

John nodded. 'It's going to be our home for the next few decades so I'm as keen as you are to see how things are going.'

The meal continued and the conversation turned to the imminent departure of the land girls.

'The girls go next weekend. They've been given two days' leave so I think some will go on the Saturday and some on the Sunday. As soon as the ladies from the village have put the house straight, I must start making enquiries at the Air Ministry about leasing this house to them for the duration,' Joanna said.

'I heard a rumour that Angus is being moved to the War Office for some senior administrative post. If that's true, we'll have a family member in the right place at the right time,' John told them.

'Sarah didn't say anything about it in her last letter but I'm sure she'll be happy to have him permanently attached to a desk.'

He hated the way her eyes filled when she looked at him. If he survived the next few months then he'd get posted somewhere safe, probably in a training capacity of some sort. He'd be safe; it was the poor sods he trained who were likely to kill themselves.

'I'd be happy to set things in motion for this house but don't want to overstep the mark.'

'Would you really? I know it's feeble of me but being pregnant seems to be taking all my energy and I just don't have the oomph that I had before.'

Elizabeth, who had been remarkably quiet this evening, finally joined in the conversation.

'You wouldn't be overstepping, young man, you would be stepping up to the mark as you should. Joanna has more than enough to think about at the moment and I certainly don't want her bothered with something as difficult as finding new tenants for this place.'

'In which case, Elizabeth, I'll look into it when I go back. They're getting it for nothing, and as the necessary changes are going to be made by the family, then I'd think they'd be delighted to have Goodwill House.'

'Do you intend to sell it to the RAF if they want to buy it?' Elizabeth asked.

'I haven't quite decided,' Joanna said. 'I know there has been a Lord Harcourt here for hundreds of years and if Peter was still alive then I'd give it to him. He was the last of the line so I can't see why I shouldn't sell the house and the estates. I don't have any emotional attachment to them.'

'Splendid. When we move it will be a fresh start for all of us,' Elizabeth said.

The twins and Tony had contributed nothing to the conversation, but that was hardly surprising. This was a decision to be made by Joanna and nobody else. Whatever she and Elizabeth thought, as far as he was concerned Harcourt business wasn't his concern.

* * *

A few days later, Dr Willoughby called in for a routine check on Joanna and agreed to remove John's stitches as they were ready to come out. They went into the sitting room that was attached to their bedroom whilst Joanna rearranged her clothing.

'Dr Willoughby, thank you for doing this. It means I can go straight back on duty and not have to faff about waiting to see the medic.'

'No problem at all, Flying Officer Sergeant. My wife, Charlie, told me that you and Lady Harcourt ruffled a few feathers the other day.'

'Her idea, not mine, but I must say I rather enjoyed it. As long as Joanna's not put in an invidious position by our marriage then I'm happy.'

'I would say that the vast majority of the village are pleased for both of you – your wife is very well thought of,' Dr Willoughby said.

'Whilst we're alone for a few minutes, I want to ask you about Joanna and the baby,' John said. 'I can see that she's blooming, but we're both concerned that she's much larger than she should be and there's absolutely no possibility her dates are wrong.'

'Sometimes it's difficult to be certain if the expectant mother is carrying twins but in this case I don't think she is. In my opinion, and I'm not an obstetrician, it's just a big baby.'

Unfortunately, Joanna hopped in as he said this.

'A big baby? I don't like the sound of that. Sarah was just over seven pounds and that was like pushing an orange up your nose but in reverse.' Both men were smiling. Joanna hadn't, as far as she was concerned, said anything remotely amusing.

'Don't scowl at me, sweetheart, you have to admit your analogy was funny.'

'Excuse me, Mrs Sergeant, I've another call to make this morning,' Dr Willoughby said.

She just nodded at him and he dashed off, looking flustered. Now that one of the culprits was vanquished she could make it clear to her husband how cross she was.

'It's all very well for you to laugh, you don't have to have this baby. It's called "labour" for a reason.'

His smile was contrite. 'I'm sorry, darling, believe me I'd change places with you if I could.'

'Good heavens, what a silly suggestion. I've no wish to be a fighter pilot. On balance, I think I've got the easier task. It's just that I hate being laughed at.'

He smiled his heart-melting smile and she tumbled into his waiting arms. This was his last full day. He had to be back at Hornchurch tomorrow. What happened next was inevitable and highly enjoyable for both of them.

They missed lunch. She was lying naked in his arms, relaxed and content when there was a timid tap at the closed door.

'We'll be down in a bit. Unless it's an emergency, go away,' John called out sleepily.

'John, there's been a phone call. They want to speak to you,' Joe said.

John sprang out of bed and was fully dressed in less than a minute. Joanna was still half-asleep and hadn't quite grasped what was happening.

'Stay where you are, darling. I love you. I'll write if I can.' He leaned down and kissed her, his lips were hard, his eyes glittering. He was as upset as she was at this sudden recall. They both knew that could be the only reason anybody was asking for him personally.

'Drive carefully, my love. I love you.'

With a brief wave, he snatched up his case and was gone. His running footsteps echoed down the passageway. How could he have been in bed with her one minute and minutes later out of the house?

The roar of his powerful bike racing down the drive moments later was a hammer blow to her happiness. The only reason there could be that he was wanted back so urgently was because something major was about to happen and they needed all their experienced pilots at readiness.

* * *

It took Joanna a while to regain her composure and be ready to face those waiting downstairs for an explanation. She was trying to be grateful that they'd had four days together when those posted far away from their homes never saw their families and wives. Indeed, servicemen who were abroad fighting might not get home until the end of the war. The prisoners of war certainly wouldn't, but she supposed they were possibly safer there than actually fighting.

Liza duly appeared and helped her hobble downstairs. She knew this was against doctor's orders but being on her own wasn't an option.

Even Elizabeth was in the kitchen, which was unusual as she preferred to remain in the sitting room or sit on the terrace. Joanna decided to pre-empt the inevitable questions and was bracing herself to be scolded for being downstairs at all.

'I've no idea why John's had to leave so suddenly as he didn't come back and tell me after speaking to whoever was on the telephone. I'm not going to talk about it, think about it or worry about it and neither should you.' She smiled brightly. 'And I want no comments about me having come down. My ankle's much better now.'

'Well said, my dear, that's the spirit. We thought we would have lunch on the terrace as it's not quite so hot today. Allow me to help you out.' Elizabeth held out her arm and Joanna took it.

'Hang on a minute, Joanna, I think you'd find it helpful to use this walking stick,' Tony said as he handed it over.

'Thank you, I should have thought of that myself.'

'I've laid the table out there already, Ma,' Liza said. 'By the time you and Grandma are settled, everything will be ready.'

The last thing Joanna wanted was to eat but she'd try to force down enough to avoid anybody commenting on her lack of appetite. She was eating for two so must make the effort.

The conversation around the table avoided any mention of the war, which was quite remarkable, and she was well aware her beloved family were doing this for her.

'I think that Charlie Willoughby might well be in a similar condition to you, Ma,' Joe said. 'She's asked me to exercise Starlight for her when I have time.'

'She might just be busy, doesn't mean she's having a baby,' his sister said.

'It's none of our business, so let's change the subject. How is that stray cat they adopted settling in?' Joanna asked.

'Lucky's a brilliant hunter, that cat keeps their larder filled with rabbits and even an occasional pheasant.'

'The two stable cats keep down the vermin here but have never caught anything for the house. It's a good thing you've turned out to be such an excellent shot, Joe,' Joanna said, 'as without the game you shoot, we'd not eat nearly as well.'

She took a few small bites from the plate in front of her and hastily pushed the ham underneath the lettuce, hoping no one would notice. Jean did and stood up and smoothly removed the untouched food. 'It's berries and cream for dessert, can you eat that?'

'I'll try, thank you,' Joanna replied quietly.

The other four around the table were looking at the huge field of early potatoes growing in front of the terrace in what had once been the rolling park attached to the house.

'I dug a root up yesterday and those are ready to be lifted,' Joe said.

'It'll be strange having land girls working down there when they're not staying with us,' Liza said.

'Whoever it is will have to cycle or walk a couple of miles to get here whereas now they only have to go a hundred yards,' Elizabeth added.

The conversation drifted over Joanna's head and she had no interest in joining in. How long would it take John to get to his base? His horrible motorbike could travel at frightening speeds and he would push it to its limits, desperate to return to his squadron with scant regard for his own safety or her happiness.

Jean interrupted her unhappy thoughts. 'Here you are, mixed berries from the garden and cream.' The bowl of freshly picked strawberries, raspberries and redcurrants did look appealing. Jean piled the finished lunch plates onto the trolley and handed round the rest of the bowls.

Joanna did manage to eat most of the fruit but was aware this wasn't sufficient to keep her, and the precious burden she was carrying, healthy. She needed to really push her worries for John's safety aside and put all her energy into staying strong.

'What I would really enjoy now is a jug of coffee,' Elizabeth said firmly. 'Miss Biggins has gone to Town to purchase some from Fortnum's or Harrods.'

This did get Joanna's attention. 'Good grief, Elizabeth, how could you have sent poor Miss Biggins all the way to London just to buy you coffee?'

'It's not just for me, Joanna, it's for you too.'

'If anything happens to her it will be your fault. Why do you think John's had to return a day early? There's going to be a big air-raid tonight.'

'Tish-tosh, my dear. Miss Biggins left long before your husband was recalled so neither of us knew there was any more risk than usual. There are shelters she can go into if necessary. She has a sister living in Romford and is staying with her tonight and will return here on Monday. I can assure you she was eager to go and it was actually her suggestion.'

'Then I apologise, if she wanted to see her sister then travelling to London for an hour or so is a small price to pay.'

Elizabeth chuckled. 'She's not paying any price, my dear. I've paid all her expenses and if she does manage to locate some coffee beans then it will be worth every penny.'

# 12

As he tore through the empty roads towards London, John regretted not having taken a few extra minutes to speak to Joanna. He was being recalled not because there'd been warning of a massive attack by the Luftwaffe but because an intelligence officer, usually known as a spy, wanted to speak to him urgently.

God knows what this was about, but nothing good, he was certain. These blokes scuttled about the place collecting information from flyers as they returned from sorties and then combined it with information from other less obvious sources. From this amalgamation they, and the bigwigs in London, came up with various schemes that were often doomed to failure from the start.

His injury had been caused by a tip and run attack, he'd nothing significant to tell about this incident and he couldn't think of anything else that might be of interest to them.

He sped through London, weaving his way in and out of the red double-decker buses and taxis, much to their annoyance. He arrived at Hornchurch late in the afternoon – just over three hours was bloody good going by his reckoning.

The guard stepped up and he gave his name, rank and number and was duly signed in. He kicked his bike onto the stand, pulled off his helmet, goggles and gloves and dropped them surreptitiously into a pannier. These were to be worn only when flying so not a good idea to appear in them now.

To his surprise, Angus – who he thought had been posted to Horse Guards – appeared from an office and beckoned him over. 'You made excellent time, John, sorry to have dragged you away. Do you need to see the medic?'

'No, local quack took out the stitches earlier today. I'm tickety-boo. What's going on? Why does a spy need to speak to me so urgently?'

'You're speaking to him – this is my new role. Let's go into this empty office so I can explain.'

A smiling young WAAF arrived before John had even sat down. 'Here are the refreshments you asked for, sir.' She put down a tray of assorted sandwiches plus what smelt as if it might be actual coffee. There was something significant going on if the real stuff was being served to him.

John shrugged off his jacket, loosened his tie and piled half a dozen sandwiches onto a plate, then poured himself a brimming mug of coffee. 'Right, let's hear the bad news, what do you want me to do?'

'I want you to volunteer for something. You've completed more than a hundred and eighty hours of sorties and are entitled to a change.'

'I don't want to be sent to some godforsaken OTU to train flyers. You wouldn't be involved if it was that, so tell me, what's this about?

'There's something called the Merchant Ship Fighter Unit being assembled at Speke near Liverpool. This has Churchill's full approval and entails fitting merchant ships with a catapult which will fire a Hurricane from the deck. This means when a bomber approaches there's somebody there to protect the convoy from aerial attack.'

'Right – sounds exciting. One thing occurs to me, Angus, what happens after being launched? It seems there are only three options – crash into the sea, bale out into the drink or hopefully find land before you run out of fuel.'

'That's a fair estimation. However, on the plus side you'll be going to the States.'

'I'm not sure what to say about this. I'll be away from Blighty possibly for months...'

'I'll tell you now, I think it's highly unlikely you'll ever be catapulted anywhere to fight anything. I know you'll be away, but you'll be a lot safer on a merchant ship than flying Rhubarbs and having dogfights every day of the week.'

John had known from the outset that he was going to agree to go, he was ready for a change and was aware that he was becoming a bit stale. This was a dangerous mindset as you stopped taking as much care and were in more danger of being shot down than when you were eager and alert.

The drawback was leaving Joanna for months, but some poor sods hadn't seen their families for years, so he was lucky really.

'Do you know that I'm your father-in-law now?' He'd spoken what he'd been thinking and Angus laughed.

'I'm also your superior officer and I think that outbids a father-in-law at the moment. And do you realise that any children Sarah and I might have will be your grandchildren?'

'Bloody hell – no, I hadn't thought of that. I'll do it, when do I leave?'

'There's an Annie, courtesy of the ATA, waiting to ferry you up there. Have you ever flown a Hurry?'

'Yes, got my initial fighter training on one before I got a Spit. I'll finish the sandwiches and the coffee, collect my kit, and then I'm ready to go. Do something for me, ring Joanna and tell her I've been posted up north for a few months. She'll think that's a safe place to be.'

'Of course.'

'The baby's due in December. I'm only doing one trip – I don't want to be the other side of the Atlantic when it comes,' John said.

'One trip it is, then you can ask for a posting in Kent. They have a squadron of Spits permanently based at Hawkinge. They work in pairs, mostly on reconnaissance and escort in the Channel.'

'That'll do. The Air Transport Auxiliary don't fly at night so let's hope we get there before it's dark. See you in a few months.'

'One more thing, you'll need your passport and civies,' Angus said. 'You can't go ashore in the States in uniform.'

'I've none here, everything's at home. Let's hope I can buy what I need in Liverpool.'

'I'm sure that's in hand. Good luck, and don't worry about Joanna, Sarah and I will keep an eye on her.'

'Obviously we can't exchange letters. It's going to be hard for her.'

'Joanna's tough, she'll be fine. You concentrate on your new post. Goodbye and good luck.'

John shook hands with Angus and headed for his billet to collect his kit. He was unsurprised to find his flying gear was waiting alongside his uniform. Angus was nothing if not efficient. Chutes were supplied by the base you were flying from as they had to be looked after and RAF bods were infamous for not looking after anything very well. He was eager to start this new adventure as it would mean he could be posted close to home when he returned. That he wouldn't return wasn't something he even considered.

* * *

The Annie, an Anson, could hold up to nine passengers and he was the last of five to get aboard. This was the first time he'd been flown by a female pilot – he'd known that there were women in the ATA and had no qualms about her being at the controls.

'Welcome aboard, sir, if you'd be kind enough to get seated quickly, I'm cleared to take off in five minutes.'

He stowed his kit under the seat, put his case between his feet, stretched out his legs and promptly fell asleep. The Annie landed smoothly twice to allow the ATA pilots and another RAF bloke to disembark. He was now the only passenger and decided to join the girl who was piloting and making a damn good job of it.

'I've not flown one of these old girls – what are they like?'

'Compared to a Spit or a Hurry? Slow, reliable and no trouble at all. I deliver fighters and have brought several to Hornchurch over the past few months.'

'Somebody told me that you girls are being trained to fly bombers – is that true?'

She nodded. 'Only a few so far, but as the war continues more of us will do it. I expect you're being transferred for something hush-hush, so I won't ask where you're going or why.'

'I had the choice of going to an OTU and training flyers or taking this. I'll get posted a few miles away from my wife when this is done, which is why I agreed.'

'You must be a very experienced pilot to be offered something non-combative.'

'Around two hundred hours– I'm lucky to still be here. I've been blown up twice but on the ground, not in the air.'

'Golly, I thought that was the safest place to be – the ground, that is.'

'Usually, I've just been unlucky,' John said. 'There's weather ahead – aren't you supposed to land?'

'I am as I mustn't fly in bad weather. However, that doesn't apply to you. If you take over you'll get to Liverpool as planned, otherwise it won't be until tomorrow sometime.'

The old kite coped with the turbulence and John informed Speke that they would be arriving shortly and that there was an experienced pilot flying her.

Twenty minutes later, through the lashing rain, he spotted the runway. The landing lights were on, he could see the green beam indicating it was safe to descend, and they touched down smoothly.

'I'm sure you could have brought us in just as well,' he said to the young woman, 'thank you for allowing me to do it.'

'I can taxi her to the apron. I hope there's female accommodation as it looks a bit sparse.'

He pushed open the exit and a blast of cold rain engulfed him. 'Bugger all here, but they knew you were coming so they must have made suitable arrangements. Cheers. Thank you for bringing me to this godforsaken place.'

* * *

Joanna wasn't sure if she was relieved or more anxious when Angus rang her to say that John had been posted to do something he couldn't tell her about in Liverpool.

'I'm sorry, Joanna, you'll have to take my word for it that John's better off where he is than flying several sorties a day with his squadron.'

'Where do I write to him?'

'I'm sorry, you can't. He'll be gone for three or four months but will be back before the baby's here. He'll then be able to transfer to Hawkinge and you'll see him more often.'

'I see. It's August in a couple of days so that means he'll be home in November at the latest?'

'That's the plan.'

'I don't suppose he had time to ask you to do something for us. I want to hand this house over to the RAF to use, preferably as a hospital and convalescent home for injured men and women. I'll pay for any changes that need to be made. I'll be vacating the house after Christmas,' Joanna said.

'I know exactly the person to speak to. If you're generous enough to foot the bill for the conversion, then I think they'll be delighted to take you up on your offer. Is this a lease or transfer of deeds?'

'I want to keep ownership of Goodwill House but don't want it returned until it's no longer needed by the RAF.'

'When I'm next in London I'll speak to the chap who deals with this sort of thing,' Angus said. 'I'll let you know what he says.'

She hung up after the usual exchange of good wishes and enquiries, almost convinced that Angus had arranged John's transfer in order to keep him safe. Why was her husband in Liverpool? The city had been heavily bombed, the people demoralised, if he wasn't going to be on active duty, what on earth *would* he be doing?

The departure of the land girls occupied her thoughts for the next few days and it wasn't until the house was empty, the bedrooms they'd used put under dust sheets, that she mentioned something that had been puzzling her. Even Miss Biggins, Elizabeth's personal maid, was now joining them for supper, so there were seven of them sitting around the breakfast table. The dining room was too large for so small a group.

'I'm wondering if any of you can suggest what John might be doing in Liverpool if he's not on active duty?'

Tony answered. 'As you can't write to each other, I think it's likely he's gone to America or possibly Canada for some reason. The ships leave from Liverpool, don't they?'

'Of course they do, why didn't I think of that? Could he be going over there to train American pilots or something like that?' The idea of him being so far way appalled her but at least he wouldn't be risking his life every day as he would have been doing in Britain.

'The Yanks don't want to enter the war,' Joe said. 'But I suppose there must be some military blokes who don't agree with Roosevelt. They might have arranged this secretly.'

'They're going to have to join in eventually. Japan's already causing havoc in the Pacific. I can't believe that they're not already preparing for war,' Tony said firmly.

'I suppose then we will be invaded by brash American servicemen,' Elizabeth said with obvious disapproval.

'Better them than Nazis, Lady Harcourt,' Jean said with a smile.

'Tony, if you can spare the time from your work overseeing the improvements to our new home, would you be kind enough to drive myself and Elizabeth over to see the progress that has been made?'

'I'll take you whenever you like. The dower house is ready for occupation. Mum and I just need to get together sufficient furniture and so on for us to move in.'

Jean saw Joanna's look of surprise and disappointment. 'I'm not moving in until we all go, you know that. Tony's going to live there on his own.'

'I thought that's what was arranged and I'm relieved that's actually the case. You can take whatever you like from the rooms that are no longer being used and I believe there are still boxes of kitchen utensils and so on in the barn. They came from the demolished Victorian wing and not everything went to the WVS or WI to be distributed to families who had been bombed out.'

'Joanna, my dear, I have a suggestion to make,' Elizabeth said. 'Why don't we walk around the place and decide exactly what we want to take with us to our new abode? Then Jean and Tony do the same and what's left over can remain here for whoever takes over the place.'

'That's an excellent idea, Elizabeth, and the sooner we do it the better.

I'm expecting to hear from Angus, or the person he spoke to in London, any day now.'

* * *

The following morning, Liza cycled off to her job at the vicarage, Joe went with Tony which left Joanna, Elizabeth and Jean to start choosing the furniture they wished to keep and the items that they didn't.

'I think tying a strand of red wool to our selection and green to Jean's is an inspired idea, Joanna. Where shall we start?' Elizabeth said.

It took all day and they still hadn't looked in the attics. 'I don't think I wish to venture up there, my dear, so I'll leave that to you younger people.'

'A wise decision, Elizabeth, and I'll designate this to Joe and Liza. The attics are full of cobwebs and probably mice as well and I'm not overly fond of either.'

The twins were delighted to be given this responsibility and gobbled down their supper and vanished to rummage about and see if there was anything they wanted or that was worth keeping.

Joanna no longer flinched every time she heard the fighters screaming overhead because she knew her beloved husband wasn't on active duty with any squadron and risking his life in the air every day to keep Britain safe.

The twins were still rummaging about in the attic when she retired at just after ten o'clock. She got tired more quickly than she used to and going to bed before it got dark was something she was unfamiliar with. The twins had been up there for three hours – high time they came down, as Joe had a morning of tutoring tomorrow and Liza had to be at work by eight o'clock.

They'd left the door open at the bottom and top of the staircase leading to the attics, so there was no need for a torch. Electricity had never been supplied up there but there was light on this floor – the nursery floor.

Joanna stood listening but couldn't hear them, so they must be somewhere at the far end of the inter-connected rooms above. The floors were all boarded and there were windows as well, as these rooms had been used for the servants when dozens had been employed by the family many years ago.

'Joe, Liza, you've been up there quite long enough. It's time that you came down and got ready for bed.' She smiled to herself, thinking it probably wouldn't be more than a few more months before such maternal instructions wouldn't be required.

There was no answer and she viewed the steep staircase with disapproval. There was no option but for her to go up and find them. Goodness knows what they were doing that had kept them here for so long.

Fortunately, as the staircase was narrow and steep, someone had thoughtfully put a stout wooden banister on both sides, therefore she was able to ascend with no danger or difficulty.

'Liza, Joe, where are you both?' Joanna raised her voice and shouted, not something she liked doing. Shouting was unnecessary in her opinion.

She heard nothing so decided to venture into the rabbit warren of rooms. She called a second time when she was somewhere in the centre of the house. There was still sufficient light filtering in through the grimy windows to make it perfectly safe to wander about without banging one's head on the beams or tripping over the various boxes and detritus left up there.

'Ma, we were just coming to fetch you, you'll never guess what we've found,' Joe yelled from somewhere to the left of her.

She followed his voice and found herself in a larger attic where the two of them were crouched on the floor over a circle of open wooden brass-bound trunks.

'It's an absolute treasure trove up here, Ma,' Liza said, her voice rising to a squeak. 'We've marked dozens of things we should take with us and we're only halfway round. What's in these trunks is the best find yet.'

# 13

John wasn't impressed with Speke, a dreary little base, and Liverpool had been devastated by bomb damage. What cheered him up was the group of interesting blokes who'd volunteered for, or been persuaded to join, this barmy project.

As he'd already flown a Hurry, he didn't have to go away to be familiarised with them. He knew these outdated kites would seem slow after flying a Spit. A few days after arriving, they gathered to be told what was happening next.

'Righto, gentlemen, now you're all familiar with a Hurricane you're going to Farnborough where you'll be catapulted in a Fulmer.'

'What's that when it's at home?' a sergeant pilot asked cheerfully.

'The Fulmar is like a small Fairey Battle,' the impressively moustachioed squadron leader replied. This meant the Fulmar was an old-fashioned and slow kite like the horrible Fairey Battle.

John was first to take this old crate up. He pootled around quite happily and landed believing he'd got it under control. He wasn't quite so sure when the mechanics wheeled him across to the catapult which had been set on a concrete pad on the edge of the drome.

'Don't worry about it, old boy. You'll get a jolt, there's a big bang and you'll see a glare and then you brownout. You'll be able to still think and in a few seconds you'll see again before staggering off and flying,' the instructor told him.

To brownout meant you lost consciousness – diving in a Spit frequently did this to a flyer, so he was used to this happening.

'That doesn't sound too difficult.'

'There's just one thing you've got to remember – whatever you do, don't grip the stick hard. You've got to hold it loosely and then everything will be fine.'

John was no longer relaxed. His hands were wet and he regretted volunteering for this bloody stupid nonsense. Suddenly he was thrown back. There was a roar and a massive sensation of movement. His vision faded and he forgot he had to keep a loose hold on the stick. As his vision cleared, the nose pointed upwards and the aircraft waffled.

Instinct made him do the right thing. He braced himself for a nasty prang. The wheels hit the grass, bounced up and then dropped down again. He was disgusted with his performance but the instructor told him it wasn't too bad.

The others were waiting to hear how it had been. He was rendered almost speechless. 'Bloody horrible. Now, we've got half an hour whilst they put things right. Shall we join the boffins sitting over there in deckchairs being waited on by civilians and drinking tea and eating biscuits?'

Somehow he'd expected everything to be at a frantic pace, after all, Farnborough was the centre of aviation in the country, wasn't it? The reverse was true and instead of every moment being spent doing something hush-hush and dangerous, there was a lot of loafing around. In the evenings, there was ample opportunity to write to Joanna.

*My darling wife,*

*I can't tell you where I am but I think we can exchange a few letters before I'll be out of circulation. Just put my name, rank and number and the RAF postal service will get it to me.*

*I'm so sorry I didn't come back and speak to you but saying goodbye once was hard enough, to have to say it a second time would have been impossible for both of us.*

*I'm just footling about learning the ropes and the other chaps are all right. Decent food, reasonable accommodation and plenty of sleep – what more could a bloke want?*

*I hope your ankle's now fully recovered but please don't overdo it. I didn't have time to speak to Angus about giving up the house but I'm sure you've got the matter in hand by now.*

*I know this is hard, my darling, but it's worth the separation as when I come back I've been promised a posting close by.*

*Angus said I'll definitely return before the baby comes. I miss you, I love you, if it wasn't for this bloody war I'd be there by your side.*

*Your husband,*

He scrawled his name, blotted the paper and addressed the envelope. He still couldn't believe his luck. How had an ordinary bloke like him come to be married to someone as beautiful, intelligent and kind as Joanna? Addressing her as his wife and signing off as her husband made it seem more real and less like a dream.

If he had his trusty motorbike with him he could explore the area, but like everyone else on this miserable base he had to rely on public transport or an RAF driver.

The following morning, they were taken into the city where a men's outfitter was waiting to equip them with suitable civilian clothes. John returned the proud owner of a lightweight suit in beige with wide lapels and baggy trousers. He also had two pairs of slacks, a single-breasted brown sports jacket, and half a dozen shirts to go with them. He refused point-blank to take a trilby – he wasn't a man who wore a hat unless forced to by uniform regulations.

He'd also been issued with a large leather suitcase in which to put everything. They would be wearing their normal flying gear when they were on duty on board the merchant ships but when they went ashore in America they would be wearing their smart new clothes. None of it had cost him a penny and he assumed he would be able to keep these things when this was over.

A week after sending his letter to Joanna, he got a reply. He found himself a quiet corner in the mess in order to read it without being disturbed.

*John darling,*

*I was so happy to receive your letter as I didn't expect to have any correspondence from you.*

*I am fighting fit and my ankle has fully recovered. I've resigned as chair of the WVS and told them I won't be attending any further meetings until after our move. I've done the same with the WI.*

*Dr Willoughby is adamant that I mustn't overdo things. I think that he means riding a bicycle or riding a horse but I'm using that as an excuse to opt out of all village activities. Now that Jean has so little to do here she is going in my stead and Liza also.*

*Jean is spending time using her skills as a seamstress to make us all new ensembles. The trunks we have discovered in the attics that are full of Indian cottons and silks will be sufficient to clothe us until the end of this beastly war.*

*Joe has now joined the Observation Corps and is thrilled to be wearing a uniform. Liza is determined to join him but they don't allow women in their ranks at present.*

*The house is quiet, which I find I prefer, but it's far too big and I can't wait to move with you and our baby next January.*

*The midwife is happy with my progress and doesn't anticipate the problems I had when Sarah was born. You might or might not be pleased to hear she thinks there's no reason that we couldn't have a brother or sister for this one.*

*I don't know what it is you're doing but I know it's dangerous even if not as dangerous as flying a Spitfire every day.*

*I love you, come back to us if you can. You mustn't worry about us but concentrate on keeping yourself safe.*

*All my love for ever,*

*Joanna*

He read it several times and it was as if she was standing next to him. They weren't allowed to use the telephone or he'd call her. This letter, and possibly one more, would have to do. He folded it carefully, returned it to the envelope and put it into his inside pocket.

He'd heard that they were to be divided into teams of two and then there would be further practice before they'd join one of the merchant ships which had had a catapult installed on its deck. They would be embarking on this perilous journey in a week or so. The sooner they left, the sooner he would be back and able to be with Joanna. Another bonus was that all the blokes would get ten days' leave when, if, they returned safely.

* * *

Joanna joined the twins, who were peering into the open trunks in the attic. Her eyes widened. 'Good heavens – a veritable treasure trove. I think most of those items are from hundreds of years ago when Oliver Cromwell was in charge.'

She dropped down beside them and Joe handed over one of the large solid silver jugs. 'I don't know a lot about silver but I'm pretty sure this is Charles I and is worth a small fortune.'

'I read somewhere that they buried their treasure during the Civil War, Ma,' Liza said as she held up a beautifully engraved two-handled dish, which Joanna thought might be called a porringer. 'I wonder why this has just been left in these trunks in the attic?'

'I've no idea, and if my previous husband had bothered to look then he would have found it himself and been able to take care of his financial worries.'

She pointed to the other three trunks, only one of which was open. 'Have you looked inside those yet? I can't believe that they can also be filled with treasure.'

'You do it, Ma,' Joe suggested.

'You'll have to undo the buckles and I think the lid might be a bit heavy for me to lift in my condition, but I'll be watching closely.'

There was a collective gasp when they saw what was in the other trunks. Liza reached in and held up what looked like the breastplate that a cavalier might have worn. 'Good thing the Roundheads didn't find all this or Goodwill House would have been handed over and the Harcourts would have been executed.'

'In which case none of us would be here because I wouldn't have married David because he wouldn't have existed. It's still a mystery why these trunks weren't properly hidden. Attics would have been the first place Cromwell's men would have searched.'

'Obviously you don't want to leave this behind, Ma, but it's too blooming heavy for us to lift,' Joe said.

'It can stay where it is for now but I'm going to donate it to the British Museum – this family doesn't need any more money so I'm certainly not going to sell it.'

'If you sold it, we could buy a couple of Spitfires,' Joe said eagerly. 'Just imagine, John might actually fly in a Harcourt fighter.'

'I'd rather not imagine him flying in anything, thank you, my dear. I came to fetch you as it's long past your bedtime as you both have to be up early tomorrow. Do you still have any more attics to rummage through?'

'We've done half of them but those over in the Elizabethan wing where the land girls were living can't be reached from here. We'll have to go up the other stairs to have a look in there. We'll do that tomorrow.'

Joanna wrote a second letter to John, even though she hadn't had a reply to her first one. He could be sent overseas at any moment but she was going to write anyway. Writing to him made him seem closer. She missed him desperately and wasn't sure how she was going to get through the next few months without any communication from him at all.

*My darling husband,*

*I don't know if you'll read this before you leave but I'm going to write anyway. Such exciting news as the twins have discovered five chests of solid silver treasure and various other artefacts from before Cromwell's reign.*

*Joe wants me to put it all in an auction and donate the money to build Spitfires but I haven't decided if that's the right option. I think they should go in the British Museum as a memorial to one of the earliest Harcourt families.*

*I wish you were here to help me make this decision. We've spent so very little time together since we met. I pray that we have the rest of our lives ahead of us.*

*The Bentley has now been put away for the duration as it doesn't seem right to be parading around in such a big car when other people have so little.*

*Therefore, from now on if I go anywhere it will be on the bus like everybody else. Joe's driving Tony's motorbike and sidecar. I honestly believe that he thinks the more practice he gets driving anything motorised the more likely he is to be accepted to train as a fighter pilot.*

*The baby's turning cartwheels and keeping me awake but I'm loving every moment of this pregnancy, whereas I was miserable throughout my previous one.*

*It's now just after eleven o'clock, the house is quiet, there have been no sirens for a few days and I'm going to try and get some sleep.*

*I love you and miss you.*

*Come home safe to me, my love.*

Joanna left the letter to dry naturally on the slope of the little escritoire she used when writing letters upstairs, carefully screwed on the top of her fountain pen to avoid it leaking and then got ready for bed. Once the bedside light was turned out, she pulled back the blackout curtains, allowing the moonlight to flood in. She pushed up the window and leant for a few minutes against the sill, breathing in the warm night air.

Was John sleeping or awake thinking about her as she was about him? She smiled at her thoughts as she was very well aware that, like all fighter pilots, he fell asleep the moment his head hit the pillow. He'd told her that he could sleep standing up if necessary but she thought that unlikely.

The next morning, determined to post the letter, she was ready to walk into the village when Liza left for the vicarage.

'You don't have to stay with me, Liza, I'm taking Lazzy for company.'

'Are you sure? If he sees a rabbit he'll pull you off your feet,' Liza said.

'He won't. He understands that I'm not as active as I used to be and will walk like a perfect gentleman beside me whatever the provocation. He's not been into the village and it's high time he did.'

Joe was ready to head off to his morning lessons with Mr Kent in the village. 'Ma's right, he might be the biggest dog in the neighbourhood but he's also the best behaved.'

'Thank you for confirming my view. If I thought he was likely to misbehave, I can assure you I wouldn't take him.' She turned to Tony, who was collecting his things ready to leave for The Manse, where the dower house just needed a final few coats of paint before he could move in.

With her dog held loosely on his lead – there was no need to hold him tight as he walked to heel without pulling – Joanna set out for the two-mile walk to the village.

Lazzy behaved impeccably and the only time he looked interested was when he saw a group of familiar faces harvesting the hay.

'No, my boy, you can't go and see them. I expect you miss all the fuss and extra treats you got when the land girls were living with us.'

The dog appeared to be listening, which was ridiculous, but then he was a very clever animal. He licked her hand and they continued, both enjoying the early-morning sunshine and being away from home.

Before this pregnancy, walking to the village was something she did quite often but halfway there she was beginning to regret her decision. Should she return or continue as she was probably about halfway between Stodham and home?

There was a rumble of an approaching vehicle. Fortunately, she was just approaching the entrance to a meadow so was able to step briskly into the space, taking the dog with her out of harm's way.

Instead of driving past, the truck rocked to a halt beside her. A familiar figure jumped out of the driver's door and came around to speak to her.

'Here, you shouldn't be walking in this heat with that dog in your condition, Mrs Sergeant. Lazzy can go in the back and you can hop in the front with me. I'll give you a bunk up if necessary.' The speaker was the builder who'd knocked down the Victorian wing a few months ago.

'How kind of you, I hadn't realised how hot it was and how unfit I am just now.'

Her dog insisted on clambering into the cab with her and it was a bit of a squash but being driven was welcome nonetheless. It was impossible to hold a conversation as her mouth was full of dog hair most of the way.

'I'm working on your new house. I'll take you right there.'

'I have to post a letter first.'

'Here, give it to me, I'll hop out and do it. Getting you and that blooming great dog in and out again is too much faffing about.'

With her precious letter in his hand, he jumped out and completed the task in half the time it would have taken her. She would ask Tony to take her back in the sidecar and Lazzy would have to run beside Joe on his bicycle when he came home for lunch later.

The Manse was progressing well and Joanna could almost imagine what it would be like when the improvements were completed. Lazzy left before her, trotting willingly beside his second favourite human. She clambered with some difficulty into the narrow sidecar and was more than ready to return home. This would be the last excursion she made until the baby arrived. She was unpleasantly hot, felt nauseous and dizzy and thought her impulse to venture away from the safety and comfort of Goodwill House had been rather foolish.

# 14

John paired up with Flight Lieutenant Thomas Shaw, known to everybody as Sandy Shaw, as he was the only other bloke who was married. They also had servicing airmen which made their team up to six. The Wing Commander, an old bloke with grey hair, explained what was going to happen but neglected to say exactly when they would be leaving.

Speke mess was at the old Liverpool civil airport and they shared it with Fleet Air Arm and RAF flyers as well as naval deck officers. The first time he'd gone there, he'd been astonished to see the perimeter and gates were guarded by airmen carrying pikes. It scarcely seemed credible that men were equipped with spears of wood with sharp metal tips in today's modern warfare.

He received a second letter from Joanna just as he was told they were leaving so he didn't have time to reply. He ferried his ancient Hurry to Abbotsinch in Scotland, where his first job was to supervise its loading onto a ship.

'Crikey, John, I'm not looking forward to this,' Sandy said after they'd been briefed as to what was going to happen.

'We have to be sitting in the cockpit so we can retract the undercarriage and the kite can be put into the catapult,' he replied. 'That bloody wire doesn't look strong enough to hold us. Let's hope the man operating the crane knows what he's doing.'

He clambered in and took several deep breaths. Slowly he was hoisted into the air more than sixty feet above the sea and his hands unclenched when some silly sod dropped something heavy, which hit the tailplane, sending the joystick forward so it smashed the instrument panel.

He swore out loud and was glad no one had heard his foul language. The Hurry settled more or less comfortably onto the catapult and his fitters and riggers assured him they could repair the damage.

On returning to Speke with his crew, they got ready to embark on the *Eastern City* which was joining a large convoy off Merseyside, its destination America.

There was no time to think about what might happen as he was too busy checking and storing the spares, tools and ammunition whilst they sailed ahead in the centre of the convoy.

For the first few days, fighters and other escort vessels constantly circled, keeping a lookout for the Luftwaffe in the air and subs under the water.

'It's up to us now, Sandy, we're too far away from shore for the land-based kites to keep up their patrol.'

He was lucky because he had Sandy so didn't have to stand to in flying kit from dawn till dusk like those who only had one flyer on board.

'How do you want to do this? Three hours on and three hours off?'

'Sounds okay to me,' John replied. 'You're senior officer here so you can take first shift.'

'In which case I should be giving the orders but I'm an easy-going sort of chap so will stand to first.'

'Do you think we'll have to deploy? If we do, let's hope it's whilst we're still within flying distance of the shore. I really don't want to ditch in the drink.'

'I think it's a crackbrained scheme and a waste of time but who are we to argue with the bigwigs?'

John left him to it and went to the bridge to watch the long lines of merchant ships. In order to keep everybody together when it was dark, each ship towed a marker which the ship behind followed. Sensible idea as that way nobody would get lost.

The entire convoy had to travel at the same pace as the slowest ship, so they weren't going nearly fast enough in his opinion.

* * *

They'd been at sea for a week or more when the captain informed John that they were out of range of the German Condors so he and Sandy could stand down.

'This is a bit of all right, isn't it, old boy?' Sandy said whilst he was removing his flying kit in the cabin that they shared. 'We've got nothing to do until we come back in a few weeks' time.'

'You've got a memory like a sieve, Sandy. Don't forget under international law we have to stand regular ships' watches as we're officially members of the crew.'

'Nobody told me that – I'm not scrubbing bloody decks, that's for certain.'

'Neither am I. Come on, let's see what we've got to do and when we've got to do it.'

Eventually, after many, many tedious days, they arrived at Halifax. John had never experienced temperatures like it and even with his cold weather gear on, it did nothing to keep out the icy wind.

The captain was less than complimentary about Halifax but John was just glad to be on dry land. He stepped ashore onto a slippery jetty and almost fell on his arse. Not a good start, but it caused a good deal of hilarity from those who were watching and had been less clumsy.

After spending a drunken week in Halifax, where he got the chance to fly a Hurricane, he rejoined the ship and the convoy gathered and then continued towards New York, which was 600 miles south-east.

* * *

He and Sandy stood gawping at New York in all its brightly lit glory. 'Bloody hell, that's the Statue of Liberty – I never thought to see that,' John said.

'The skyline of Manhattan's everything I'd been told. I'm going to enjoy every minute here. Piece of cake this posting, old boy, isn't it? We better get into our civies and put our uniforms away. Do you think we need to bring them with us?'

'I'm taking mine – I'm proud of being a flyer in the RAF and hope I get the opportunity to wear it,' John said.

He and his five compatriots headed into New York and after days of junketing he was beginning to feel guilty that he was having such a fantastic time when Joanna would be at home worrying about him.

John was the only one pleased when they were recalled to their ship and the long tedious journey back to Blighty began. The Hurry was rearmed and everything carefully checked just in case it was needed.

During a vicious storm, the kite was damaged but the airmen soon fixed it and as they sailed into the danger zone, John put on his Sidcot suit, Mae West and silk scarf. This time he was taking the first three-hour shift.

There were a few ships sunk but fortunately the one he was on remained intact. It was with considerable relief that he and Sandy were stood down when shore-based fighters arrived to protect them.

He and his friend had filled the ammo panniers with smuggled liquor, well protected with nylons and other things that were no longer available in Britain. They tossed a coin and he was the one who was going to be catapulted from the ship in Liverpool Bay and the others would disembark in a less dangerous way.

'I'm not going to take the parachute, Sandy, if I crash it'll be in the bay and I'll soon be picked up. We'll be able to get more contraband into the country if I fill up the parachute case with it.'

'We've got enough fags, booze and flimsies for the ladies to make us very popular when we get home,' his friend said.

'Don't forget the chocolates and coffee – my wife will be happier with those than the alcohol and lingerie.'

'Good show – you keep the coffee as I can't stand the bally stuff. The only thing I didn't like about America was that they only drink coffee and you can't get a decent cup of tea anywhere.'

'We'll share the booty when we can. When I've got it at Goodwill House, I'll telephone you. We can arrange how I'm going to hand your share over then.'

'It's not that far from Brighton to Ramsgate – I'm sure we can organise something. It's been a grand few months, old boy, I hope we remain friends.'

'When this bloody war's over, travelling will be a doddle.' They shook hands and he scrambled into the cockpit of the Hurry.

There was the expected roar, a bang, blinding light, and he was airborne. Some impulse made him turn and beat up the *Eastern City*. Flying low like this was strictly forbidden but he didn't care, he was so glad to be home. In a few days, he'd be with his beloved wife.

She would be enormous by now, as the baby was due in five weeks. The weather was grey and dull, which was only to be expected in the middle of November. He should have been landing at Speke airfield where customs officers would be waiting, and he had no intention of giving up any of his contraband to them.

He flew across Mersey water and after dodging a balloon barrage he threaded his way out across the Dee and landed at Hawarden.

'Welcome back, Flying Officer Sergeant, you deserve your ten days' leave,' the Wing Commander said as he shook his hand.

'Can I leave my parachute bag here for a few days, sir?' As John spoke, he placed a bottle of bourbon on his desk.

'Certainly, I'll take good care of it.'

Message received and understood. This Win Co was a good sort.

Three days later, John was able to fly across to Speke and collect the bag. He'd already got his ill-gotten gains from the ammunition panniers. Getting it home was going to be difficult as he could hardly clank about with it in his suitcase.

Before he was dismissed from this posting, he bought himself an ancient trunk from a second-hand shop and transferred everything into that. He arranged for a carrier to take it to the station where he would leave it to its fate. He caught a bus to the station where the station master said things were rarely lost but they were often delayed so his trunk would be at Ramsgate eventually.

'As long as it gets there, there's no rush.'

There was a telephone kiosk outside the station and he checked his pockets to see if he had sufficient pennies to make a long-distance call to Joanna. As he waited for the operator to connect him, his finger poised over Button A, for the first time he had a flicker of panic. Whilst he'd been enjoying himself, things might not have gone as well at Goodwill House.

# 15

## NOVEMBER, GOODWILL HOUSE

Joanna was sure she looked like a beached whale and if the baby arrived before John got home that would be a bonus. She hadn't seen her feet for weeks, needed help to get out of a chair and even lying down was no longer comfortable.

'Joanna, John's on the telephone. Shall I tell him...' Jean said from the open sitting room door.

With a Herculean effort, Joanna regained her feet and was trundling to the grand hall before Jean had finished speaking. She snatched up the receiver.

'John? Darling, I can't tell you how happy I am to hear your voice.'

'Not more than I am to hear yours, my love. I'm safely back. Are you well?'

'The size of very large tent but apart from that absolutely splendid. The house is all but finished and we can move immediately after Christmas.'

Why were they talking about houses when this was the first time she'd heard his voice for more than three months?

'I've missed you, my darling, and I'm hoping to get a flip to Manston instead of Hornchurch in the next couple of days. Sod it – I haven't got any more coppers. I love you.'

There was just enough time before the line disconnected for her to answer. 'I love you too. Come home to me as soon as you can.'

Tony had put a comfortable, wide-seated chair next to the telephone especially for her as standing for any length of time was difficult. She flopped into it, the receiver still in her hand.

'Here, Ma, let me put that back. When's he going to be home?' Joe asked.

'In a few days. I'm desperate to see him but now I know he's safe and won't be on active duty again for two weeks I can relax. I've avoided making several important decisions in the hope that John would be here so I can discuss them with him.'

'That toffee-nosed RAF officer from London is waiting for you to give him your answer about handing over this place when we move.'

'I've also not done anything about the trunks of precious silver that you found in the attics.'

'Tony and I hid it in his new house and I guarantee nobody will find it. Liza and I are thrilled with our rooms at The Manse. They might be smaller than the ones we've got here but warmer, more comfortable and we've got a bathroom to ourselves.'

'You've also got a shared sitting room where you can entertain your friends if you wish.'

Joe frowned, something he didn't often do. 'Jean and Tony won't be living with us, Grandma has rooms downstairs and now Liza and I have our own space too. I don't think we'll see as much of each other.'

'We're still eating together and will gather in the drawing room to listen to the wireless most nights. I don't think hearing a new baby crying during the night would be good for either of you. Having us on opposite sides of the house means you and Liza can enjoy an undisturbed night's sleep even if I can't.'

'Grandma thinks you should employ a nanny and not look after the little one yourself.'

'That's what happened with Sarah and I'm determined to do things differently this time. I'm looking forward to being a full-time mother for this baby.'

He grinned. 'I don't reckon John will be as enthusiastic about crying babies as you are, Ma.'

'I've thought of that, there's a spare bedroom he can sleep in if he wants to. But he told me several times he wants to be involved as much as he can with his son or daughter.'

'He's a good bloke, has got a really modern outlook about women and marriage, but I doubt that he'll want to get involved with stinking nappies – I certainly wouldn't.'

'I should think not. I wouldn't dream of asking him to do anything like that.' Joanna smiled up at him – he was turning into a very handsome young man. She was aware that he already had a young lady in the village who he was taking to the cinema and out for rides in Tony's motorbike and sidecar.

'Please give me a hand standing up. I'm worried that the weight I'm carrying in front might tip me forward onto my face and then four strong men will be needed to get me up again.'

Safely on her feet, she returned to the warmth and comfort of the small sitting room. The only rooms they used now were the breakfast parlour, kitchen and their bedrooms. The house was far too big for so few of them and certainly unpleasantly cold.

Elizabeth looked up from her newspaper as Joanna tottered in. 'I swear, my dear, you look ready to burst. Is your midwife quite sure that you're not having triplets at least?'

'I'm definitely only carrying one, a big one obviously, and Dr Willoughby assured me there's as much water as baby.'

'When I first met you, I would have said that a woman of your age shouldn't be pregnant at all but that's not how I feel today. You might be closer to forty than thirty now, but you look ten years younger.'

'Thank you, that's kind of you to say so. I am conscious of the age gap between myself and John and hearing that I look to be in my twenties is reassuring. My biggest fear is that somebody younger—'

'Poppycock! That young man will never leave you. He's besotted with you. Even I have to admit that you could not have found a better husband.' Elizabeth smiled and continued. 'Mind you, he might not be around to watch you grow old. Did you know that people call pilots the walking dead?'

Jean walked in with the coffee tray and overheard this last remark. 'Lady Harcourt, Joanna doesn't need to hear things like that, not in her condition.'

Elizabeth chuckled, completely unrepentant. 'He's like a cat with nine lives – he'll be the exception that proves the rule. Hasn't he already been blown up twice and survived?'

Joanna collapsed onto the chaise longue and with a sigh of relief put her feet up in front of her. 'He's also just returned from a highly secret and dangerous mission unscathed so I think you might be right. He's used up three of his lives, but he's still got another six in hand.'

'This is the last of the real coffee, Joanna, so don't let it go cold. Rock cakes with butter and jam to go with it. The fact that several of the land girls left without having paid what they owed you means we get gifts of cream, butter, cheese and other things on a regular basis.'

'I told all of them as far as I was concerned the debt was settled,' Joanna said. 'This is their way of saying thank you and it's much appreciated. Now the chickens, ducks and geese have been transferred to the new house it's even quiet outside as well as in.'

'They've settled in well and Tony loves taking care of them. Most of the things stored in the barn have gone, including the petrol stored in the cans and the Bentley.'

Joanna sipped her drink, appreciating every mouthful, knowing it might be years before she tasted this bitter aromatic brew that she loved so much. 'I've left all that to Joe and Tony – I've heard a couple of lorries coming and going so assumed it was to clear the outbuildings.'

Elizabeth helped herself to a cake. 'There's very little to move when we go after Christmas. Only the things we're donating to the RAF – or whoever has the house after us – is left in the unused rooms.'

'Actually, very little of what's left will accompany us. Our bedrooms there are fully furnished and it will be just personal items that have to be moved.'

The *Light Programme* was on the wireless, an orchestra playing classical music of some sort – Joanna thought it might be Mozart, but wasn't sure. Whatever it was, it made a pleasant background to their conversation.

'Joanna, my dear, as this is to be the very last Christmas there will be a Harcourt at Goodwill House, do you think we could decorate the rooms that we are using? Perhaps we could have a farewell party combined with a welcome for the new baby before we leave?'

'We've already talked about that, Elizabeth, and the twins have brought all the festive decorations down and they're currently stored in the dining room waiting to be put up. Joe's selected the tree he wishes to cut down and will do that in a week or two.'

Jean joined in the conversation. 'There's absolutely nothing Christmassy to be had in the shops this year – not that there was much last year. There will be no orange in the bottom of a stocking for any of the children as you can't get one of those for love or money.'

Elizabeth sniffed. 'I'm sure if you and I went to Fortnum & Mason or Harrods, Jean, and are prepared to pay an exorbitant price, then we can get everything we want.'

'Well, I certainly won't be going to London but if you take Tony with you, Elizabeth, then you have my blessing,' Joanna said. 'I know we should do without when everybody else is having to, but I think my husband deserves to have the best Christmas possible, don't you?'

* * *

John said his farewells to the blokes he'd been stationed with for the past few months and with his belongings piled into the panniers on his motorbike, two suitcases securely attached to the pillion, he was ready to leave Hornchurch.

As he had to cross London, he decided to call in and see Angus, who was now working from the War Office in Westminster as an intelligence officer. He found a willing WAAF who agreed to stand guard over his bike for an hour.

'I need to see Squadron Leader Trent on a matter of urgency, but I won't be long.'

'Yes, sir, I'm happy to keep watch. Out of the wind it's not too bad today.'

'Thank you, much appreciated.' John bounded up the steps and into the cavernous foyer. He headed for what looked like a reception desk of some sort and explained who he was and what he wanted. The girl sitting there made the necessary telephone call.

'Squadron Leader Trent is on his way down. If you would care to take a seat over there, sir.'

He nodded his thanks but didn't bother to sit down. He'd obviously come when Angus was busy or he'd have been invited up. Angus appeared a few minutes later.

'Welcome back, John, I'm glad you didn't have to...' he hesitated and then smiled, 'didn't have to do anything you didn't want whilst you were away.'

Angus couldn't refer to the catapults on the ships as it was highly secret. They shook hands vigorously. 'Good to be in Blighty again. Everywhere seems so dull and dark here after my trip.' He was careful not to mention any actual places.

'Not surprised. Was this a social visit or have you something you need to ask or tell me?'

'Actually, I've brought you something. I won't hold you up.' He pulled out a bottle of bourbon from the inside pocket of his greatcoat and handed it over. 'My thanks. I'll get off now, as I'm eager to see my wife. Is Sarah well?'

'Splendid, thank you. Up to her ears in work and exams and I think she might be qualified a year early because she's so far ahead of the others in her cohort.'

'I'm not surprised. I hope you and Sarah can come down sometime before we move. We want you to meet the new member of the family and say a final farewell to Goodwill House.'

'Definitely. I've already put in for some leave and so has Sarah. We're both excited about the baby – we don't want any of our own at the moment, so we'll be taking a close interest in your infant when it arrives.'

They shook hands again and Angus marched off cradling the bourbon and John delved into his other pocket, where he'd hidden a packet of nylons to give to the girl for helping him out. When he handed them over, she was overjoyed.

'Blooming heck, are you sure, sir? These are like gold dust. I'll be the envy of my mess.'

'I am sure, thank you.'

He kicked the bike into life and headed for Kent and his much longed for reunion with his darling Joanna. London was depressing, which was hardly surprising considering the pounding it had taken over the past few months. If there was any Christmas cheer, he didn't see it and was glad to leave the city behind and head for Stodham.

Fog was rolling in from the sea, making driving more difficult, but he'd flown in worse conditions when his instruments were down and had made it safely to base. There was little civilian traffic on the roads, petrol was in short supply, and he had a horrible feeling someone in authority might confiscate the stash hidden behind the barn if they discovered its whereabouts.

* * *

It was dark by the time John turned into the drive but he could find his way to the house from there with his eyes shut and he might as well have done so as he could only see a couple of feet in front of him.

Nothing would be flying tonight, which was a relief as whenever any kite was in action there were bound to be fatalities. He had to report at Hawkinge in December which gave him almost two weeks at home. The baby was due on the 21st of next month and part of the deal, when he'd agreed to the ridiculous catapulting excursion, was that he would have a substantial block of leave when the baby arrived.

Despite having on his Irvin suit, jacket and trousers, his knee-length flying boots and his greatcoat over the top, John was cold, but didn't care. He was home. He rode the bike into the barn and as the noise of the engine died, he sat for a few moments, listening and breathing in the familiar scent of home.

The chickens would be shut up, the dog sensibly inside, so he wasn't sure what he was expecting to hear. No self-respecting bird would be singing in the middle of winter in the dark.

He had gifts for everybody – not all his bounty was travelling in the trunk. He couldn't manage everything in one trip. With a suitcase in either hand, he groped his way to the back door.

He put one bag down between his feet and turned the knob. The kitchens were more modern than the Georgian front and Elizabethan wing so didn't have latched doors.

There was no one to greet him, not even the dog, but then he hadn't told anybody he was coming today just in case he couldn't make it. He dumped the cases inside the door and returned to fetch the bulging panniers.

Still no sign of anybody – in fact, he wasn't sure there was a light coming from under the kitchen door, which was unusual as Jean should be in the final stages of preparing the evening meal. His stomach gurgled loudly, reminding him he'd not eaten since breakfast.

A flicker of unease ran through him. He'd spoken to Joanna three days ago and everything had been fine, but things could change in an instant. Had something dreadful occurred? He dropped the panniers and raced down the passageway, past the boot room, flung open the door and erupted into the kitchen.

Jean dropped the saucepan she was holding. Joe spilled his tea. Liza screamed. Tony's chair crashed back as he surged to his feet. Joanna stared at him as if he was a ghost. The only person not upset by his dramatic appearance was the dog, who rushed over to greet him.

'God, I'm so sorry. I'm back...'

Joanna recovered her voice. 'That's patently obvious, John. I hardly think we missed your arrival.' She wasn't smiling but staring at him through narrowed eyes. This wasn't going well. 'Indeed, my dear, it's fortunate Jean wasn't holding a saucepan of boiling water. I shall be unsurprised if your ridiculous behaviour precipitates the early entrance of our baby.'

He looked around the room, nodded and backed out without another word. From outside the closed door, he spoke. 'I'll do this again. Excuse me. I promise next time I won't scare the crap out of all of you.'

He heard someone laugh and smiled. When he returned with his gifts, they would forgive him – at least the others would. He wasn't so sure about Joanna. He should have telephoned to let her know he was on his way. Pregnant women obviously didn't appreciate surprises.

Ignoring the case, which held nothing interesting, he snatched up the two panniers and this time he called out as he approached the kitchen door.

'Hello, it's me, I'm back and so pleased to be home.'

The door swung open. Joanna stood there, her smile radiant. She'd never looked more beautiful despite being the size of a small house. He put the panniers down and she walked into his waiting arms.

A very satisfactory few minutes later, he raised his head and smiled down at her. 'Good thing I've got long arms, my darling, or…'

'Please don't tease, I can barely stand up and can't even put my own knickers on.'

'I'll be delighted to assist with that.'

She laughed as he'd hoped. 'Don't be an ass, John. Come in. Supper's almost ready and we tend to eat in the kitchen now.'

'I've got presents for everyone. Where's Elizabeth? I hope she's all right.'

'She has a head cold and has decided to remain in her rooms so she doesn't pass it on to me.'

'That's thoughtful of her. Go in, sweetheart, I'll bring the pannier.'

He'd got chocolate for everyone, coffee for the adults, nylons for the ladies and strong liquor for Tony. The second pannier had things for the baby and Christmas gifts. He's spent every penny, or cent to be more accurate, and was confident no one would be disappointed this year by inadequate gifts and the lack of luxury items.

The gifts didn't signify, he was home and that was all that mattered.

# 16

Joanna spent the evening in a daze and couldn't keep her eyes from John; she could scarcely believe he'd come home looking so well and would be with her for the next two weeks. There was so much they had to talk about but that could wait – tonight he was regaling the family with his exploits in New York, and she was as entertained and amused as everybody else. He'd warned them not to divulge any of it to anyone else.

'I'm sorry to break up the party but it's time we retired. I've not slept for twenty-four hours and Joanna's falling asleep despite the fact that my anecdotes are absolutely riveting.'

'I was, as Elizabeth would say, just resting my eyes. Goodnight, everybody, don't expect us to be up early, we'll see you later in the day.'

John had his arm around what used to be her waist and she was glad of his support. Going up and down stairs was becoming increasingly difficult. If she didn't have this baby soon, she might have to resort to sleeping on the chaise longue in the sitting room.

They were almost at their bedroom when she realised that something she'd just said might well be misconstrued by those who had been in the sitting room with them.

'Oh dear, do you think they thought that my saying we wouldn't be up early meant we would be otherwise occupied?'

His rich, deep laughter echoed down the freezing passageway. 'I think that highly unlikely, darling. I love you and even with you the size of a barrage balloon, I think you're the most beautiful and desirable woman in… in Stodham, but even I am not going to—'

She interrupted him. 'In Stodham?' She laughed and playfully punched his shoulder. 'A few months ago, you told me I was the most beautiful woman in the world – and referring to your wife as a barrage balloon is hardly encouraging or complimentary.'

Their bedroom was pleasantly warm, all the bedroom fires were lit at lunchtime so nobody had to undress in the cold. A luxury the majority of the population didn't have.

'If you sit on the bed, sweetheart, I can act as your personal maid.'

'As long as you don't undress me as speedily as you undress yourself then please go ahead. In my delicate state, I don't think I could cope with anything but a leisurely disrobing.'

Her nightgown had been hanging on the rail in front of the fire and was deliciously warm when he slipped it over her head. She now had a commode behind a screen – like Elizabeth – as staggering out of bed and trekking to the WC during the night was too much for her.

'I'll use the bathroom – I take it the arrangement behind the screen isn't for my use as well?'

For a moment she thought his question serious and was about to tell him in no uncertain terms that he was a man, not pregnant, and used to the cold, when she saw his smile.

'It's quite humiliating to be obliged to have a commode like Elizabeth but—'

'It makes perfect sense. It isn't safe for you to totter about the place in the dark, on your own in the middle of winter. If you wish to use the WC or bathroom whilst I'm here then I'll be happy to escort you.'

Joanna carefully regained her feet, shaking her head as he reached out to help her. She preferred to do as much for herself as she could. 'I notice, Flying Officer Sergeant, that you didn't offer to carry me. I shudder to think what I weigh now, certainly more than you can manage safely.'

Before she could object, he was at her side, slipped one arm under her knees, the other under her arms, and she was lifted easily. He walked across the bedroom and put her gently on the chair behind the screen where there was a jug of warm water and a basin ready for her night-time toilette.

'You still don't weigh more than I can manage, my darling, I'll carry you up and down stairs every day if that's easier for you.'

'It would be easier, but the midwife has said that I must keep active as much as I can as that's good for both me and the baby. Thank you for your kind offer but I'll continue to use the stairs, with your assistance.'

He vanished and she heard him strip in less than a minute and she hoped he'd remember to put on his dressing gown as to wander about the house in his birthday suit might not be appreciated by the others.

She was settling beneath the blankets, revelling in the warmth from the two hot water bottles Liza had put in earlier, when he returned – thankfully with his dressing gown on.

The main light was already off, only the bedside light on his side remained. He flicked it off as he climbed in beside her. His normal method of entering their bed was to vault in but tonight he got in cautiously. This was kind of him, but it just emphasised that he was treating her differently.

Instead of his naked limbs – usually freezing cold – enveloping her he was wearing both parts of his pyjamas.

'You really don't have to behave any differently just because I'm pregnant, my love.'

John put his mouth next to her ear, his hot breath sending shivers of desire rippling through her distended body. 'It's for your protection and mine, sweetheart. I know we mustn't make love but I'm sure we could manage it if it wasn't against medical advice.'

'I love you for saying that, darling, it makes me believe that beneath this massive mound there's still an attractive woman hiding.'

'I love you and there's nowhere else I'd rather be. I still can't believe my luck that someone like you agreed to marry me.'

She relaxed into his embrace. 'I'm the lucky one, my love, to have you as my husband.'

* * *

For the first time in several weeks, Joanna slept soundly and didn't wake up until the welcome rattle of early-morning tea disturbed her slumber.

She opened her eyes to find him, fully dressed, not in his uniform but in smart civilian clothes, smiling down at her. He put the tray on the bedside table.

'Good morning, darling, I've brought your tea. Shall I open the blackouts?'

'Gosh, is it light enough to do that?'

He grinned. 'It's just after ten o'clock so even on a miserable November day it's light enough to see.'

She pushed herself upright. 'Thank you, the tea's very welcome. Where did you get those smart clothes? I don't recall you having anything like that in your closet.'

'Another benefit of having to go to America was that we couldn't go ashore in uniform, so a complete wardrobe was supplied and paid for by the War Office. I look very dashing, don't you think?'

'You look handsome in everything as you very well know so stop fishing for compliments. One of the benefits of marrying someone as attractive as you means that we're bound to have a stunning child.'

'That's true – will the infant have my different coloured eyes or your blue ones? All my family have black hair – I think we've got Italian blood somewhere in our ancestry – so I wonder if black hair and blue eyes is a possibility.'

'I'm hoping that if we have a son then he'll be your image and a daughter will look like me – Sarah certainly does.'

He hooked a chair leg with his foot and moved it across so he could sit down next to her whilst he drank his tea. She was impressed that he didn't spill a drop whilst he did this.

'Do you know when you're likely to have this baby? Could it be earlier than we expect?'

'Anything's possible, but until the baby drops into position the birth isn't imminent. I can't wait for that to happen as having the bump so high gives me shocking indigestion.'

'So I'm not likely to become a father during this visit?'

'I'm afraid not. The only good thing about the baby being under my bosom is that he or she isn't pressing on my bladder, making me want to spend a penny every five minutes.' She stopped and shook her head apologetically. 'I'm sorry, I'm sure you don't want to know that sort of detail.'

He put his cup and saucer back on the tray and then took her hands and raised them to his lips. He kissed the knuckles whilst his extraordinary eyes were holding her captive. 'I want to know everything, however mundane, however intimate. I know it's not a man's place to be involved with pregnancy or birth and that children in your world and babies are relegated to the nursery and packed off to boarding school as soon as possible. I want this to be different.'

'Good lord, the last thing I'd want is for you to be there when I deliver this baby. I can't imagine any man feeling quite the same about his wife if he had to witness that.'

His smile was wicked and she laughed with him. 'Well, maybe in our case nothing will stop us wanting to be intimate.' Was it wrong to want to make love to him at this late stage in her pregnancy? She dragged her thoughts away from this and changed the subject. 'We've already discussed this; you know I intend to feed the baby myself and don't wish to have a nanny. Our child is absolutely not going be sent away. Possibly not educated at the village school, but definitely attending any school we select only on a daily basis.'

* * *

John was waiting for her to question him about his three months away but supposed she'd learned more than enough last night when he was telling the others about the time he'd spent in New York. He'd not mentioned the drinking and nonsense as that would be rubbing their noses in it. Joanna had been worrying about him when he'd been having the time of his life. Of course, for a month he'd been at risk, but he couldn't talk about that as it was hush-hush.

'I'll take the tray back to the kitchen whilst you start getting up. Do you want me to take you to the bathroom?'

She shook her head. 'Absolutely not, I can make my own way there when it's light without any danger to me or the baby. I do wish you'd stop fussing.' Her voice was sharp, and she waved her hand at him as if dismissing a servant.

'In which case I won't come back to offer my assistance but will wait for you in the kitchen.'

He was halfway down the passageway when he reconsidered. He'd got no right to stomp off like a child at the slightest upset. He was a grown man, a fighter pilot, why the hell had he let such a small thing get to him?

He was aware that he was sensitive about his background, that he came from working parents, and that people might well think that she'd married beneath her and that he was a fortune hunter.

This wasn't her fault – he'd just got to get over it. When he'd received that letter asking him to come back to her, he hadn't hesitated. Joanna was irreplaceable, he'd never love another woman, and whatever other people thought about the match, if she was happy to give up her title for him, then that should be enough to reassure him.

He'd left the door ajar and pushed it open, half-expecting to see her sitting on the bed crying because of his behaviour. However, she was in the process of collecting the items she needed to take to the bathroom and looked around in surprise at his reappearance.

'Did you forget something, my love?'

He'd overreacted – made something out of nothing. Until that moment he hadn't realised how insecure he was in this relationship.

'I just wanted to doublecheck you don't want me to carry you down the stairs or hold your arm whilst you negotiate them yourself. I know you want to remain independent, but I'm here if you need me. There's bugger all else I can do for you at the moment.'

'I do wish you wouldn't swear so much, darling, what if the baby can hear?'

This was so ridiculous, he laughed, shook his head and lounged against the door jamb. 'Imagine the consternation if our baby is born able to repeat a string of swear words. It'll be the wonder of the century.'

With remarkable speed and accuracy, she threw one of the pillows from the bed, which hit him full in the face.

If he hadn't been securely propped against the door, he might well have fallen backwards into the corridor.

As he reached up to remove it from his face, she arrived at his side and shoved him. This time he did lose his balance and slithered to the floor. He could hear her laughing as he untangled himself and jumped to his feet.

He tossed the pillow onto the bed and then stretched out on it. He had his shoes on and had no intention of removing them. He wanted to see her reaction when she returned. He didn't know much about pregnant women – in fact he only knew what he'd learned from Joanna – but guessed swings of mood might well be normal.

He heard her coming back and put his hands behind his head and closed his eyes as if asleep and waited. Again, she surprised him.

'You look very comfortable there, I'm tempted to come back to bed myself but I'm ravenous and want my breakfast.'

He sat up and swung his feet to the floor. 'I'm waiting for an apology, wife, as I didn't appreciate being knocked to the floor so violently.' He tried to sound cross but failed.

'Did you not? I thought it funny. I take it you've no objection to being hit by a pillow? I'll make a note of that.'

'You're impossible, adorable and I don't know how I'm going to deal with not being able to make love to you for months.'

'Cold showers and long walks should solve that problem.' She was behind the screen and he was sad that she no longer wanted him to see her unclothed. He wasn't going to invade her privacy but he would talk to her about it.

John made the bed whilst she was dressing – another skill he'd learnt in the RAF when he was still obliged to take care of himself.

'Goodness, so domesticated! I'm impressed, Flying Officer Sergeant.'

He moved towards her and leaned in and kissed her tenderly. 'Jean's an amazing seamstress. I love the maternity dress that you're wearing. Blue suits you perfectly.'

'Thank you, I don't deserve your kind words,' Joanna said. 'I'm sorry if I've been grumpy and for throwing things and pushing you over.'

'Don't apologise, it's who you are, and I don't want you to change. Is throwing things and knocking people over normal for women in your condition?'

'I certainly didn't do either when I was expecting Sarah. I wouldn't have dared. I don't think you realise just how happy you make me. I never knew that marriage could be so wonderful, so liberating, and I thank God every single day for bringing us together.'

Her eyes glittered and he slipped behind her and gathered her close. 'Being married to you is better than flying a Spitfire and I can't say fairer than that.'

She turned her head and looked up at him. 'How kind of you to say so, I'm sure Elizabeth will be equally impressed by your wonderful comparison and compliment.'

He kissed the top of her head and then picked her up as he had before and marched through the house, down the magnificent carved wooden staircase and put her carefully on her feet. The dog was waiting to greet his mistress.

'Good morning, lovely boy, I hope Joe has already taken you out.'

'I'm sure he has. I can smell bacon – I'd forgotten how good it tasted until I had it served with pancakes and maple syrup. Although rationing hasn't affected the RAF as badly as it has civilians, we still don't see bacon very often.'

'I can smell coffee brewing – I'd be happy never to eat bacon again if I could have coffee every day.' Her smile made him feel ten foot tall. 'You couldn't have brought me a better gift than four tins of coffee.'

* * *

After a belated breakfast, they retreated to the study to talk. 'What do you think, John? Should the treasure go to a museum or be sold to buy Spitfires?'

'Fighters, definitely. It will still end up in a museum somewhere, it won't be melted down, will it?

'I doubt it. How many aircraft would it pay for?'

'Haven't the foggiest. What's it worth, do you think?'

'Tens of thousands of pounds.'

'Then maybe three. I think you'd get four or five Hurries for the same amount.'

'Then two Spits and two Hurries. Will we be able to have them called after Goodwill House?'

'I've seen other kites that have been donated by families and villages and they have the family name, or the name of the village, painted on the side. I'm sure if you make that a stipulation, they'll be only too happy to agree.'

'Now the other thing that I can't decide is whether to give the house to the RAF or lease it.'

'If you hand over the deeds, then don't pay for the refurb; if it's a lease, agree to pay for the changes. Has whoever you've been speaking to confirmed it will be used as a hospital and convalescent home?'

'No, that's another thing that has made me hesitate. They won't commit. Air Commadore Berkhamsted passed on my suggestion to a local businessman, one Sir Cecil Hadley, and he doesn't have a good reputation. I remember David saying he couldn't be trusted.'

John decided this was too much for Joanna to deal with so late in her pregnancy. He'd try to sort it out before he had to leave for his new posting.

# 17

Joanna waited to hear John tell her she was imagining things because of her condition but he did the reverse.

'Berkhamsted? I've heard that name before. I think he's infamous for avoiding any work. Passing on your request sounds exactly like him. Why is this other bloke not trusted?'

'I've no idea – David didn't tell me directly; it was something I overheard him saying on the telephone. He sounded quite animated, which wasn't like him at all, and that's the only reason I remember the name.'

'If that's all, I don't think there's much to worry about. That said, I'll make some enquiries before you decide.'

'Before *we* decide – being married to me means that you have equal responsibility for everything that goes on with the estate and the family finances.'

'I'm happy to do what I can whilst I'm here. Once this bloody war's over, I can shoulder far more of the work.'

Reassured by his response, Joanna told him what Tony had found out already. 'Sir Cecil has an unsavoury reputation and I think he might have been a Mosley supporter. All fascists are now incarcerated so I suppose he must have wriggled out of it somehow. Of course, this was never proven and he appears to be a pillar of respectability nowadays.'

'The more I hear about this man, the less I like the sound of him. Why in God's name would the Air Commodore think he was a suitable person to deal with your offer?'

She shook her head and ignored the question, assuming it was rhetorical. 'Tony has been asking around and the builders, who worked here and then on The Manse, told him something interesting.'

He raised an eyebrow and she smiled. 'I know, I do tend to ramble nowadays.'

'Shall I guess?' She nodded and he continued. 'Hadley's hoping to get hold of the place but not to turn it into a hotel or hospital. No, from what you've told me he's more likely to make it into a funk hole.'

'What's that? I've never heard that term.'

'It's a house or hotel where rich people come to hide and avoid doing anything useful for the war effort.'

'That can't be what's being thought of for here. It's too close to Manston, Ramsgate and Dover, to be considered safe, isn't it?'

'No, it's ideal. Plenty of woodland and gardens to hide in and far enough away from the village to avoid prying eyes. Now the windows in the drawing room have been replaced, it's perfect. I know you're not using the boiler, but having working central heating would be a plus to the people wanting to get this set up. This house could have two dozen cowards living in it and nobody would know who they were.'

'Surely you're not suggesting the Air Commodore is involved? I can't believe he'd agree to the house being used in this way instead of as an RAF hospital and convalescent home.'

'If you hand over the deeds to this Hadley, he can then do what he wants. Have you spoken to Angus about this?'

'No, he's away. I spoke to a WAAF initially, explained why I was telephoning and was put through to Berkhamsted. He told me that the RAF were delighted, thanked me for my generosity and said this Sir Cecil would deal with everything.' She frowned. 'I feel rather silly now. I really should have written and not relied on telephone calls as I have nothing at all on official headed paper.'

'Don't worry, I'll take over if you'd like me to? I'm pretty sure there's something about this Hadley that's dodgy and you're right to be suspicious,' John said.

'Thank you, darling, I'm very happy to leave it to you. Can you also organise the sale of the family treasure and have the proceeds turned into fighters?'

'I'd be happy to. I'm going to have a run across to The Manse to see our future home and will call in at Manston on the way back. I'm sure someone there can set the ball in motion.'

'I've not been to Stodham to see the house for months. The twins and Jean are over there all the time. Most things have already been transferred and when we move after Christmas, we'll not need more than a small van. I'm surprised you haven't noticed how empty the rooms are.'

'Blokes don't notice that sort of thing. The lack of chickens, ducks and geese I was immediately aware of. Also, that the Bentley has gone – have you sold it?'

'No, it's been in the family for years and I'm hoping after the war we can use it again. Elizabeth's given up a lot and she really loves that car.'

'Given up? You've taken her in and made her an integral part of this family. She's lucky to be here. I don't think many women in your position would welcome their ex-mother-in-law.'

'There's something you don't know – it never occurred to me to tell you,' Joanna said. 'After David died, those villains at the bank were going to foreclose as we couldn't pay back the money they'd stolen. Elizabeth cashed in all her trust fund and paid the debt and has refused all my offers to repay it.'

'Crikey – that puts a different complexion on it. Don't get me wrong, sweetheart, I love the old bird, she always made me welcome even before we were officially together.'

'There's an excellent auction house in Ramsgate and I'm pretty sure it's still functioning. Why don't you call in and tell them about the silver? They wouldn't sell it there but I'm sure they'll have connections to both Sotheby's and Christie's in London.'

John got to his feet and kissed the top of her head – an affectionate gesture but one that was starting to grate. It was something one did to a child, not one's wife. Joanna ignored the flash of irritation and smiled.

'It's still very foggy, wouldn't it be better to leave it until the weather improves? There's no real rush as you're here for another ten days.'

'*Carpe diem,* my love. You know what could happen. I might get a telephone call at any time be told to report immediately even though I've been given almost two weeks off.'

'True, but I'm hoping that won't happen this time.' She put on a brave smile. 'If it does, then at least I know you're only an hour away and not the other side of the world.'

'I'd better change into my uniform. Against the rules to be seen out of it even when on leave.'

He smiled but she could see he was already thinking about what he was going to do. He had a disconcerting tendency to be able to compartmentalise his life most of the time. When he was with her, she had his full attention, but as soon as he left, she was certain he didn't think of her nearly as much as she thought of him.

* * *

Despite the fact that Joanna had decided not to have the boiler lit this winter, they still had fires in all the rooms that were used, including the study. Liza no longer had lessons with Mr Kent in the village as she'd completed all the work she needed to take her school certificate next summer. Joe, who intended to do his higher school certificate when he was seventeen, still had the occasional morning with his tutor.

Joanna was comfortable sitting with her feet up on the sofa in front of the fire and decided to stay there. If somebody telephoned who required to speak to her then Jean would come and find her.

She was woken by Jean's arrival with the tea trolley, closely followed by Elizabeth. She yawned and stretched. 'Goodness me, I didn't realise I'd been asleep so long. Tea and cake – perfect.'

Joanna glanced at the mantel shelf where a clock had always ticked noisily but that too had been moved to its new home at The Manse.

'It's three o'clock, my dear, and you will be delighted to know that the fog has mysteriously vanished as suddenly as it appeared two days ago,'

Elizabeth said. 'I expect the beastly Germans will be coming over in force now they can see where they're going.'

'Obviously, John's not back yet. I can't tell you how happy I am to know that he's just driving around the countryside on his motorbike and not doing anything dangerous in the sky.'

'It's odd in here without the large desk that dominated this end of the room,' Elizabeth said as she sat on a comfortable, but somewhat dilapidated, armchair opposite the sofa. 'I know you said we should remain here until after Christmas so your baby can be born at Goodwill House, but as he or she isn't a Harcourt, I can't see that it makes any difference where they are born. Why can't we move before? Everything will be ready by then so Jean and Tony tell me.'

'To be honest, Elizabeth, I have been thinking the same.' Joanna paused to gather her thoughts, not wanting to alarm her mother-in-law but believing it was time to tell her what had been going on with the possible transfer of the house to the RAF.

She explained her doubts and that John had gone to make some discreet enquiries. When she finished, Elizabeth nodded.

'All very havey-cavey, Joanna. However, I don't see that this would make it impossible to move.'

Jean handed around the tea and cake and then joined them. 'Lady Harcourt, if the house's empty it would be simple enough for someone to move in and claim possession. I agree with Joanna that we should remain where we are until things have been legally finalised.'

'Take possession? Whatever do you mean, Jean? I cannot believe that squatters would have any legal rights over the house. Even if they did, I'm certain there are men in the village who would be only too happy to live here and keep any intruders at bay.'

Both of them had valid points. 'It's still five weeks until Christmas so we don't have to decide immediately. As only our personal possessions need to be packed and taken, it would be simple enough to leave early if that's what we want.'

She should have said the decision was hers and John's, nothing to do with either of them, but arguing and confrontation was too much effort.

Growing this baby had apparently taken away her ability to make decisions and the sooner it was born, the happier she'd be.

* * *

John had no difficulty finding the auction house and when he explained the reason for his visit he was ushered into the office of the senior auctioneer.

'Please sit down, Flying Officer Sergeant, I'm sure my company can help you with this sale.' The speaker had introduced himself as Jonathan Faulkner and was a man in his fifties, immaculately dressed in a dark suit and, apart from his wild head of grey curls, looked and sounded like any other toff.

John explained what was involved and what they wanted to do with the proceeds of the sale. He'd politely refused refreshments as he had several visits to make and didn't want to be out after dark and worry Joanna.

Faulkner was glancing down the list of the items he'd been given and at the end of his perusal was almost licking his lips at the thought of how much commission his company was going to make from the sale.

'Excellent, excellent. Despite the fact that we're in the middle of a war there are still collectors, museums and so on who will be interested in such a magnificent collection of artefacts.'

'I need to make it very clear that none of the items are to be melted down. My wife and I are well aware that the value of the silver is immense but any sale at auction or privately will only be agreed if the purchaser signs a legal document accepting our terms.'

'Absolutely, absolutely. I will have my legal department draw up something for you to approve.'

'Good. You said that museums would be interested but I thought everything of value had been removed from the major museums and put somewhere safe for the duration. I can't believe the curators of those establishments will be buying anything new at the moment.'

'That's a valid point. However, there are various trust funds attached to these places and trustees who can access the money. I can assure you, sir, that something as important as this collection will be of relevance even in the current situation. I can think of two individuals with vast wealth who have an interest in such antiquities so even if the museums don't bid, one of these gentlemen will.'

'Obviously, we'd prefer the collection to be available for the public to see but as long as it remains intact, isn't split up, then we've no objection to it going to a private buyer as long as it remains in the country,' John said.

He cut the meeting short. Faulkner wanted to see the collection for himself before he started the process of its sale and that was fair enough. As it was hidden somewhere at The Manse, he'd have to speak to Joe or Tony and make sure they had it on display when the valuers from the auction house came to view it in a couple of days.

* * *

Visibility was improving rapidly as the fog was drifting out to sea. This made driving a pleasure rather than a hazard. He turned into the short drive of what would shortly be his family home in watery November sunshine.

He was astonished to have Lazzy bounce up to him. 'Where did you come from, you daft dog?'

Joe peered out of a window on the first floor of the handsome Georgian building. 'He travelled in the sidecar; he's taken a fancy to it. The front door's open – would you like to come in and have a look around?'

John straightened from fussing the dog and stared directly at the boy. 'As it's my house, I don't think I need your permission to do anything here.' He kept his tone neutral but from his expression his feelings were clear.

The boy vanished, hopefully to come and meet him and apologise. The sooner John established his position in the hierarchy, the easier it would be for everyone. He was the man of the house and now was as good a time as any to make that fact clear.

There were two village women, their hair tied up in cotton turbans, wraparound aprons around their ample waists, polishing the wooden staircase.

'We'll get out of your way, sir, you won't want us flapping about when you get your first look at your lovely new home,' the older of the two said with a friendly smile.

'No, carry on, ladies, it doesn't bother me.'

Normally he would have looked around the ground floor first, but he wanted to speak to Joe or rather hoped that Joe would be waiting to speak to him. He wasn't disappointed as the lad was hovering nervously in the bedroom where he'd been hanging out of the window a few moments ago.

'I'm so sorry, sir, I spoke without thinking. You're my stepdad now and...'

'Apology accepted, Joe. As long as the situation's plain.' He smiled, making it clear he wasn't cross. 'I'm John, not sir.'

The boy grinned. 'What about Pa?'

'I'm not ready for that. Now, show me around. As you've been involved with the renovations whilst I've been elsewhere, you'll make an excellent guide.'

At the end of the tour, John was delighted and impressed in equal measure. 'Elizabeth's eager to move in immediately and I can't see any reason why not.'

'Ma wants to have the baby and this last Christmas at Goodwill House. It's become a bit of an obsession with her, John, and Grandma knows that. She sometimes forgets that she's not the most important person in the family.'

'She's the only one with a title. Hardly surprising at her age that she gets a bit confused.'

'Blimey, she's no more confused than I am. She's sharp as a tack and is quite prepared to use her age to cajole Ma into doing what she wants. Don't you give in, John, if my ma wants to have my brother or sister at Goodwill House and to spend Christmas there then that's what must happen.'

'Well said, Joe. I've got to call in at Manston before I go home – do you want to come with me?'

The lad's eyes lit up at the thought of being allowed onto an RAF base. 'That would be amazing. I'm going to volunteer as soon as I'm old enough. Do you think the war will still be going on in two years' time?'

'God knows, but I've a nasty feeling it will be. Do you follow the news?'

They were chatting as they headed outside to his motorbike. 'What about the dog? Will he try and follow you?'

'No, he only comes for the ride. He'll wait until Tony comes back for supper later.'

John kicked the bike into life and rocked it off its stand. 'Right then. Hop on the back and we'll get going. Before I forget, the treasure has to be put out to be inspected by the valuers and auctioneers the day after tomorrow.'

'Okay. Tony and I'll have it ready.'

As it was only three miles to the base, they were there in minutes. He cruised to a halt at the barrier and showed his ID and gestured behind him. 'This is my stepson, Joe Harcourt, he's planning to sign up as soon as he's old enough.'

'Good for you, lad. There's some of your old squadron from Hornchurch here today, sir, I reckon they'll be pleased to see you.' The corporal pointed to the far side of the massive runway. 'They're at readiness, but not been scrambled.'

The guard waved them through. John could see a couple of blokes standing outside in their flying gear, no doubt keeping an eye out for the NAAFI van. The rest of the squadron would be in the warm inside the newly built dispersal hut. The old one had been blown up last year.

He accelerated across the runway. You never knew when a kite might be coming into land or be about to take off so it didn't do to hang around. He slowed as soon as he was across and glided to an expert stop beside the dispersal hut.

'Well, as I live and breathe, if it's not the wandering hero returned to visit us lesser mortals,' one wag called out on recognising him.

'Smithy, I thought I'd drop by and buy you all a char and a wad.'

Joe slid off the pillion and stood in awe, gazing at the neatly parked kites. 'Does your lad want to sit in one?' Smithy asked.

'Yes, please, sir, I'm going to be flyer when I'm old enough.'

'So I've heard. Come on, you can have a dekko at mine, it's the nearest.'

'Thanks, Smithy, you've made his day.'

'Made my year, John, this is the best day of my life.'

Sergeant Pilot Bert Smith grinned, saluted and strolled off with Joe hanging on his every word. John watched them go and hoped Joe would never become a flyer and cause his beloved wife extra anxiety. One pilot in the family was more than enough.

He reached into one of the panniers and removed two cartons of fags. Giving the flyers bourbon when they were at readiness wasn't on. His gifts were appreciated and he left two quid with Smithy when he returned with Joe to pay for the tea and buns when the NAAFI van eventually turned up.

'I sat in the cockpit, John, I don't know how you do it. When the lid was closed I couldn't breathe.'

'It's a tight fit, Joe, but you get used to it.' He was surprised the boy's previous enthusiasm had evaporated so quicky. He'd expected the reverse would be true.

'I've changed my mind about being a fighter pilot. I'm going to fly a bomber instead.'

'Don't tell your ma that! Anyway, if you do pass all the exams and tests to be a flyer, you don't get the choice. You'll be sent to Fighter, Bomber or Coastal command. You don't have a say in the matter.'

# 18

The two weeks' leave passed too quickly for Joanna. Tomorrow would be 1 December and in just over three weeks' time, not only would it be almost Christmas, but her baby should be here. He or she was due the week before and Sarah had arrived only a couple of days late. Would this one do the same or was it possible it would actually be a Christmas baby?

Moving about was becoming increasingly difficult as the baby had now settled into the eagerly anticipated – by her, at least – pre-birth position. This meant the pressure on her digestion was alleviated but she was now in permanent danger of having an embarrassing accident.

'We haven't really decided on names, sweetheart, I suppose it will have to be Noel or Holly if our child arrives Christmas week,' John said.

'I rather like the name Geoffrey John for a boy and Charlotte Joanna for a girl.'

They were in the sitting room after supper listening to *ITMA – It's That Man Again* – on the wireless. Elizabeth had already retired, the twins were engrossed in the other side of the room in a lively game of Monopoly ably assisted by Tony and Jean. It was a happy family scene but in twenty-four hours everything would change as her beloved husband would be leaving for his new posting.

He considered her choices of names and then, to her annoyance, ruffled her hair and kissed the top of her head. 'I'm happy with your choices. By the way – I'm glad that my parents have decided to come after we've moved. There's no point in them seeing this house now.'

She ignored his reply and told him, not for the first time, that she didn't like being kissed on the head. Instead of apologising, he smiled in what she thought was a patronising manner, which only aggravated her annoyance, and stood up.

'I'm going to make the cocoa – can I raid the biscuit tin, Jean?'

'Not for me, thank you, John, I'm going up.' This was ungracious but the closer it got to his departure, the more wound up she was becoming. She forced a smile. 'You stay and drink yours down here. Don't wake me if I'm asleep.'

He was at her side immediately and offered his arm for her to hang on to so she could heave herself to her feet. 'I'll come up with you and then come back and make the cocoa.'

* * *

The next day, Joanna was out of sorts and Dr Willoughby called it a bilious attack. He suggested she stay in bed and just eat only lightly.

'You've been incredibly fit throughout this pregnancy, Mrs Sergeant, and although things are rather uncomfortable at the moment this is nothing to worry about. Remain in bed, read and listen to the wireless.'

'I'll do that, thank you for coming so promptly. I can assure you that it wasn't me who wanted you here but my husband. I'm dreading his return tomorrow and think that might have something to do with this.'

'I'm sure you're right. Worrying isn't going to change anything and isn't good for you or the baby.'

She heard John talking to the doctor in the corridor outside the bedroom and smiled. He was probably as upset as she was about the fact he had to leave tomorrow afternoon.

He put his head round the door and his flashing smile even now still made her heart skip a beat. 'I'm going to get the wireless from the kitchen and bring it up here so we can listen together. I won't be long.'

By lunchtime, she was perfectly well and insisted on going down even though she only had soup and toast and not the rabbit stew that everyone else was eating.

As John was due to report to his new base, Hawkinge, by midday they retired early in order to give them some time for private conversation. Joanna was also considerably more comfortable in bed with her feet up than sitting on the chaise longue.

They were stretched out on top of the bedspread; her head was resting on his shoulder and he was running his fingers idly through her loosened hair.

'This is the longest we've spent together since we met, my love. I truly believe that we've finally got to know each other. We've spent so much time talking…'

'I think not being able to make love is the answer to that,' he said as he yet again kissed the top of her head.

'Don't do that – it's patronising and I really don't like it.' She hadn't meant to snap but she'd been on edge all day thinking this could possibly be the last night they might ever have together even though he kept reassuring her that his new posting wouldn't involve being scrambled. Also his unromantic reference to their love life had upset her.

'Don't like what? Me touching your hair or kissing you?'

'You know very well what I mean and you're just being deliberately obtuse. Children are kissed on the head, not wives.'

John withdrew his arm and with casual deliberation rolled away from her and stood up. 'I've no idea you didn't like it or I wouldn't have done it.'

'I've told you twice at least so you obviously don't listen to me. I know you're a dashing pilot, everything you do is of far more importance than me, but it would be good to have your undivided attention whilst you are here and not be treated like a child.'

'I apologise if my affection was misconstrued. Excuse me, I'll leave you to get ready for bed. I'll be up later.' He nodded and walked out. His words were inoffensive enough, but his tone was cool. She really should go after him, apologise, but didn't have the energy.

Why didn't he understand that she was anxious about him going, anxious about having this baby without him, and this was making her sharp and shrewish?

Her intention had been to apologise when he came to bed, she didn't want to fall asleep with any bad feeling between them. However, by the time she'd washed, got into her nightgown and climbed into it she was yawning and fell asleep with him still missing from beside her.

* * *

Joanna woke the next morning feeling guilty and reached out for him but the space beside her on the bed was cold and empty. Wide awake, she sat up and looked around. His suitcase and kitbag had gone and so had he. The blackouts had been drawn back and weak December sunshine was filtering through the shutters, which were still closed.

The clock on the mantel shelf above the fire showed that it was just after ten – how could she have slept in so long on his last morning? More importantly, why hadn't John woken her to say goodbye?

How could he have done that? Her throat thickened, tears trickled unheeded down her cheeks and she flopped back against the pillows. By the time she was up and had waddled through the house and got downstairs, it would be too late.

She didn't doubt that he loved her but she just didn't understand why this time he'd been so insensitive. Her stomach growled, the baby was moving restlessly and painful lumps were appearing as the infant tried to get comfortable. Seeing and feeling these bumps which were, she thought, elbows and knees, was uncomfortable but she loved it.

Could unborn babies sense when their mothers were upset? She tried to stem her tears but the more she mopped with the corner of the sheet, the heavier they fell.

* * *

John had joined Joanna in bed half an hour after leaving her to get over her snippy mood, he was disappointed that she was already asleep as he'd wanted to put things right between them.

He usually slept well but tonight he was the one who was restless. This wasn't how he'd expected to spend his last night with her and it was as much his fault as hers. It was 1 December today. Last night he and the others had come up with an idea that would make his departure less painful for both of them. He was lucky to have had so long at home. Some poor buggers hadn't seen their wives and families for years.

At just after six, he was up, dressed, and with his flying gear and suitcase he left her sleeping and headed downstairs. He met Joe and Liza in the kitchen.

'Is Ma asleep?' Joe asked.

'Out for the count. Come on, let's get this done.'

'I need your help to bring in the tree – it's the biggest one I could find that had roots but would still go in the pot. If we'd brought in one without roots so early it would be bald by Christmas.'

'I'll come with you now as I want to put my stuff on my bike.'

'Why have you brought that down now?' Liza said. 'Ma will think you've gone without saying goodbye if she wakes up.'

'Sod it! Should have thought of that. I want to get the bike packed so I can spend longer with her when she's awake.' He shrugged. 'No point in carting it back, I might wake her. I'll stow it away, bring in the tree with Joe, and then we can get on with it.'

Lazzy was happy to come out in the freezing darkness, not even a glimmer of moonlight to help. John found his motorbike by the small beam of his torch and had his belongings safely packed away in minutes.

'The tree's in the corner – I'm surprised you haven't noticed it. As Ma doesn't come out any more, I didn't need to hide it.'

'Let's hope Lazzy hasn't been watering it for you. Come on, dog, get out of the way, we've got work to do.'

They took the tree in through the front door Liza had opened for them. 'Jean said to put it by the door, then it won't shed its needles so quickly as it won't be near the fire or the radiators if Ma agrees to put them on for Christmas.'

'Right, it looks perfect there, don't you think?' John said as he and Joe positioned it where Liza had directed.

Jean came in to check they'd got it right. 'That'll look lovely when it's decorated. Tony's coming over soon so we'll have a cup of tea when he gets here. I'm just going to get the breakfast parlour ready and then I'll decorate the tree.'

'Right – the three of us can start here.' He pointed to the half a dozen tea chests spilling over with glittery tinsel, sparkling glass baubles and rolls and rolls of brightly coloured crêpe paper. 'There'll be more than enough in those boxes to make the place look festive.'

Tony joined them and, between the four of them, soon the place was looking spectacular, there wasn't a surface or corner that wasn't festooned with twisted crêpe paper, tissue paper bells and glittering tinsel.

Jean had got the range going and put the kettle on to boil and after an hour they stopped for tea. 'I don't think Goodwill House has ever looked so Christmassy – certainly not since I've worked here,' Jean said happily. 'And we've just got the sitting room to do now.'

'Joanna will love it. I want her to spend the next few weeks surrounded by colour and joy so she doesn't worry about me or the baby.'

'Hadn't you better check if she's awake?' Liza suggested.

He went up with a tray of tea, but Joanna was still sleeping. He opened the blackouts and then left her. She needed her sleep. Carrying a baby was hard work.

At nine the fog was clearing and the sun was attempting to shine. John looked around the grand hall and smiled at his helpers. 'We've done well. The greenery from the garden with the candles is the finishing touch.' He grinned and hugged each of the twins. They hugged him back. 'Thank you both. Joanna will love it.'

'Having the fire lit in here makes it even better. The sitting room's looking lovely too and the breakfast parlour's dressed in the best china ready for breakfast. I put a note through Miss Biggins's door last night asking her to bring Grandma down today,' Liza said.

'The paper chains and other things you found in the attic are perfect. I don't think even Harrods will look better than our house this year. This will be a December to remember.' The tall clock in the corner struck the hour. 'Bloody hell – it's ten. Christ, I hope she hasn't woken up and thinks I've buggered off without saying goodbye.'

Elizabeth spoke from the stairs. 'Moderate your language, young man, it's inappropriate for Goodwill House. I could hear Joanna crying as I walked past so you had better go to her.'

He took the stairs three at a time and burst into the bedroom. 'Darling, please don't cry. I'm so sorry. I wouldn't leave without saying goodbye.'

Her lovely face was blotched and tear stained. She stared at him as if he was an apparition. He was across the room and gathering her into his arms before she could answer.

Joanna cried against his shoulder for a few more minutes before pushing him away. 'Where were you? Your things have gone.'

'Stupid of me. Let me help you get dressed. We've been busy downstairs and even Elizabeth's come down today.'

He picked her up and carried her through to the WC in the passageway. 'I'll leave you here and run a bath for you.'

He filled it with more than double the allowed amount of water and sprinkled in some lemon-scented bath salts. The room was warm, the steam rising from water and condensing on the mirror.

'Goodness me, I've not had a bath for months. Are you quite sure you'll be able to get me in and out safely? I really don't want to be stuck.'

'Absolutely certain, darling.'

'Help me put my hair up as it takes so long to dry.'

He removed her nightie and lifted her into the water. She lay back with a sigh of satisfaction. 'This is absolute bliss. If you hand me my mug of tea, that will make this perfect.'

Whilst she drank her tea, he watched the strange lumps come and go on her distended stomach. 'Doesn't that hurt?'

'Not at all, a bit uncomfortable perhaps but I love to feel our baby moving about inside me.'

'Promise not to drown whilst I'm gone – I'm going to fetch you something to put on. It's much warmer in here than your bedroom. The boiler's now alight and the house will be warm everywhere until we move. Bugger the expense and the fuel.'

'Using bad language demonstrates a paucity of vocabulary, my dear.'

He chuckled and said something even ruder. She scooped her empty mug into the bath and was about to throw it at him. He saw her intention and was able to move swiftly to one side.

'Behave yourself, wife, whilst I fetch you something suitable to wear.'

Twenty minutes later, he carried her down the long passageway, marginally warmer now the radiators were on, and paused halfway down the stairs.

'Look, my darling, what we've done for you. It's why I was up so early.'

Her reaction was all that he'd hoped. She clutched his lapel, her mouth rounded and her eyes were wide.

'My word! How lovely the hall looks. I can't believe you did all this for me.'

'Not just me, sweetheart, we all worked to decorate the house. I know putting all this up so early is unusual, but we hope having so much colour around you will make the weeks go more swiftly.'

He gently put her on her feet, being careful that she was securely on a step, and then bent his head and they kissed. She didn't need to say anything else. Her kiss told him all he wanted to know.

Joanna insisted on wandering around examining everything and loudly exclaiming at all she saw. 'Darling, breakfast's waiting. Jean's made a special effort this morning. You've got weeks to look at it all.' He didn't say that their time together was short, but she understood immediately.

'Such indulgence for the house to be so warm. Our baby will now be born in absolute luxury.'

He kept his arm around her waist as they strolled down the vast hall and into the beautifully decorated breakfast parlour.

'Oh my, this is so pretty. I'm so sorry to have made you wait for your breakfast.'

Elizabeth beamed and gestured expansively at the ribbons, baubles, candles and streamers. 'I am not as a rule a lover of such falderols, but I must admit that even I admire what has been done.'

Jean arrived with Liza and a groaning trolley. 'Here we are; please sit down, Joanna, John, we're all more than ready to eat.'

'Can I smell actual bacon?' Tony asked eagerly.

'Yes, and scrambled and poached eggs as well as fried bread and sauté potatoes. Followed by toast, real butter and strawberry jam.'

'I've got coffee and tea here,' Liza said.

Joanna squeezed his hand. 'This is perfect. I was dreading today but you've managed to make a difficult morning for both of us more bearable.'

Whilst the plates were being piled high, John spoke quietly to her. 'I'm so sorry about last night. I should have woken you when I came to bed. I hate to think you went to sleep unhappy with me.'

Her enchanting smile as always touched his heart. 'To be truthful, my love, I fell asleep immediately and it wasn't until I woke up and thought you'd gone that I was upset.'

There was no further opportunity to talk as they were presented with a truly exceptional breakfast. Bacon and butter were a rarity and there was an appreciative silence around the table.

Liza and Joe went off to make the toast whilst Jean topped up everybody's cup with their chosen drink.

'I went into Ramsgate the other day and there's absolutely nothing to be had in the shops to cheer up anybody's Christmas. The kiddies will be lucky to get any sort of toy in their stocking this year,' Jean said.

'Didn't you say that the WI and WVS have been unravelling old woollies and re-knitting them into dolls and teddy bears?' Joanna said as she sipped her favourite drink.

'No wrapping paper at all – it's a good thing I saved it all from last year and the year before,' Jean said happily. 'I've already ironed it and you wouldn't know it wasn't new.'

'My newspaper has half the pages,' Elizabeth informed them. 'Miss Biggins told me this is because paper is made from wood and all the wood is needed for the war.'

'Everything's needed for that,' John said. 'I used to have an orange, a silver sixpence and sweets in my sock. I've not seen an orange over here this year.'

'It must have been like walking into another world when you were in America, my boy. I've almost forgotten what it is to see the brightly lit streets, the shops full of everything you want and jolly news on the wireless instead of what we hear every night at the moment.'

'They don't have rationing, my lady, the blackout, or anything else but believe me, they're well aware that war's heading their way. At least we're not fighting on our own now that Russia has changed sides,' he said and there was a chorus of agreement.

'Do you think the Yanks are going to help us?' Joe asked.

'They already do – we're getting most of our armaments and so on from them on a loan-lease agreement. If Japan attacks America then they'll be coming over here in droves. Maybe the Americans will ask to requisition Goodwill House.'

'Americans living here? I should think not,' Elizabeth exclaimed loudly. 'If we must give the house up, it should go to help our boys, not American invaders.'

The freshly made toast arrived and that was more important than the possible – no, probable – arrival of thousands of American servicemen in Blighty. Any attempt to take back Europe from the Nazis would have to start on this coast and inevitably there would be Yanks all over the shop flashing their money and seducing the local girls with gifts of chocolate, nylons and other things that weren't available here.

# 19

Joanna interrupted the conversation to share with them something that had occurred to her whilst the others around the table were busily discussing the deprivations of rationing and other depressing subjects. Her mind did tend to wander nowadays.

'I have an idea that I hope everybody will agree with.' She smiled at John. 'This excludes you, my love, as you'll have other more important things to do with your time.'

Even Tony was looking at her with interest. 'The thought of so many children in the village and in Ramsgate, where a lot of them are living like troglodytes underground in the tunnels, being without gifts this Christmas is most upsetting when we have so much here. I've been thinking—'

'Joe and I saw several boxes of discarded and broken toys in the attics when we were looking at the furniture. We can bring those down and see if we can mend them.'

'Liza, that's exactly what I was going to suggest! Everybody's having to "make do and mend" and we must do the same. Second-hand toys are better than none at all,' Joanna said. 'Tony, you're a skilled engineer, I'm quite certain there's a barn full of bits and pieces you can manufacture into toy wheelbarrows, trains, and push-along toys of various sorts.'

Joe didn't look quite as convinced as his sister. 'Don't forget that we've cleared out everything metal and handed it in to be made into fighter planes. The gates at the end of the drive went months ago for the same reason.'

'I know that, but I'm sure there are still bits and pieces that didn't go that could be used. What do you think, Jean? Couldn't you make teddy bears and dolls from scraps of material?'

'I certainly could – in fact I'd already decided to do so. I've had another thought too. Just a minute and I'll show you.' She jumped to her feet and rushed to the kitchen to reappear with an empty National Dried Milk tin. Jean waved it triumphantly and it rattled.

'I've got several of these and thought that by putting stones inside, painting them gaily and attaching some sort of handle made with string or knitted wool a toddler could have endless fun with one.'

Joanna was delighted with this suggestion. 'That's exactly the sort of thing I was hoping for. Ingenious...'

John laughed. 'I'm not always airborne – there's a lot of time sitting about – I'll get the blokes to start whittling. Wooden toys are always popular.'

Joe nodded. 'I save the feathers from the game birds that I pluck and I reckon I've got a sackful. Wouldn't they be useful for stuffing a cushion or something?'

'Good idea. I could make bedding for a doll's pram and the feathers would be perfect for that,' Jean said.

Tony had been silent up to now. 'The previous owners of The Manse kept canaries and we found half a dozen birdcages. I think I could make them into dolls' houses.'

Joanna smiled. 'I can't imagine how you'll do that but I trust your skills. I can make dolls' clothes, stuff teddies and rag dolls, but that's about my limit.'

Elizabeth had been listening and now chimed in. 'Miss Biggins is a resourceful lady and has been collecting old, knitted garments from jumble sales for weeks. She's washed them herself and then together we've been unravelling each item and rewinding the wool.'

'You've been doing what? I never imagined you doing something so... so practical,' Joanna said.

'I must say that I surprised myself. When my maid explained why she wished to do this, I was impressed by her kindness. Surprising as it might seem, I assure you that I am an accomplished needlewoman and can knit as well.'

'Then we'll work as a team and see if we can't produce gifts for as many children as possible in the village and in Ramsgate.'

'We can hardly go around to each house and give the things to the parents,' Liza said. 'What about if Tony and Joe dress up as Father Christmas and hand out the gifts that way?'

'Didn't you say, Jean, that there's no wrapping paper available this year? I'm sure you don't have enough put by to wrap up all the gifts I'm hoping we can make. Therefore, the only way our small presents can be a surprise for Christmas morning is by hand delivering them to the houses with children.' As Joanna said this, she understood such a task would be all but impossible, however willing they were.

'I'll talk to the ladies at the next WI and WVS meetings, Joanna,' Jean said. 'Between us we can work out how to do this. Every parent and grandparent wants to be able to fill their little one's stocking.'

* * *

John touched Joanna's arm and her heart sank. He was warning her he'd have to leave soon and wanted to say goodbye in private.

She gripped the edge of the table and levered herself upright. 'Thank you for agreeing to do this. It's going to make the next few weeks pass more quickly.'

She led the way into the hall which, with the radiators warm and the huge fireplace filled with crackling logs, was a delightful place to spend a few minutes. 'The tree's quite lovely this year. I never knew that there were all those stunning glass baubles hidden away in the attics.'

'It looks wonderful. Before I go, I wanted to tell you not to worry about the house and its new tenants. Angus is now taking care of it and this Sir Cecil is no longer in the picture. No one will bother you until after the baby's here.'

'Thank you. That's a relief. I hate to say goodbye.' She swallowed and tried not to cry. 'It's only an hour for you to get back here. I'll make sure someone telephones the base when the baby has arrived.'

'I want to be told when you go into labour.'

'No, better to wait. You might only get a couple of days' compassionate leave and I don't want to waste a minute of it with you pacing up and down outside the bedroom whilst I give birth.'

'I love you, darling, and next time I see you we'll be a real family.'

'We're that already. Take care, my love. Drive safely.'

They exchanged a final kiss and John strode through the front door. Joanna didn't go outside to wave goodbye but remained by the Christmas tree, watching through the window as he bounded down the steps that led from the end of the terrace to the drive.

He didn't look back so didn't see her watching. She supposed that was the only way a fighting man could do his duty. He had to put aside his personal life and concentrate on firing his gun, flying his aircraft, or driving his tank. She shuddered. In her opinion, having been born a woman was the better option.

No one came in to check if she was coping and for that she was glad. It took a few moments to compose herself, put on her usual smile and waddle back to the breakfast parlour. There was still a lively discussion going on about the toys and other items that they proposed to make as their contribution to Christmas for those less fortunate than themselves.

'I've been thinking, everybody, that what we need to do is collect everything we've got that might be suitable to turn into toys for children or gifts for adults. The study's the perfect place to put it all and for us to work,' Joanna announced with a forced jollity.

'Tony, if you and Joe bring down my sewing machine and set it up in there then I can get started,' Jean said.

'We'll do it now, Mum,' Tony said as he pushed back his chair. 'Come on, Joe, we've got a devil of a lot to do at the house today and need to get cracking.'

'Liza, shouldn't you be at work?'

Her daughter shook her head. 'I've been meaning to tell you, Ma, they don't need me any more as the children's grandma has come to live with them. I don't think Mr Evans could really afford to pay me – a vicar doesn't seem to get much in the way of wages.'

'I'm sorry to hear that but am delighted to have you home at the moment when there's going to be so much to do. The layette for this baby is done, everything's prepared in the bedroom where he or she will be born so having this Christmas project to organise and complete will keep both of us happily occupied until the big day.'

Jean and Liza quickly cleared the table, leaving Elizabeth to make her way into the sitting room where she would spend the morning reading whatever newspaper was delivered. The *Daily Mail* and the *Evening Standard* were her choice but over the past months she'd been obliged to read whatever arrived as sometimes there just weren't enough of her chosen titles to go around. Joanna was sure that her mother-in-law quite enjoyed receiving a copy of the *Daily Mirror* or the *News Chronicle* occasionally.

* * *

John completed the formalities at the guardhouse and headed for the admin block. After parking his motorbike, he reported his arrival a second time and was directed outside again to find his way to the officers' accommodation block.

There was the usual to-ing and fro-ing on the strip, all very relaxed and not at all like the frenetic activity he'd become accustomed to at Hornchurch. There squadrons were constantly screaming into the sky after being scrambled for one party or another. Here, so he'd been told, the squadron didn't fly in two flights of six but in pairs. He would be doing reconnaissance over France, escort duty up and down the Channel and the only dogfights would be if he and his partner were attacked by *Messerschmitts* and needed to fight to escape.

His room was a bit smaller than the one he'd had at Hornchurch and the other bed was obviously occupied. An orderly appeared and saluted somewhat sloppily.

'Welcome to Hawkinge, sir, I'll unpack for you.'

'Right, thanks.'

The spotty young man grinned. 'You'll find everybody at dispersal.

Visibility's rubbish so nothing much going on today. Flying Officer Jordan shares this room with you, sir, and he's a nice enough bloke.'

There was an odd, vaguely familiar smell pervading the room. Not pleasant at all. John thought this an odd thing to say but would reserve judgement until he'd spoken to the chap himself. As he was already wearing his flying boots, Irvin jacket, helmet and goggles, he just dumped his greatcoat on the bed and was ready to report for duty.

He used his bike to get to dispersal and the racket it made attracted plenty of attention. He was greeted cordially enough by the other men but the Wing Commander Flying acknowledged him with a curt nod.

'About bloody time, Sergeant, I've been running one short for the past ten days. I suggest you check in with your ground crew as you'll be going up next with Jordan.'

John snapped to attention and saluted smartly – this sort of nonsense seemed appropriate. 'Yes, sir, I'll grab a chute on the way.'

The three blokes looking after the Spit that would be his were friendly and seemed pleased to see him. They might well have been hanging about doing nothing much for the past ten days. 'All tickety-boo, sir, ready when you are.'

'Great. Is that Jordan's kite next to this one?'

'It is, sir, not sure where he is though, you'll usually find him having a fag behind the hut.'

Again, this comment raised alarm bells. Most flyers smoked, so why had they bothered to mention it? He walked to the rear of the dispersal hut and sure enough found two officers propped against the wall. They weren't smoking, they were drinking from hip flasks. He could smell the alcohol fumes from where he was standing.

They were the same rank as him so he couldn't order them to stop. However, he wasn't about to fly with Jordan if the man was drunk.

'Put that bloody flask away, you cretin, or I'll make a formal complaint to the Win Co.'

His sudden appearance and snarled command had the desired effect. The fact that he was over six foot and broad shouldered added to the impact of his words. If it hadn't been such a bloody awful thing to have discovered, what happened next would have been funny.

Jordan literally left the ground, dropped his flask and the other bloke stepped back, treading on the silver and crushing it. Jordan recovered and wailed plaintively, sounding like a small boy, not a young man about to fly a Spitfire. 'That belongs to my pa, he'll flog me for ruining it.'

'Don't be such a drip. I'll bally well punch you if you—' the other chap began to mutter in response.

'I'll kick both your arses if you don't sober up and get back to dispersal.' These two were exactly the sort of privileged chinless wonders who'd made him originally refuse a commission. He'd not wanted to be forced to share a mess with them. 'Do I make myself clear?'

All would have been well if another bod hadn't arrived and called, 'Sergeant, Win Co wants a word.'

Jordan straightened and exchanged an outraged glance with his friend. 'How dare you threaten us. We'll have you court martialled. Threatening an officer is an—'

John didn't bother to correct them. He turned his back and marched off to see what the CO wanted. He'd been under the misapprehension that this posting was for experienced, decorated flyers, so how in God's name had those two imbeciles ended up here?

'Where the hell have you been?'

'Trying to talk some sense into Jordan and his companion, sir.' John stood ramrod stiff in front of the grey-haired officer. 'They were both drinking behind the hut. I'm not going up with either of them until they sober up.'

'Not again. I've warned my boy about being inebriated on duty, but does he bally listen?'

Warning bells rang loudly. 'I take it Jordan's friend is your son, sir?'

'Unfortunately, that is correct.' The Win Co rubbed his eyes and suddenly looked too old to be in charge of a squadron. 'Do you want to make a formal complaint, Flying Officer?'

'I just want them removed from duty. They are likely to kill themselves or whoever has the misfortune to fly with them.'

The two drunken flyers burst from behind the hut, full of indignation at John's apparent insubordination.

But before they could make even bigger fools of themselves, the Win

Co yelled at them. 'Flying Officer Sergeant insists that you be removed from duty. You are both a disgrace to your uniform. You will be posted somewhere you can do no harm. God knows what your mother will say when she hears about this latest escapade, Charles.'

'He's an officer? We thought he was a sergeant and he threatened to hurt us,' Jordan complained. Then he turned green and vomited over his boots, much to the amusement of the watchers and the disgust of the Win Co.

'I'm not drunk, Pa, I can take Nigel's place.'

This had escalated far further than John had intended. It didn't do to alienate his commanding officer so thoroughly. 'Jordan's in no state to go, sir, but I'll fly with this chap if he's sure he's sober.'

He really should have found out the name of his superior but it was too late to do more than remain at attention and pray his offer was accepted and that he was right to think this other idiot would be safe in the cockpit of a Spit.

'Good man. The spy wants to talk to you. I'm not happy about anyone being up in this visibility. It's less than 2,000 yards and getting worse.'

The intelligence officer was insistent that the operation should go ahead despite the worsening weather conditions.

'There's a convoy proceeding north up the East Coast and at present it's in Barrow Deep moving at seven knots.'

They were standing in front of a map pinned to the wall and he and his pale-faced co-flyer silently pencilled in the coordinates on their maps. John now knew he was going up with Nigel Reynolds, the only son of his commanding officer. Reynolds's parentage didn't bother him but the fact that the boy was half-cut did.

Back outside, the rain was heavier and John had a bad feeling about this operation, especially with the man accompanying him. He headed for his waiting kite, his parachute over his shoulder, helmet on and oxygen mask dangling to one side.

This was going to be a bloody awful sortie. If they both came back unscathed he'd be surprised. His ground crew were quiet but that was only to be expected in the circumstances.

'How long will you be up, sir?'

'An hour, possibly an hour and a half.'

John took off first, keeping a close eye on the other Spit which to his surprise was being flown with as much confidence and expertise as his was. This young man had probably flown half-cut before and was able to pull himself together once he was in the cockpit.

By the time they'd escorted the convoy, the clouds were lifting, the wind blowing the bad weather away. They'd maintained RT silence but now he told control they were returning after successfully completing their escort duties.

As he was approaching the strip, John noticed the giant metal 'T' on the runway outside the control tower, which showed wind direction, had been turned 180°. This meant that his approach had to be made in the reverse direction. You always landed and took off into the wind.

He touched down smoothly, the tail dropped, but he couldn't see ahead because the nose of his kite obscured his view. Halfway down the runway, he was suddenly hurled forward with such violence one of the straps tore from its mooring. His head jerked forward and there was a hideous bang as metal tore. His windscreen and canopy shattered. His engine screamed and died.

What the bloody hell had just happened? John's hands were shaking, his legs trembling and he couldn't release the buckles of his harness. He could hear the siren and bell of the fire engine and ambulance racing towards him.

The canopy was wrenched off and somebody reached in and released him. He wasn't hurt – just shocked and shaken.

'Out you come, as quick as you like.' There was urgency in the voice of the speaker and this jolted John from his inertia. The biggest fear of any flyer was being burned alive in his cockpit and there was a definite whiff of fuel.

He was heaved out and then saw what had happened. Reynolds hadn't seen the wind had changed and had crashed head-on into him. As he was assisted to the ground, he nodded towards the other wrecked kite.

'Poor bugger's gone for a Burton. Bloody bad luck – his harness failed and he broke his neck on impact.'

'Christ, I should never have let him fly.'

'It's not your fault. Wing Commander Reynolds made that decision. The poor sod has lost his only child and it was entirely down to his own error.'

John then realised he was being supported by a squadron leader – not a member of the rescue squads. 'I'm not for the high jump then?'

'Absolutely not. I'm Billy Williams. You're on my squadron now.'

John shook his head, trying to clear it. He could have died because of some other idiot's error and his unborn child would never have known their father. Joanna would have been a widow for the second time. God, how he hated this bloody war.

# 20

Joanna was amazed by the number of interesting items the twins had carried down from the old nursery floor and the attics. 'Good gracious, I'm so pleased with these. I can see several jack-in-a-boxes as well as tattered teddies, velvet rabbits, building blocks and tin cars. They can be laundered, repaired or repainted and will make splendid gifts.'

'There's still quite a lot of things we can use left up there. Bits of material, old books and so on. Tony's found some paint and Grandma and Miss Biggins have bags of clean, freshly wound balls of wool for making clothes, new hair and so on for the soft toys and dolls,' Liza said.

Joe had discovered some interesting gift-related information. 'Ma, the milkman and postman are going around to houses with lists of requests from their customers and if they find a match then the two families get in touch.'

'What a good idea. When we've got our toys and things ready, perhaps we can use both of them to distribute them for us.'

'No, Ma, we can't. They're just passing on the information, not the actual toys. Maybe we could ask them to let parents know what's here and then they can come and collect it.'

Jean was busy at her treadle-sewing machine, the needle flashing up and down at speed. There was already a colourful pile of finished items on the table next to her. Bedding for dolls' prams and cots as well as items for actual babies.

'We've only been doing this for three days and look how much we've accumulated already,' Joanna said.

Lazzy, who was roaming about outside, started to bark which was unusual – someone he didn't know must be arriving. Joe immediately went to investigate.

'I do hope it it's not the midwife as she really doesn't like him.'

'He wouldn't bark at her, Ma, he's got better manners than that. I'm going to see who it is just in case.'

Joanna wasn't sure it was wise for both her children to be outside when the dog was obviously on full alert.

'Don't worry, Joanna, I'll go as well. It's a pity my son isn't here as nobody argues with him.' Jean removed her feet from the treadle and rushed off. Now everybody was outside apart from Joanna and Elizabeth and no one would have stopped to put on a coat.

She was feeling too lazy to follow them so continued with the miniature patchwork quilt she was making from some of the pretty scraps of material. Jean had said it would do for a doll's pram or a tea tray so could be given to an adult or a little girl.

The door had been left open and hurrying footsteps approached – she recognised them as belonging to the elderly maid who took care of Elizabeth.

'Miss Biggins, were you looking for me?' Joanna called from her comfortable position in the armchair with her feet resting comfortably on a pouffe.

'Oh, Mrs Sergeant, there's a kerfuffle going on outside. There are two men and a lorry and they've come, they insist, to collect the petrol you've illegally stored.'

'Goodness me, I suppose I'd better speak to them.'

Miss Biggins kindly handed her a shawl to put around her shoulders and Joanna headed for the front door. This was closed, so the others must have gone out through the back.

'I'd be grateful if you'd accompany me, Miss Biggins. It could well be icy out there and I've no intention of falling over as I fear

I'd never get up again without the assistance of half a dozen burly men.'

'Good heavens, Joanna, you shall not go out to brave the intruders alone. I shall accompany you.' Elizabeth, also wrapped in a woolly shawl, appeared from the passageway that led from the sitting room.

'I'm not sure who you should be assisting, Miss Biggins, so I think it might be better after all to use the back door which doesn't require going down slippery steps.'

The look of relief on the maid's face was comical. Joanna smiled at her mother-in-law. 'I'm sure having an actual Lady Harcourt confronting these people will be sufficient to rout them.'

As they stepped out into the freezing December afternoon, the matter was decided for them. Lazzy, now a fully grown dog the size of a small pony, stopped barking and growled. Before Joe could grab his collar, the dog launched himself at the nearest man and sank his teeth into his leg.

The man screamed in a most satisfactory manner. 'Good dog, send the nasty men away.'

Hearing Joanna's encouragement and approval, the animal released his hold and turned his attention to the other man who was desperately trying to scramble back into the cab of the lorry, leaving his unfortunate friend collapsed in a moaning heap on the ground.

The dog was quicker and managed to take a lump out of the man's ankle before he could retract it to safety.

Joe caught hold of the dog. 'That's enough, Lazzy, the bad men are going now.'

The one on the ground, still whimpering, threw himself into the back of the lorry. In order to get the lorry engine started, one of them would have to put in the starting handle and turn it and this would require them to brave the snarling dog a second time.

Joanna called the dog over. 'Come on, silly boy, let's go inside and have a biscuit.'

At the magic mention of the word biscuit, a ferocious beast turned into a docile and friendly domestic pet.

Elizabeth and Miss Biggins had already retreated now the excitement was over and Jean offered her arm to Joanna, which she took gratefully.

'My word, that was exciting. Who do you think those men were? They certainly weren't anybody official.'

Her son answered from close behind her. 'I'm coming in to get my shotgun, Ma, and will stand guard until they go. You'd better keep the dog inside as I doubt they'll dare to get out to start the lorry if he's around.'

'No, there's no need for that, Joe. I'm sure once we're inside they'll be only too happy to get away without being savaged a second time.'

'It's a good thing the fuel's no longer behind the barn or they might still try and steal it whilst we're indoors. There are still a couple of cans, but I doubt that they'll find them.'

Thinking he'd agreed not to go out with a gun, Joanna headed for the kitchen and the warmth and comfort of a much-needed cup of tea. The dog followed her and only when he got the promised treat did he leave her side and take it under the table to his blanket.

Joe hadn't joined them. 'Liza, where's your brother?'

'I don't know but I expect he's making sure those two villains are gone.'

Joanna could hardly send Liza or Jean outside so would have to trust the shotgun wouldn't be needed.

Elizabeth had returned to the sanctuary of the sitting room but Miss Biggins remained to take a tray of tea through. 'Master Harcourt is a sensible young man, Mrs Sergeant, he won't do anything untoward.'

'Thank you, I hope you're right. He acts and looks a lot older than he actually is and I don't think a boy of fifteen should be outside guarding the house with a gun in his hand.'

'There were boys that age fighting in the last war, Mrs Sergeant, not that they should have been, of course.'

There was no need for a reply as the sound of the lorry backfiring as it drove away made it obvious the danger was over.

'After all the excitement, Joanna, I think you need to put your feet up. Are you going to join Lady Harcourt in the sitting room or go back to the study?' Jean asked as she busied herself at the range making tea. The precious coffee that John had brought back from America had been put away and wouldn't reappear until Christmas.

'The sitting room, I want to make sure Elizabeth's not upset.'

Even Miss Biggins smiled. The last person in the house to be put out by a couple of ruffians in a lorry was the redoubtable Lady Harcourt. Joanna found it difficult at times to be just plain Mrs Sergeant and no longer a lady like her ex-mother-in-law.

The chaise longue in the sitting room was her preserve and she collapsed on it gratefully. Elizabeth was already settled in front of the roaring fire and greeted her with a raised eyebrow.

'Well, my dear, I think your dog has more than paid for his supper today.'

'He certainly has.' Joanna stood up immediately. 'It's too warm in here for me. We don't really need the radiator and the fire. I'm sorry, I'll have to sit in the study and leave you to boil.'

'I am luxuriating in the warmth. I am an old lady, almost an octogenarian, and I do not want to spend my final years shivering in a shawl.'

'Eighty next birthday? We'll have a party, that's if you'd be kind enough to tell me when your birthday is. You must have had two since you've been here and we've not marked either occasion as you haven't seen fit to tell us the date.'

'It is Christmas Day, Joanna. I have always hated having my name day on the same one as our Lord. That is why I don't celebrate it.'

'Well, now that I know, you have no choice in the matter. I'm certainly not allowing your eightieth birthday to go unmarked. Forgive me, I'm beginning to perspire, I'm going to retreat to the study. Miss Biggins will be along with your tea shortly.'

Later that day, plans had been put in hand for a celebration of some sort for Elizabeth on Christmas Day. Jean was excited at the prospect.

'Actually, it's the perfect day for a party as we already have things put by for Christmas. Do you think Lady Harcourt would like us to invite the ladies that she visits occasionally?'

'I'm sure she wouldn't. You do realise, don't you, that I might be confined to my bedroom, having just produced this baby?'

'You should have had it by then and be up and about at least for part of the day. Looking at you, I think you could go into labour any day.'

'The sooner the better. I'd love to be able to see my toes again.'

* * *

John's new CO insisted that he go in the ambulance to the small medical centre to be checked out.

'Best to be sure, old boy, could have a spinal injury.'

John was about to protest but something about the look Billy gave him made him reconsider. A very senior officer's only son had just died in a prang involving his kite. The dead man was at fault, he'd landed in the wrong direction, but blame could be thrown his way and some of it could stick.

'Feeling a bit grim, actually, sir, we both could have been killed. I'll get checked out.'

'That's the ticket. No more jollies today, weather's closing in again. Join us in the mess when you've got the all-clear from the medic.'

They both knew he was just bruised and shaken and had a few superficial cuts from the shattered cockpit. A pretty young nurse cleaned him up, the medic gave him a cursory once-over.

'You'll be stiff tomorrow and will have some spectacular bruises on your shoulders and chest from your harness, but should be fit for duty.'

'Thanks, Doc, I'm going to have a stiff drink and hopefully find something to eat.'

John was putting his shirt and jacket back on, with some difficulty, as moving his arms was becoming increasingly difficult. The doctor frowned.

'Humph! I'm reconsidering my decision. You can hardly fly a Spitfire if you can't move your bloody arms.'

'I'll be okay tomorrow.'

'You won't, you'll be worse. No, you're having a sicknote whether you like it or not.' He pointed to the large white scar that ran across John's stomach. 'How did you get that?'

'I was a fire fighter at Manston and got blown up during a raid.'

'Nasty. Any gut problems since?'

'None. Can I go now, sir?'

'You do know there's going to be a hell of a stink about his crash? That boy was an excellent pilot as is his pal, Jordan. Making that sort of fundamental error isn't like him at all.'

'He and Jordan were drinking behind dispersal. Jordan was too pissed to fly so Reynolds came with me instead. He missed the "T" and landed in the wrong direction.'

'Jesus. I'm not a friend of the Win Co but knowing he's killed his own child by his mistake will be hard for him.'

'I know. I should have refused to fly with him...'

'Not your fault, Sergeant.' The doctor grinned. 'Bet your name causes great hilarity in the mess. "What's a sergeant doing in the Officers' Mess?" and all that guff.'

'Even worse when I was Sergeant Sergeant. Only reason I accepted a commission was to avoid the confusion.'

'Right, enough banter. Take this. It gives you two days' light duties and you have to see me before you fly again. Got that?'

'Yes, sir.' John turned at the door. 'Can you direct me to the mess? Only arrived a few hours a go and haven't had a conducted tour.'

'Turn right and keep walking. Can't miss it even in the fog. The racket you flyers make is second to none.'

John now knew that he wouldn't have gone anywhere but his bed if he had the choice. The invitation to go for a drink with his new CO had been an order thinly disguised as a suggestion. After being involved in a fatality, the sensible thing was to do as he was asked.

The heavy rain had become a steady, miserable, freezing drizzle and by the time he reached the mess, none of his limbs seemed to be working as they should. He edged his way in, trying to avoid doing further damage to his shoulders.

It was a relief to get out of the rain. He'd got his Mae West over his shoulder but was still wearing his helmet and goggles. His oxygen mask must still be in his kite as it certainly wasn't attached to his helmet as it had been before.

He could hear loud voices and the clinking of glasses coming from behind a closed door just ahead. Might as well get it over with – the sooner he made an appearance, had a swift drink, the quicker he could find his bed.

The bogs were on his right and he thought he'd better go there first and see just how bad he looked. He stood in front of one of the mirrors hanging above the wash basins and stared at the stranger he found in it.

Although he had no stitches, his face was speckled with small cuts, he had an impressive bruise on his forehead, and his shirt collar was red, no longer blue. Maybe going in to join the others looking as he did was a bad idea. He didn't want their sympathy – it wasn't him that had died in such a bloody stupid way.

He'd heard someone come in but ignored them. 'Do you feel as bad as you look?'

John turned slowly to face Billy. 'Worse, if you can imagine that. I can't fly for at least two days.' He was still holding the slip of paper given to him by the doctor and it was sodden and almost illegible from the rain. He handed it over anyway.

'The last thing you need is to be slapped on the back and commiserated with. I'm surprised you managed to walk so far. If you go out of the door at the end of this hallway, it leads into our accommodation. Do you need me—'

'No, I'll find it myself, thank you, sir.'

'I'm Billy, or Skip – never sir to any of my men.' He grinned. 'My name's George, but I'm known as Billy.'

With a surname of Williams, the nickname made perfect sense.

'Right, thank you, Billy.'

Somehow, John managed to walk in a straight line and push his way through the door without stumbling. As last time he'd entered from the other end of the building, he was disorientated and had no idea where he was supposed to go.

'There you are, sir, I've been looking everywhere for you. Come along, what you need is a nice hot bath, and some scoff.'

John didn't recognise the speaker but the bloke obviously knew who he was. 'No bath, but tea and scoff would be most welcome.'

* * *

When John woke up the next morning, everything above his waist hurt. With some difficulty, he heaved himself upright and swung his legs to the floor. He'd no recollection of undressing and supposed that his orderly had helped him.

His stomach rumbled loudly. He couldn't remember eating anything either last night so his first task would be to get some clothes on before going in search of breakfast. Blackouts were still drawn and he'd no idea of the time.

He groped his way to the light switch by the door and switched it on. The other bed was occupied and the unexpected illumination wasn't appreciated.

'Turn the bloody light out, it's the middle of the night.'

'God, I'm sorry, I thought it was morning.' He was about to plunge the room back into darkness when the lump under the blankets poked his head out.

'It is morning, mate, but I like a lie-in. You don't look too clever – not surprised you didn't join us for a jar or two last night.'

'You know who I am, but—'

'Right, Flying Officer Albert White – better known as Chalky. Pleased to meet you.'

John looked around for his clothes.

'What you took off last night will have gone to the laundry. Your things will be neatly arranged in your chest of drawers or hanging in that wardrobe over there.'

Chalky flopped back into bed and pulled the covers over his head but didn't ask for the light to be turned off. It was early – just after six o'clock – but not disastrously so. At Hornchurch they'd have been at their forward base and eating their breakfast by now, not lolling around in bed.

Once John got moving, it was easier, and by the time he was dressed, more or less correctly, he hurt less. 'Are you getting up, you lazy sod, or shall I turn the light out?'

'Leave it on, mate. Had a few too many last night – most of us did – raising a glass to our departed comrades.'

This comment stopped John in his tracks. He walked over to the bed and pulled back the covers so he could see Chalky's face.

'Comrades? Did somebody else die?'

'No – but Jordan's been posted elsewhere along with our erstwhile commanding officer. Not sorry to see any of them go, to be honest.'

'That's harsh considering what happened to the Win Co's son.'

'Those two should never have been on our squadron. Nepotism gone mad. Jordan and Reynolds could fly all right but nobody wants alcoholics on the squadron and having two of them was just an accident waiting to happen.'

Chalky yawned loudly and bounced out of bed. He was a wiry bloke a few inches shorter than John with unkempt hair and three days' growth of beard. Obviously, standards were much lower here than he was used to.

John grinned. He was going to like it here.

# 21

Joanna was surprised and delighted when John telephoned only two days after he'd left.

'It's so wonderful to hear your voice, my love, I really didn't expect to hear from you so soon. How do you like your new posting?'

'Different to my last – and I'm not talking about my excursion abroad – but they're a decent lot of blokes and after a difficult introduction, things have settled down.'

She didn't ask what had happened and he didn't tell her. It was probably better not knowing the sort of risks he had to take and the near misses he certainly had.

'I'm absolutely spiffing and we're all keeping busy with our Christmas preparations. Have you managed to persuade any of your comrades in arms to make toys for our collection?'

'I have and as at the moment we have more time on the ground than in the air, everyone, including our squadron leader, is whittling away. Some with more enthusiasm than skill but I'll have a bag full of toys to bring with me when I come next time.'

'I'm quite sure whatever you bring will be appreciated. Elizabeth will be eighty on Christmas Day and we're going to have a double celebration.'

'Let's hope it's a triple celebration and our baby has arrived by then.'

'The midwife's coming every week until I deliver and will be here tomorrow. Shall I write to you or will you be able to ring me again?'

'We're the only squadron permanently based here so after the others have returned to their home bases, we've got the place to ourselves. I'll ring you at seven o'clock when I can. Don't worry if I don't, it will just mean someone else is using the telephone.'

There wasn't anything else they could say as he couldn't talk about his work and her life continued in a leisurely fashion with nothing new to report. Knowing that someone at the local exchange could well be listening to their call was also a factor in what was said.

'I love you. Goodbye.'

Joanna replaced the receiver, thankful that she was one of the lucky wives. Her husband was able to talk to her, to visit, would be coming back when the baby was born. There were people in the village who hadn't seen their husbands since they were posted overseas and there were at least three families who'd lost a son or husband in the fighting.

Ramsgate had been bombed more than once and the casualties had been light considering the amount of damage done to the town. However, there had still been over a hundred fatalities and more than double that number of injuries.

All the unwanted furniture from the Victorian wing had been donated to those who needed it before the building was demolished after the fire last year. Housewives had been asked to contribute their aluminium saucepans and anything else that could be used in the manufacture of fighters and this meant there was now a national shortage of cooking utensils.

Everybody, including Elizabeth and her maid, was gathered in the study. The wireless that had been in the kitchen was now installed in there so they, like the factory workers, could listen to light music whilst they sewed, painted or glued.

'Has John settled in, Joanna?' Elizabeth asked.

'He has and he thinks he'll probably be able to ring me every couple of days. He also told me that his squadron are having a go at making toys for our collection.'

'Apart from the unpleasant aroma of the hot glue being used by Joe and Liza to stick things together, it's really rather pleasant in here. Less cramped than the sitting room, don't you think?'

'I suppose I should have told them to do the carpentry, painting and gluing outside but they are at the far end of the room and have the window slightly open during the day,' Joanna said. 'I must admit that the smell of the glue isn't enjoyable.'

Her children had wandered up to hear what news John had had and Joe laughed. 'It's made from horses' hooves, Ma, so bound to smell nasty.'

'I'd no idea and wish you hadn't told me. As you're both on your feet, would you make the cocoa for everybody tonight?'

'I'll find something a bit more exciting on the wireless first,' Joe said as he began to twiddle the knobs. The large room was filled with a lively tune that was new to her.

'Glenn Miller's band and "Chattanooga Choo Choo" – I heard it the other day. It's just the ticket, isn't it?' Joe asked.

Joanna was about to ask him to turn it down as she didn't think either Elizabeth or Miss Biggins would appreciate this new music, but both were nodding and smiling. They listened to this very enjoyable concert with their cocoa – if that's what one called an evening of band music – and then Joe adjusted the set so they could, like every other family in the country, listen to the nine o'clock news.

With considerable relief, the wireless was switched off. Tonight, for a change, there'd been nothing appalling to report. The twins and Jean started tidying up the study before they retired.

'At least the bad weather is keeping the RAF on the ground,' Elizabeth said.

'More importantly it's keeping the Luftwaffe away from our cities too.' Joanna looked around the room, wanting to be sure there was nothing left out, that the workspaces were tidy and ready for another day's work tomorrow. There was a sudden spasm in her back which made her gasp.

Jean was at her side at once. 'Do you think you've started?'

Joanna waited to see if another contraction gripped her, but nothing did. 'No, just a practice twinge. I do recall having them last time. I spent the last two weeks in the very expensive clinic in London because of them. David wouldn't let me come home until Sarah arrived.'

'Maybe I should sleep in the sitting room next to your bedroom just in case.'

'No, that won't be necessary, thank you, Jean. I'm not due for another three weeks and was a few days late with Sarah. The midwife's coming in the morning so will know at once if things are starting.'

'Do you know, you're walking a bit better than you were last week. That's odd, isn't it?'

'The baby's shifted and I'm more comfortable. I'm just relieved my ankles haven't got more swollen.' Joanna smiled. 'Mind you, as I've not seen them myself for weeks, I have to rely on you and Liza to keep me informed.'

As she slowly undressed, the baby heaved and she smoothed her hands down her stomach. 'Settle down, baby, Mummy needs her sleep. You mustn't come for another few weeks.'

There were no more practice contractions and Joanna slept well. She was woken by Liza with her very welcome tray of early-morning tea.

'The fog's really bad, Ma, we won't get any post nor milk today and Grandma won't get her paper.'

'I'm sure we'll manage. I actually like the fog as it means no plane will be in the air so none of our boys will die. Also, no bombs will be dropped on civilians anywhere.'

'You wouldn't like the peasoupers they get in London. Thick yellow stuff, you can't breathe or even see your hand in front of your face.'

'I have read about it but have no wish to see it for myself. Thank you for the tea. I'll drink it at leisure and then get up. I'll remain up here until the midwife has visited.'

'She'll not be coming in this weather, Ma. She'll only go out to deliveries today, I reckon.'

'How silly of me – of course she won't come to a routine appointment. I'll be down as usual for my breakfast then.' Liza handed her the tea. 'I'm looking forward to resuming our gift-making efforts, aren't you?'

'Not half, it's like Father Christmas's workshop down there. Jean's going to run up lots of stockings from any bits of material that are big enough and then we can fill them ready for the kiddies when they get up on Christmas Day. The parents can hang them in front of their chimneys.'

'That's an excellent idea. The adults will be able to take them home and the contents will remain a secret. Jean told me someone in the village managed to buy a Meccano set weeks ago and because it wasn't wrapped the neighbours saw it and her son knew before she got home. Rather ruined the surprise.'

'If he's getting Meccano, he probably doesn't believe in Father Christmas any more so it won't matter.'

Joanna nodded. 'That's true. You don't have to wait; I can get myself organised and down the stairs safely.'

'Are you sure, Ma? John was carrying you up and down when he was here.'

'He did that because he wanted to, not because I really needed to be carried.' This wasn't strictly true as walking had only become easier in the past couple of days.

* * *

After spending another day in the study, which was now called 'The Grotto', Joanna was pleasantly tired. The midwife had telephoned to apologise and said that she would come as soon as the weather allowed.

Tony had managed to ride his motorbike and sidecar from Stodham and had brought milk and a newspaper. Sensibly he was staying the night and not risking the return journey.

'Do you think that John might ring you tonight, Joanna?' Elizabeth asked when they were all gathered around the table in the breakfast parlour eating a tasty rabbit stew.

'He said every other day so I'm not expecting him to call. After all, we're constantly being told not to use the telephone unnecessarily and to send postcards, not letters or parcels, this Christmas.'

'How ridiculous – I'm sure it has to be as much work for the Post Office to deal with a postcard as it is for a letter,' Jean said forcefully.

The lively debate about the postal services continued until Liza and Jean cleared the plates and cutlery and went to fetch dessert from the kitchen. Joanna noticed that Elizabeth had scarcely touched her food and this was unlike her. Neither had she joined in the conversation and usually she had plenty to say.

'Are you feeling well, Elizabeth? You've not eaten your meal tonight.'

This question was ignored and the answer Joanna received was odd.

'I do hope we're not having a stodgy pudding again tonight,' Elizabeth complained. 'Something light would suit my digestion better.'

Jean overheard this remark as she was coming in with the tray. 'Then tonight you'll be happy, my lady. It's stewed apple and custard – can't get much lighter than that.'

'No, even spotted dick would be preferable to that.'

It was unlike Elizabeth to speak like this. Joanna was now concerned there was more going on than a bout of dyspepsia.

Jean was unbothered by the criticism and smiled. 'What about tinned peaches and custard? There are still a couple of tins left from the store sent over a few months ago when we had those spies staying with us.'

'No, that doesn't appeal,' Elizabeth said. 'Miss Biggins, I wish to retire.'

Her maid now joined them for meals and although everyone had to be extra careful not to use any bad language or, even worse, blaspheme, she was a welcome, if quiet, addition to the family group.

'Miss Biggins hasn't finished her meal, Elizabeth.'

'I can see that, Joanna, I am not senile or blind. I am not suggesting that she misses her dessert, she can assist me and then come back for it.'

The unfortunate lady was already standing behind Elizabeth, ready to help her to her feet. There was an uncomfortable silence as the two of them left. Joanna watched carefully and Elizabeth, apart from not eating and being bad-tempered, seemed to be walking briskly, showing no signs of faintness or ill-health.

'Oh dear, that was very unlike Elizabeth. Do any of you know what might have upset her today? Usually, she loves stewed apples and custard and I know that tinned peaches are a favourite of hers. Her behaviour's rather odd, don't you think, Jean?'

'She's almost eighty, Joanna, I'm sure when we reach that grand old age that we'll be cantankerous occasionally too.'

'Don't look so worried, Ma, Grandma's a game old bird, she'll go on for another ten years, you'll see,' Joe said as he devoured his apples and custard with relish.

'Whilst she's not here and we're all together, shall we discuss what plans we have to celebrate her special birthday?'

* * *

John spent his two days' sick leave getting to know Hawkinge and the members of his squadron. There were no light duties to perform so he was free to wander, chat and explore without restraint. He smiled wryly. This wasn't quite true as the weather made doing more than exploring the immediate vicinity impossible.

Chalky was proving to be a good friend. He'd learned that Billy and himself were the only married blokes, although a couple of others had fiancées. Folkstone was a small busy fishing port and the locals were friendly. As they were grounded, and it was too filthy to explore on his motorbike, his roommate had been happy to give him the local gen. The Officers' Mess was where the bods spent their leisure time. Although there were WAAFS and other civilian females on the base, they had their own quarters and weren't invited to their den.

John wasn't a heavy drinker but there was tea and ersatz coffee available on demand so he was happy to waste time with the members of his new squadron in there. He would have a frighteningly large mess bill to pay at the end of the month. Being the new chap had meant oiling the wheels of communication with a few rounds of drinks initially. What he didn't like was the permanent blue fug of tobacco smoke as most of the blokes smoked fags or pipes. He wasn't one of them. Thankfully this morning the room was relatively clear of smoke as he and Chalky were the only men in there.

Billy was at a meeting with the spy and John was lounging in a comfortable armchair that had seen better days.

'Tell me about the set-up here before Billy took over. Nobody seems bothered about the change.'

'Seeing the back of the Win Co and his two blue-eyed boys is something we've all wanted,' Chalky said. 'The flyers on this squadron are here as a reward for being bloody brilliant for far too long. How many ops have you flown?'

'God knows, but more than a hundred.'

'Me too. Reynolds and Jordon had completed thirty, if that. They were posted here because the Win Co pulled strings. The pair of them were LMF and should have been sent somewhere to clean latrines for the duration.'

LMF meant lacking moral fibre and was to be avoided at all costs. 'Is that why they drank? Because they were scared?'

'They drank because they were allowed to do as they bloody well pleased. Win Co sent you up because he wasn't happy with your arrival. He'd tried to get another of his cronies' relatives as the replacement.'

'Then why did he want me to go up with his son?' John asked. 'Why wasn't I told to go up with whoever my new partner is?'

'That would be me and I was doing something for admin.' Chalky scowled into his warm beer. 'Believe it or not, the stupid old sod didn't seem to realise how much those two were drinking. He probably hoped his son would show you up. The boy was an excellent flyer when sober.'

John drained the dregs of his revolting coffee and thought longingly of the real stuff he'd left at home. Chalky kicked his foot.

'Don't nod off when I'm talking to you. Moving on, as you know we fly in pairs, no dogfights unless attacked, and are here for escort and reconnaissance duties. Last time I had to photograph some German bases in Northern France.'

'Spying?'

Chalky raised his half-empty glass. 'It's not called that but that's what it is. We often fly under the radar, sea level, and you're replacing my partner, Dave, who went for a Burton in the drink.'

'I was flying regular Rhubarbs from Hornchurch before going to the States.'

He told Chalky about his eye-opening trip and ended saying that he thought it wouldn't be long before the Yanks were in the war.

'Have you got any of your smuggled goods with you?'

John grinned, glad he'd tucked a bottle of bourbon into a pannier where it was still located. 'If I can find my bike in this fog, I'll go and get what I've brought. I was intending to keep it until things improved.'

They both knew he wasn't referring to the weather but the fatal crash and the reasons for it.

Billy wandered in as John was leaving. 'Met Office say the fog's clearing and will be all systems go by tomorrow. I need everyone in the briefing room.'

'Okay, Skip, but there's only Chalky and me in the mess. Haven't the foggiest where the others are.'

'Ha, bloody ha. I've found most of the blighters, just you two and Smiler to go.'

Chalky chimed in. 'Smiler's got the trots, Skip, you'll find him in the bogs.'

'Then there he can stay. Come on you chaps, the spy awaits.' Billy nodded at John. 'You'll be cleared to fly tomorrow so you come too. Meeting starts in ten.'

This was John's first visit to the briefing room as he was still officially on sick leave. Not that anybody had done anything for the past two days, so he'd not missed much.

It was a select group of blokes who made up the squadron. There were only fourteen members but they had twelve kites, so this meant there were two spare bods floating about. If Chalky had had to go on a mission of some sort, one of the spare blokes would have accompanied him. Obviously, with the demise of Reynolds and the removal of both the Wing Commander Flying and Jordan, they were two short.

The briefing room was spacious – a dozen or so battered wooden chairs roughly lined up in the centre and plenty of space around the walls for those that preferred to stand and lounge.

The intelligence officer – John still didn't know his name – was the one who'd insisted that he and Jordan fly the other day. This officer was standing at the front with the skip and the discussion the two were having was animated – almost an argument.

Today, as there were so few of them, all the blokes had chosen to sit and he and Chalky joined them. Birdie Starling, Flight Lieutenant, and second-in-command, swivelled on his chair.

'You're the only chap here without a nickname. From henceforth you'll be known as Encee.'

John looked blank, then twigged. NC, short for NCO, because of his surname.

'Flying Officer Encee Sergeant it shall be. Did you know you're up for another promotion?'

'I'm quite happy as I am – there are plenty here with more experience and better credentials. I don't want to be rewarded because some idiot could have killed me.'

'Fair enough. Right – eyes front, chaps, our revered leader's about to speak.'

It had taken longer to gather everybody than the time spent on the actual briefing. The men wandered off to discuss what they'd been told, which wasn't much, away from their senior officers.

'Blimey,' Chalky said, 'I'm not sure I'm any the wiser. What about you, Encee?'

'It's obviously all very hush-hush. Can't see the point in having us in the briefing room if we weren't going to be properly briefed. All we know is that we're doing some sort of reconnaissance across the Channel.'

'And only half of us will be going and we won't know that until tomorrow either. You'll have Jordan's kite – do you want to go and inspect it?'

'No – I'm sure the aircrew have everything under control. Do you want to come for a spin on my bike? I assume we're allowed off base.'

Chalky's answer was drowned out by the arrival of a squadron of Hurries. They would stay at Hawkinge, on readiness, and then return to their home base when it got dark.

John watched them land and mentally crossed his fingers that they wouldn't be scrambled as the visibility was still poor. Being involved in a dogfight in these conditions would be miserable and more dangerous than usual.

'To be honest, I'm not feeling too clever. I have a nasty suspicion whatever Smiler's got he's kindly given to me,' Chalky said.

'Could be something you ate as I'm tickety-boo.'

'Smiler nipped out and got fish and chips and half of us had them. You didn't.' He grimaced, shook his head and dashed off.

John thought he'd ring Joanna now when it was quiet. Probably better during the day as she would definitely be downstairs.

He returned to his room to collect the loose change he'd put in a chipped saucer on top of the chest of drawers. For ten minutes, he'd need all of it.

His orderly met him as he was heading the admin building. 'Half the squadron have got the squits, sir. Seems the fish and chips were the culprit.'

'At least we know it's not contagious. I didn't have any.' John was jingling the change in his hand and the bloke grinned.

'There's a telephone you can use without them coins, sir, it's in an office no one uses. I'll show you if you like.'

'Thank you, but I prefer to pay my way.'

He dialled the operator, gave the number for Goodwill House, and waited eagerly to be connected. He could hear the telephone ringing and was becoming anxious when nobody answered it immediately. Then Liza picked it up.

'It's John, can I speak to Joanna?'

'She's not here. She's at the hospital.'

His stomach plummeted. 'What's happened? Why didn't you contact me?'

'Oh, no, it's not Joanna who's unwell, it's Grandma. The doctor thinks she might have had a stroke. The ambulance left half an hour ago and Tony's driving Ma to the hospital in the Bentley.'

'I'm so sorry to hear that,' John said. 'Please send my love and best wishes and ask Joanna to let me know how things are.'

'Miss Biggins wanted to go with Grandma but as she's not family she wasn't allowed. We didn't want Ma to go at all, not in her condition, but she insisted.'

'What did Dr Willoughby say?'

'About Grandma or Ma?'

'Both. Hang on a minute, I've got to put in some more money.' He quickly shoved the change he had into the slot and bought himself another fifteen minutes. He hoped that would be enough and that the news wouldn't be as bad as he feared it might.

'Tell me exactly what happened, Liza.'

The girl sniffed and cleared her throat. 'Grandma was a bit grumpy last night, didn't eat anything, but went to bed and said she had a headache.'

'Go on.'

'She was asleep when Ma and Miss Biggins looked in on her during the night, but she seemed to be all right. No one realised until this morning that she wasn't asleep but unconscious. She looked ever so peaceful but very pale. Oh, John, we're that worried about her and about Ma. Can't you come home?'

# 22

Joanna hadn't asked Dr Willoughby's permission to go to the hospital and he hadn't offered an opinion. He was well aware that she'd have ignored him if he'd said she shouldn't go. He was following the ambulance and would see that Elizabeth got the best possible treatment when she arrived at the hospital in Ramsgate.

When Miss Biggins had come down last night and told them that Elizabeth had taken two aspirin because she had a headache, they were all relieved. Having a bad headache apparently explained why Elizabeth had been so out of sorts. Everything had appeared to be fine until Miss Biggins couldn't rouse Elizabeth a couple of hours ago.

The Bentley had been fetched from The Manse whilst they waited for the ambulance. The doctor, who only lived a few miles away, had been there fifteen minutes after the frantic phone call.

The family car was comfortable and Tony was an excellent driver. Joanna didn't often pray but had been sending constant messages to the Almighty to spare Elizabeth today. At least the fog wasn't so bad that driving was dangerous.

'Lady Harcourt's a strong old lady. If anyone can get through this it will be her, Joanna,' Tony said quietly.

'I pray that you're right. I keep thinking that we should have realised there was something seriously wrong and called an ambulance last night.'

'You checked on her, she looked as if she was sleeping peacefully so why would you have suspected that she wasn't asleep but unconscious?'

'I know, but I still feel guilty. I suppose I should have rung John and told him what's happening but I've no intention of distracting him – his job's dangerous enough without adding to it with such dreadful news.'

'Do you think he'd ask to come home if he knew the situation?'

'I doubt it – Elizabeth's not really any connection of his and if he uses up his leave now he might not be able to come back when I have the baby.'

Tony drove slowly through the village and she was glad it was murky so anybody shopping would be unlikely to recognise her or the car. Then she shook her head. Of course they'd have heard the ambulance clanging through the village, seen the doctor's car close behind, and would be expecting the Bentley to be following.

'I don't think there's anything they can do for somebody who's had a stroke apart from keep them comfortable,' Joanna said.

'She looked peaceful, she's obviously not in any pain. If this is her time, then it's how she'd want to go. It's how anybody would want to go.'

'Should I have kept her at home so the family could be with her?' She rubbed her eyes. It was all very well talking about Elizabeth having had a good life, but she would be so missed by everyone.

'I think the doctor would have suggested it if he didn't think there was anything the hospital could do to help,' Tony said. 'Having her transferred at speed must mean he thinks that something can be done.'

He pulled up outside the steps leading into the hospital. 'I'll find somewhere to park then join you. Can you manage those steps?'

'Of course I can. I might be three weeks away from giving birth but I'm not ill and I'm still quite capable of climbing a set of steps without assistance. Pregnancy is not an illness, it's a normal part of a woman's life.'

She wasn't sure if he'd heard her because he was already at her side of the car and opened the door as if he was really a chauffeur and not part of the household. When he offered his arm, she took it; she might be independent, but she wasn't stupid. Tony jumped back into the driver's seat and she made her way slowly and carefully to the main entrance.

A helpful student nurse held the door open for her. 'Goodness me, someone should be with you. I'll get a wheelchair and take you to the maternity wing.'

'I'm not in labour. Lady Harcourt, a member of my family, was brought in a short time ago with a suspected stroke. Please direct me to where she's being looked after.'

'I beg your pardon, it's just that you're...'

'I know, I am large and the baby's ready to come but I've got another three weeks until my due date,' Joanna said. 'Now, where do I go?'

The girl, she looked not much older than Liza, smiled nervously. 'I'll show you, my lady, but I really think you'd be better in a wheelchair.'

'Firstly, my dear, I am Mrs Sergeant. Secondly, I just need directions, not an escort, and certainly not a wheelchair.'

Tony arrived at her side. 'I'll take it from here, thanks, nurse.'

The girl hurried off without having told Joanna where she was supposed to be going. 'She said it was too far for me to walk. I'm sure I can manage, especially now I've got your arm to hold onto if I need it. Look, there's a doctor. He can tell us where we have to be.'

The harried young man gave directions and it was a ten-minute walk to the side room in which Elizabeth had been put. There was a bottle of clear fluid dripping into her arm and Dr Willoughby was talking to an older man who presumably was the consultant in charge of the case.

They both looked round as Joanna and Tony walked in. 'I'll leave you to explain things, James.' The other doctor avoided eye contact and left without speaking to her.

One look at Dr Willoughby's expression was enough to tell her the news was very bad.

'I'm glad you've got here, Mrs Sergeant, Lady Harcourt's slipping away. If you'd been much longer you might have been too late. When I examined her earlier her vital signs were stable. I knew that she'd had a stroke but believed she could, with expert nursing, make a good recovery. I'd never have suggested moving her if I'd known she'd deteriorate so quickly.'

Joanna's eyes filled. 'It's not anybody's fault. Is she aware of anything?'

'I don't think so, but sit with her, hold her hand, tell her how much you love her and how much you're going to miss her, just in case.'

'How long?'

'Hours, possibly less. It's a gradual process. She won't be feeling any discomfort. Her organs are slowly shutting down and she'll slip away peacefully.'

They'd been standing away from the bed to talk and Tony had been listening. 'I'll ring home and let everybody know what's happening. I could drive back and collect the twins – it sounds as though there's time for that.'

She nodded. 'Yes, go now and hurry. I think Liza and Joe would really like to be here when she passes.'

He left and Dr Willoughby went with him – she could hear them talking quietly in the corridor.

Elizabeth didn't look as if she was dying. It was hard to believe someone so vibrant, so full of life could be about to die. Seventy-nine was old but not impossibly so and they'd all been so looking forward to celebrating her eightieth with her on Christmas Day.

There was a hard wooden chair at the side of the bed and that would have to do. Joanna moved as close as she could and took Elizabeth's cold hand in hers. 'I'm here, I love you and I'm so glad that you came into our lives so unexpectedly two years ago. You saved us from eviction with your generosity and that was a wonderful thing to do.'

She squeezed the limp hand gently but there was no response, not a flicker of an eyelid, nothing to show that this wonderful old lady, who had become so important to her, was aware of her surroundings or anything that was happening.

She wished with all her heart that they were at Goodwill House. Then, to her surprise, both Tony and the doctor reappeared.

'I'm going to arrange for the ambulance to take her home. You travel with her just in case. I'll follow in my car and stay until I'm needed,' the doctor said. 'Of course, there's a risk she could die in transit but you'll be with her and that's all that matters.'

Tony had vanished and Dr Willoughby explained where he'd gone. 'He's telephoning the house so they have everything ready. He's getting a bed put up in the grand hall so she's surrounded by the lovely decorations.'

'Thank you, I appreciate you helping us at this very difficult time.'

* * *

The ambulance men were courteous and respectful and handled Elizabeth with great care. Her breathing hadn't got any worse in the ambulance and Joanna had continued to talk, reassure her, tell her that she was coming home where she was loved and wanted.

The blackout had been ignored, as on their return the front door was wide open and light spilled out into the darkness. Joe was there to help Joanna scramble down from the ambulance and then assist her to ascend the stairs and go into the hall.

Miss Biggins, Jean, Liza and Joe were waiting. They were sombre-faced but not crying and watched sadly as Elizabeth was placed lovingly into her own bed, with her own lavender-scented sheets.

'There, my lady, you're better off here with us.' The maid looked at Joanna. 'Can I say a prayer for her?'

'Yes, yes, that would be lovely. Then, Liza, could you sing for your grandma like you did for Betty?'

'As it's almost Christmas, Ma, why don't we sing carols? Grandma loved "Silent Night" and "Good King Wenceslas", we could start with those.'

The prayers were moving and absolutely the right thing to do. Then Liza led the impromptu choir. Her daughter had a beautiful voice and it filled the huge space.

Joanna remained seated in a comfortable armchair, holding Elizabeth's hand, and as they sang 'O Come, All Ye Faithful', Elizabeth's eyes flickered open. She looked around at those she loved singing to her and she smiled. Then she was gone.

* * *

John hovered in the hall outside the admin office, anxiously awaiting a second call from home. Joe had rung and told him Elizabeth was coming back to die and that her death was imminent.

'Sir, there's call for you,' a sympathetic young WAAF called out.

He didn't have time to greet her as Joanna burst into speech. 'John, darling, she's gone. I can't believe that last night she was here and now she's dead. It doesn't seem real.'

'I'm so sorry, sweetheart. I know how much you loved her. I can't come back now but will come to the funeral if I can. How are the twins coping? What about Sarah?'

'I haven't contacted her. Elizabeth's in the hall with us. She looks as if she's asleep. The doctor has written the death certificate and we're waiting for the undertakers.'

'Where will she be buried? Is there a Harcourt plot somewhere?'

He thought talking practicalities would help her as she was finding it difficult to talk.

'There's a section in the village churchyard where she'll go to join her ancestors. Well – I suppose they're not really her ancestors, are they? Poor David should have been there but... but...' She couldn't continue and it was killing him not being there to hold her when she needed him.

There was a clatter as she dropped the receiver, then Jean picked it up. 'It's difficult, John, because Lady Harcourt's in here with us. It'll be easier when the undertakers have been.'

'Take care of Joanna for me. I'd be there if I could.'

He hung up and stood for a few seconds gathering his thoughts. If half the squadron weren't down with a bilious attack, he'd ask for a day off. As he was part of this secret operation tomorrow, there was nothing he could do about it.

During the rest of the evening, whilst he and Chalky were playing a desultory game of darts, his mind was whirling. What if he went for a Burton tomorrow? He wasn't sure Joanna would get through it. Elizabeth's death couldn't have come at a worse time. Fortunately, Chalky hadn't been too unwell and was now fully recovered.

'Crikey, Encee, that didn't even hit the board,' Chalky said. 'Look, mate, it doesn't do to dwell on things you can't do anything about. Your wife will deal with things – it's what the womenfolk do.'

John collected his dart from the wall and dropped all three of them into the pot on the shelf. 'Sorry, I can't concentrate.' He flopped into a vacant armchair and his new friend sat opposite.

'This squadron has been doing what it does for the past five months and we've only had one fatality. The odds of it being you tomorrow are very slim.'

'You're right. You know, I was just thinking that Elizabeth picked a really bad time to die then realised any time's a bad time – especially for the person concerned.'

'Let's eat. You'll feel better when you're full.'

As they were flying the next morning at dawn, neither Chalky nor John had a drink before retiring. Their orderly would bring them tea around at five which meant they then had half an hour to eat and get themselves to the dispersal hut by half past.

* * *

It was a freezing morning with no glimmer of dawn on the horizon but at least it wasn't foggy. Whatever they were going to be doing, he was damn sure they wouldn't be doing it until there was better visibility. Spits weren't good in the dark.

He and Chalky, in full flying gear, scrambled into the waiting lorry along with the other four bods who were part of this operation. Normally there was chatter, blokes exchanging jokes, pipes and cigarettes being lit for a last puff. Nothing personal was allowed to fly with them, not even photographs of loved ones, but fags didn't count as far as the flyers were concerned. This morning – possibly because there were only six of them in the lorry – there was no conversation.

John jumped down from the tailgate. As he was first out, he shone the beam from his torch ahead so they could follow. The dispersal hut was only a few yards from where the lorry dropped them off. He waited until they were all by the door before pushing it open – nobody bothered with a blackout curtain out here.

The intelligence officer was waiting as he had been on John's first sortie for this squadron. The map with various pins in it was on the wall. The six of them, breath condensing in clouds, knew the drill and got out their notebooks and pencils.

He and Chalky were being sent on a recce to Flanders. They were to fly at sea level on the way in and remain low as they completed the sixty miles to their destination. Information had reached headquarters that the Germans were building a fighter airfield there and they wanted confirmation of this.

'Do a circuit of your area, gentlemen, and then get the hell out of there. Make your visit quick. Don't hang about and come back however the hell you want. You'll probably have the Luftwaffe on your tails. Bon voyage.'

Billy spoke to them afterwards. 'No engaging the enemy unless attacked. It's vital that you get back safely with the information that's needed. Do your best to stay together, stay off the RT and good luck.'

He nodded at John. 'I'm sorry to hear about Lady Harcourt. You'll get a compassionate day to attend the funeral but I'm afraid no more than that.'

'I've got two weeks' entitlement left for this year and I'm keeping it for when my baby arrives. I can get there and back and attend the ceremony in a day as I don't have to use the trains.'

'Good show.'

His ground crew were waiting and attached his chute to the rings on the rear of his harness. 'Bloody horrible weather, sir, but at least the Nazis won't see you coming and going,' one of them said cheerfully.

Fighter pilots had their chutes attached to their harness at the rear so they sat on them. Aircrew in a bomber attached their own by two clips on the front and it was stored beneath their feet or beside them. He preferred to have his permanently joined to him, as he doubted there would always be sufficient time to grab the chute in an emergency.

John scrambled onto the wing and stepped into the cockpit, making sure the chute was under his backside before he sat. Then he plugged in his oxygen and his RT lead. After adjusting his goggles, putting on his mask, he was ready for them to start the engine.

This was done with a battery on a trolley and the Merlin engine roared into throaty life immediately. The Perspex canopy was closed over his head. Fighter pilots rarely had the luxury of being able to do a preflight check – usually they were scrambled and in the air in minutes and had to rely on the ground crew to have got everything shipshape.

As they were to maintain radio silence, he and Chalky would have to rely on visual checks to see if they were together. They were first to taxi from the apron onto the strip.

Flying in the almost darkness was second nature – they'd been chosen for their experience and expertise, after all. The G force pinned him into the seat as he soared into the air. He had Jordan's kite as the one he'd flown a few days ago was still being repaired somewhere on the base. It would be back in use by the end of the week at the latest.

The sea was choppy, a dismal grey and very uninviting. At this time of the year, anyone who ditched in the drink would die from hypothermia very quickly if they weren't picked up promptly.

He pushed these unwelcome thoughts aside and concentrated on the task at hand. As his trusty Spit skimmed above the waves, responding to his lightest touch, for a few minutes he was able to forget the reason he was there and just enjoy being in charge of this fabulous silver beast.

They encountered no flak, no German fighters dropped down from the sky above them and the race across the Channel and then over Belgium was accomplished in minutes. They reached their objective safely. This was the point when things would get unpleasant. As they skimmed across the airfield, obviously under construction, they were going to be seen and heard.

How long would it take for the *Messerschmitt* he saw on the ground to get airborne? Minutes probably, so after a single circuit which had told him all he needed to know, he pulled back the stick and climbed at full throttle, hoping to get into the clouds before he was shot down.

Chalky was close behind him as by some miracle they'd managed to complete their mission and remain close enough to keep visual contact. Radio silence was no longer necessary, and he switched on the RT.

John climbed to 10,000 feet and headed for home. He was smiling. He had the information the spy had asked for and would be rewarded with a twelve-hour pass to go to the funeral.

The radio suddenly crackled into life. 'John, John, on your tail. Look behind you,' Chalky screamed into his ear.

John had lost concentration for a second and in that moment hadn't seen the three 109s almost on him.

Dive or climb? Spitfires were very manoeuvrable – more so than the *Messerschmitt 109* – he decided to climb first and if that didn't shake them off, he would dive.

# 23

Joanna hadn't been able to watch the undertakers remove the body yesterday and like a coward had hidden in the sitting room until it was over. Being in there had been almost worse than remaining in the grand hall as she'd expected to see Elizabeth sitting in her usual chair, looking up from her journal with a delighted smile on her face.

Jean had stayed with her, but the twins stoically remained at their adopted grandmother's side until the very end. Lazzy sensed something was wrong and remained by Joanna with his head in her lap.

After a miserable night, she got up and made her way downstairs. The house seemed emptier. How was it possible that the absence of a person could be as tangible as their presence?

Miss Biggins said that as soon as the funeral was over, and she'd done what she could to help with any arrangements, she would be leaving. It appeared that she had an unmarried brother somewhat older than herself who'd asked her several times to come and look after him and now she was free to do so.

Jean laid up for breakfast in the kitchen and her friend looked round with a sad smile as Joanna entered.

'How are you this morning? You look as though you had as little sleep as I did.'

'I'm glad that Tony and Joe put the bed back upstairs. The hall's easier to walk through now but I don't think I want to be in the sitting room at the moment.'

'We'll be getting on with our Christmas preparations in the study, and there's no reason why we can't sit in there in the evening as well, especially now we've got the wireless to listen to.'

Joanna's eyes were dry, her throat scratchy. 'I don't want to give in to tears, Jean, because it would be so bad for the baby to cry. I'd only known Elizabeth for about two years but I loved her dearly and she's going to be sorely missed.'

'She wouldn't want you to be sad, Joanna, she loved you and your children. She'd tell you, if she could, that she'd had almost eighty years on this earth and was content to meet her maker.'

Joanna stared at her friend. 'You know as well as I do that she'd want us to be as miserable as sin, to think about her every day for the next year. She certainly wasn't in any hurry to depart this mortal coil. I know she was so looking forward to meeting the baby and moving to Stodham next month.'

Jean shrugged. 'Of course I know that, too, I was just trying to cheer you up.'

'You did – she had a peaceful and dignified death. Elizabeth didn't suffer and at the end I think she regained consciousness briefly and heard us singing.'

'I'm not frightened of dying, Joanna, but in the manner of it. You're right, Lady Harcourt didn't suffer and let's hope she's in heaven.'

'Good grief, are you suggesting that she could have gone to the fiery pit?'

Jean's mouth dropped open in horror. 'No, no, nothing like that. I was just indicating that I'm not sure anyone goes anywhere at all. I don't think I'm an atheist like John, but I'm certainly not completely convinced there's a supreme being taking care of us all.'

'To be honest, I think a lot of people who attend church, say their prayers and so on, are doing it because it's expected of them and not because they actually believe it. I don't disbelieve but like you I'm not absolutely certain we're not talking to ourselves.'

Joanna helped herself to tea but ignored the toast. 'There's so much to organise and I suppose I should have started letting people know yesterday but I just couldn't face it.'

'Shall I speak to Mr Evans? You'll want to get the funeral over before the baby comes.'

'I certainly will. Surely the undertaker will have informed the vicar for us? We can hold the wake here in the grand hall where she died.'

Jean laughed softly. 'Probably better not to tell anybody that. I'll ring Mrs Thomas as well – being the chair of the WI, and also the WVS since you resigned, means she can let everybody else know. People will want to send condolence cards.'

Joe and Liza wandered in and overheard this last remark.

He grinned. 'They can combine it with a Christmas greeting and save postage and paper.'

'If they wait another week or two, they can add congratulations for the baby, Ma,' Liza said.

The two of them seemed fully recovered and as cheerful as always. Coming from the East End as they had, they'd had to become tough and resilient, and she was going to try and emulate them and not give in to her grief.

'I was just saying to Jean that we could have the wake here. It should be a celebration of her life, not a miserable occasion.'

'Have you spoken to Mr Evans yet, Ma?'

'No, I'm going to finish my tea and then do it, Liza.'

'There's no need. The three of us can take care of everything if you want us to.'

'It would just be feeble of me to allow you to do that. If my husband was here then I could legitimately leave it to him, but he's not, so I must pull myself together and do what's necessary.'

'John said that he's going to be here for the funeral. I expect he'll ring when he gets back from whatever op he's on today,' Joe said, sounding so much older than his years. He already knew the RAF jargon and would be able to volunteer in two years. She just had to hope this wretched, beastly war would be over by then.

After speaking to the vicar, Joanna couldn't face ringing the solicitor or the bank in London that handled Elizabeth's financial affairs. Instead, whilst the others were sewing, gluing and painting, she sat at a table pushed up against the far wall, and wrote letters to all those who needed to be informed.

They had soup and baked potatoes for lunch and she forced herself to eat. She must put the health of this unborn baby before her lack of appetite. Tony had returned to Goodwill House as soon as he'd completed his tasks at The Manse and then kindly returned to the village to post the letters. These would already be on their way to the recipients. No doubt there would be a flurry of telephone calls from these official bodies, but not for a day or two, she hoped.

The house was horribly quiet, the wireless turned off out of respect, and instead of the previous happy chatter in the study, everybody was subdued. Joanna looked up from the book she was attempting to read, she rather thought she'd read the same page several times, and spoke to Jean, who was nearest.

'It's the sixth tomorrow, so that means we've got a week until the funeral. And then I'll only be a week away from my due date. I was going to go upstairs and have a rest this afternoon as I didn't sleep at all well last night, but I want to be available when John rings. I didn't think any of these sorties, operations, or whatever you call them would continue for so long.'

'I'm sure he'll ring when he gets a moment. It's possible he's been busy all day.'

Later she was becoming anxious and decided to call Hawkinge. She would just ask whoever answered the telephone to relay a message to John, telling him about the funeral.

'I'll do it, Ma,' Joe offered. 'You stay where you are with your feet up. You hardly ate anything at lunch so Jean said tonight that we're having the rest of the soup followed by omelettes and sauté potatoes as they're your favourites. She's opening two tins of peaches as we all need cheering up.'

'How nice. I was going to refuse your offer to ring Hawkinge for me, my dear, but actually I'd be grateful if you would do it.'

Her heart was thudding uncomfortably, her head throbbed. Why hadn't John rung her himself? She closed her eyes and tried to think of summer days, blue skies, happy thoughts, but it was impossible.

Jean was in the kitchen, Liza had gone out into the hall with Joe, and Tony had gone to The Manse to shut up the chickens and ducks. Why was it taking Joe so long to make the telephone call?

Joanna pushed herself upright, put her feet firmly on the floor and was about to go out and see for herself what the delay was when Jean came in, her face ashen.

'Oh, my dear, I don't know how to tell you this. You have to be brave and believe they will find him.'

The words made no sense to her for a moment. 'What do you mean? What's happened to John?'

'His squadron leader was about to ring. John didn't return from his mission this morning. They are still searching. They haven't given up hope and neither must you.'

* * *

John felt the fuselage quiver as bullets hit his kite. He slammed the stick forward and for a second his Spit was pointing downwards. His Sutton harness held him in his seat and the canvas straps were biting into his chest.

He was vertical, plummeting towards the sea thousands of feet below. Airspeed was astronomical. He had ammo and decided to take the attack to the attacker. He was still miles from home and if he bailed out, it was unlikely he'd be found in time – before the icy water killed him.

He pulled out of the suicidal dive, opened the throttle and with the emergency boost on, began to climb. There was no sign of Chalky. The RT was on. 'Chalky, I need your help. Two bogeys on my tail and I'm hit.'

There was a crackle of static but no response. He tried calling control. Again zero. What a bloody awful time for his radio to pack up. He was on his own – he wasn't going to give in easily as he had too much to live for. Joanna and the baby needed him.

John spiralled upwards until he was above the clouds. There had been no further attacks and the kite appeared to be functioning as it should. He was frantically swivelling his head, looking out for the ME 109s that had bounced him a few seconds earlier. There – just below him – a glint of silver.

Without hesitation, he dived towards the glimpse he'd had and opened fire. Despite being enveloped in thick grey cloud he saw the flash of orange and seconds later the German kite exploded.

One down – one to go. As he was pulling out for the second time, his poor little Spit received a massive dose of bullets from one end to the other. The engine stopped. Then the dreaded flicker of fire told him it was time to bail out.

Automatically he ran through the procedure in his head. First – release his Sutton harness, disconnect his helmet, slide back the canopy and roll the kite so he was upside down. Then push the stick forward and he'd be out of the kite and on his way down.

He completed this manoeuvre successfully and seconds later was out of the cockpit. It was like hitting a brick wall – one minute he'd been travelling at 300 miles an hour and the next was stationary.

He counted as instructed and then pulled the D-ring. Immediately his chute opened and for a few seconds he felt like he was travelling up rather than down. The sea was invisible and he wasn't sure how far he had to fall before he ditched into the drink.

His radio had been on the blink so nobody knew his coordinates. There would be no rescue boat screaming out from Ramsgate to find him. In fact, he wasn't sure if he was even near his home base. It was hard to believe that after living a charmed life he was now to die from hypothermia.

Vaguely he recalled being told by the instructor it would take about ten minutes to travel 10,000 feet – plenty of time for the other ME 109 to find him and shoot him if it wasn't for the blanket of cloud surrounding him.

Should he kick off his boots before he hit the water? They would fill up immediately and drag him under. He was supposed to dump his chute before he hit the sea as being shrouded with yards of silk might well pull him under.

Suddenly he was through the thick clouds; visibility was dire, the wind moving him violently from side to side, the rain lashing his face, and he couldn't see how far away he was from the water.

He misjudged it horribly and before he could press the quick release button and set his chute free, he was in the icy sea. He'd not even kicked off his boots as he'd intended. He took a deep breath so when he submerged he didn't swallow a gallon of water. The Mae West did its job and he bobbed back to the surface. He was a lucky sod as the chute had landed beside him, trapping air inside a balloon of silk and giving him extra buoyancy.

The drill was to float on your back, not try to swim as that would expend energy and you needed to keep every ounce for as long as possible. Anyway, swimming in a Mae West was all but impossible – you could kick your legs and flap your arms but not make much progress, however hard you tried.

John was being tossed up and down by the waves and he knew he had only the faintest chance of being rescued. If Chalky had been with him, he could have circled until help came but they'd become separated in the cloud and God knows where his friend was now.

As he'd failed to contact control and give his coordinates, they would have to search for him in the most likely location. If he knew where the hell he was, he might have some inkling of his chances of survival.

Every time a wave broke over his head, he swallowed salt water. He kept his eyes and mouth closed in the vain hope this would help. He tried to cheer himself up with the thought that at least he wasn't injured and most blokes who bailed out had been shot or burnt.

The good thing about the rain was that it washed the salt from his face and he could lick it from his lips. He could no longer feel his extremities. All flyers knew that it was essential to stay conscious, not drift off to sleep, as that inevitably led to death.

He thought about his beloved Joanna, the baby they were having, how happy he was to be married to her and how lucky. His parents were overjoyed and even his father, a dyed-in-the-wool socialist, was pleased. They were coming to stay when the baby arrived if they could manage to get to Kent.

He could see the white silk balloon bobbing about beside him and he thought it looked pretty, magical even. Then, belatedly, it occurred to him that it would also be visible even in this bloody horrible weather to any passing vessel.

Maybe he wasn't going to die today – or at least not just yet. He was still afloat, still more or less awake, and wasn't drowning, which was a bonus. Even now when he was in such peril he didn't waste his energy on praying to a non-existent deity. If he survived it would be because he was lucky, not because someone had said prayers.

If the weather was better, maybe he might hear the approach of a boat, see a search aircraft overhead and then that would mean they would be able to see him. However hard he tried to fight it, a strange lethargy was slowly overcoming him. His last thoughts as he fell asleep were of his wife, the love of his life, and his unborn child.

From a distance, John heard somebody talking to him. 'Come on, don't die on us now. It's a bleeding miracle we picked you up at all.'

He couldn't open his eyes, couldn't speak, but understood he'd been rescued. Vaguely he was aware of being stripped naked, rubbed vigorously with something rough, and then cocooned in something warm.

'Here, get this down you. It's hot and sweet and got a slug of rum in it. It'll help warm you up.'

Obediently John opened his mouth and swallowed what was offered. It immediately came back again along with half a gallon of seawater.

'Better out than in, old son, but a shocking waste of rum. Let's try again, shall we?'

This time John kept it down and felt better for it. He still couldn't open his eyes, didn't have the energy to speak, couldn't tell these men who he was as he didn't know himself.

He was safe, wasn't going to die, and that's all that mattered.

The next time he woke, the boat wasn't rocking as violently as it had been before. An overwhelming smell of fish told him what sort of vessel he was on and who these men were.

'Look, Jimmy, the bugger's awake. Here, get your clothes back on, we'll be docking soon and you ain't decent. We've had your uniform drying on the engine and you'll be snug as a bug in a rug with that back on.'

He saw his salt-encrusted clothes in a heap beside him and they were indeed warm and dry. 'Did you radio ashore and tell them that you picked me up? My wife will be beside herself.'

'Told them we fished a pilot out but as you don't have your tags, we couldn't say who you were.' The speaker, a grey-haired bearded man in his forties, smiled. 'Don't look so worried, they know we picked up a pilot and there can't have been that many fished out now, can there?'

John instinctively put his hand to his neck and his tags were missing. 'How long have I been on board your boat? When did you pick me up?'

'Yesterday morning. We was on our way out so as you was asleep, we finished what we came out to do before turning back. Lovely lot of cod we've got.'

'My God, my wife's expecting a baby any day and her mother-in-law died two days ago. If she thinks that I'm dead too...' He couldn't finish the sentence.

# 24

Joanna heaved herself to her feet. 'Is the officer still on the line? I need to speak to him myself.'

'He is. I was just going to tell you that,' Jean said.

Joe was holding the telephone receiver and handed it to her. 'Mrs Sergeant speaking. Please tell me at once what you know.'

'Mrs Sergeant, I'm Billy, John's squadron leader. He ditched sometime this morning and we've been searching for him. We do know a pilot has been picked up by a fishing boat, but he's unidentified.'

'Then he's safe.'

'He very well could be. But there are five men missing and only one, so far, has been found. Until the boat docks…'

'Why can't they read his dog tags?'

'This pilot doesn't have them on. They said he's a young man with black hair.'

'Tell them to look at his eyes. John has one green and one brown.'

'I would do that, ma'am, but they have gone out of range. They'll be back with their passenger at dawn tomorrow. I'm so sorry, but you'll not know for sure if it's John until then. It sounds as if it is, but I can't say for certain.'

'It is him. I'd know if he was dead. Will you let me know as soon as you have any information of any sort?'

'As soon as there's any definitive information, someone will telephone.'

'Yes, it doesn't matter what time it is, there will be somebody waiting for the call.'

'I'm sorry for the other wives and mothers as they won't have good news.' There was no need to say that she was referring to the other missing men. Her beloved husband was well and in the fishing boat and tomorrow he would be home.

'By the way, I don't suppose you knew that any chap who has a prang gets a week's crash leave.'

'That's good to hear,' Joanna said. 'Thank you for ringing me yourself. I do appreciate you taking the trouble to do that.'

She turned to the others, who were grouped around her, listening avidly. 'I'm convinced that he's safe, but we won't know for certain until the fishing boat that has picked him up returns to...' She frowned and shook her head. 'How silly of me, I forgot to ask where this fishing boat will be docking.'

'As we don't know exactly where John was flying from when he went down, he could have been picked up anywhere in the North Sea or the Channel,' Tony said.

'It doesn't really matter as he'll have to go back to Hawkinge to be debriefed before he can come home. All pilots who crash get a week's leave – isn't that splendid?'

Joanna was determined to keep cheerful as there was already enough grief in the house. 'I think I'll remain downstairs so I'm here when the telephone call comes. I'll be perfectly comfortable on the chaise longue if Joe and Tony would be kind enough to bring it through.'

'We'll do that after supper – we might very well get a telephone call before then,' Jean said, trying to look cheerful but not succeeding.

'I'm going to help Miss Biggins upstairs,' Liza informed them. 'She's packing Grandma's things before she leaves. I know you'll want to take them with us when we go next month.'

Surreptitiously, Joanna wiped an errant tear from her cheek, hoping that nobody had noticed. 'Thank you, my love, that's kind of you.' She turned to the others still standing behind her.

'Shall we return to the study and get on with our work? We've got more to do now that we don't have Elizabeth or Miss Biggins in the workshop.'

'I'll not stay with Miss Biggins for long, Ma, and will come back and do my share in here,' Liza said.

There were half a dozen telephone calls but they were all of condolence and with offers to help – although what exactly these kind people thought they could do, Joanna had no idea.

They moved to the kitchen for supper, something they'd never done when Elizabeth was with them. She refused to eat in there and always insisted that they ate in the breakfast room.

'That was delicious, Jean, exactly what I wanted. Thank you so much for everything you're doing for me,' Joanna said as she replaced her spoon in the dish after finishing the last morsel of peaches and custard.

'I'm making coffee tonight, Joanna, for Tony and us, and cocoa for the twins. People have been arriving with little gifts all day so we've got plenty of milk, cream and so on. Considering how poor the weather is, it makes these gestures even more kind.'

Lazzy suddenly jumped to his feet and rushed to the back door, wagging his tail. Moments later, there was a loud knock on the door.

'I'll go,' Joe said. 'It must be somebody we know.'

Joanna hurriedly got to her feet as she really didn't want to see anybody just now. She found it easier to walk with both hands supporting her belly, even if it made her look quite ridiculous. She was just settling comfortably on the chaise longue when Joe came in with Dr Willoughby.

'Mrs Sergeant, I just heard that your husband's missing at sea. I'm so sorry. I thought I'd better come and check on you myself as too much upset might cause you to go into labour a little earlier than expected.'

'How kind of you, Dr Willoughby. We believe that he's been picked up safely by a fishing boat but won't know for sure until the boat returns with its catch tomorrow morning. I'm as well as can be expected in the circumstances and absolutely no unwanted twinges.'

He nodded professionally, collected a bentwood chair and placed it next to her. 'I'll just check you out now I'm here.'

Joanna was about to protest that she had no intention of exposing her tummy where she was when he picked up her wrist and began to take her pulse. Then he got out his stethoscope and listened to her heart without asking her to move any garments.

Next he checked her ankles, again without comment. 'Excellent, absolutely nothing to worry about.'

'I'm not worried, I told you that I'm tickety-boo. Forgive me for asking, but where did you hear about John?'

'It's all over the village. My wife told me and I thought I'd better come at once. Two shocks so close together isn't good for anyone and especially not a woman so close to term.'

'John will be coming home for a week at least as he gets statutory leave because he crashed. I don't know the details, so don't ask. His dog tags were lost somehow but the description the fishermen gave was definitely of John.'

'I take it your husband wasn't in any condition to tell them who he was if he'd been in the sea for a while.'

'I believe that's what happened. As you seem to have your finger on the pulse of the village, Doctor, could I ask you to let people know the funeral's on the thirteenth and everybody is welcome to come here afterwards to celebrate Lady Harcourt's life?'

'Good God, I'll do no such thing. You'll be a week away from the arrival of this baby and having hordes of villagers here is the last thing you need.'

For a moment, Joanna was rendered silent. This was not his concern – or was it?

'Perhaps you're right. We'll keep it just close friends and family – of course you and Charlie must come. Could you kindly ask her to see if Daphne and Sal would like to join us too? Those three got on very well with Elizabeth and it would be good to see them again even in these circumstances.'

'Now that I'd be happy to do,' Dr Willoughby said. 'I'm sure that Charlie will tell you when she sees you, but we are expecting a happy event ourselves next spring. Hopefully our children can be friends and grow up together as they'll be living so close together.'

'That's the most wonderful news and has cheered me up immensely.

Thank you so very much for coming without being asked to see if I was dealing with all the difficulties. I promise that whatever happens now or in the future I'm strong enough nowadays to cope. That wouldn't have been the case three years ago but I'm a different woman now.'

'Then I'll take my leave, Mrs Sergeant...'

'Please, will you call me Joanna, as I feel we're already friends and such formality is rather tiresome, don't you think?'

'I'd be delighted to. And you must call me James. After all, if my wife calls you by your first name then it is rather odd that I don't. Goodbye, Joanna, don't hesitate to call me if you need to.'

He strode out, swinging his bag in his hand, and she was glad to have him as a friend. Perhaps it would have been better to wait until after the baby was delivered before being on first-name terms – it might be a little awkward for both of them if he was needed at the delivery and would see rather more of her than she wished any male friend to do.

His visit had cheered her, made things seem a little less grim. She just had to get through the interminable time between now and when the fishing boat was likely to dock and she would hear that her beloved John was indeed safe and well.

* * *

John struggled into his underwear and then added his shirt. He didn't remember them being quite so snug. He thought it was probably the long immersion in salt water that had caused them to shrink a bit.

He no longer had any socks but didn't want to disturb the two fishermen, who were busy navigating into port, to ask where they were. He pushed his hand into one of his flying boots and was unsurprised to find the interior still sopping wet. His Irvin jacket seemed okay when he touched it.

His next task was to get into his uniform. He ached all over, had a filthy headache and was so fatigued he could scarcely move, but he was alive – it was a bloody miracle he'd been picked up.

He tried to pull his trousers up his legs. They were dry but they were now three sizes too small. Drying them on the engine had been a brainwave but the woollen material had shrunk disastrously. The thought of stepping out of the boat in his underpants wasn't a happy one.

One of the blokes heard his struggles and ducked back into the cabin. 'Bugger me – they ain't much good to you now, are they? Sorry about that, we didn't know they'd shrink.' He held out a hand. 'Give them here, I'll cut open the seams. Be a bit draughty but at least you'll be covered.'

John grinned. 'If you could do the same with my jacket then I can put that on.'

'Your socks are buggered, sorry, mate. Your boots and flying jacket are still a bit damp but I reckon they'll fit you all right.'

'Are we close to shore? It's not as bumpy now.'

'No, but we'll be in range of the Coast Guard in a few minutes. We'll let them know who you are. Here, tea and toast. Bit salty but better than nothing.'

John was so hungry he would have eaten raw fish but that wasn't offered. With the side seams of his trousers split open, he was able to pull them up but they wouldn't fasten. He just had to hope they'd stay in place and not slither down to his ankles when he stood up.

His uniform jacket was little better. It was no longer long enough to cover the discrepancy of his trousers. When they docked, he'd put on his wet Irvin jacket. Better to be uncomfortable than embarrass the ladies.

He heard the radio crackling and one of the blokes talking but was too damn tired to go and ask if the message had been sent to Joanna. He stretched out on the bunk, narrow and smelly, but he could have slept on the floor he was so tired.

He was dragged from his slumbers by being shaken.

'Righto, up you come, there's a welcome party on the hard.' The fisherman didn't offer to help John to his feet but left him to stagger up his own.

The boat bumped against the quay and he lost his balance and fell onto his knees, knocking his shin painfully on something metal and sharp. Somehow he shrugged into his Irvin jacket, shoved his bare feet into his boots and was ready to clamber up the ladder to the deck.

It had been warm in the cabin but outside it was bitter. The rain stung his face and his cut trouser legs flapped around in the wind. He no longer had his helmet or goggles – God knows what happened to those.

The tide was on the rise but in order to get off the vessel he'd still have to climb a few rungs of a metal ladder fastened to the side of the dock. He viewed it with alarm. How the hell was he going to scramble up that without falling into the water for a second time?

Then his rescuers stepped in to help. 'Here, I'll fasten this rope round your waist, I'll go up first and then can haul you up. I won't let you fall. Blimey, you've done enough to keep us safe. It's the least we can do.'

With the rope being held securely above him, John was ready to attempt the climb. Between one man holding the rope like grim death and the shoulder of the other bloke under his arse, he was able to achieve the impossible. He tumbled headfirst onto the cobbles and had never been more grateful in his life to be on dry land.

For some reason, he didn't have the energy or inclination to get to his feet. He was safe. He'd just have a bit of a kip as it was comfortable on the ground.

* * *

John woke up in a hospital bed. Lounging beside him was Billy.

'Good afternoon, old boy, glad to see you back in the land of the living.'

'What the hell are you doing here? In fact, where the hell is *here*?'

'Margate and District Hospital as it lives and breathes. The quack said you just needed to sleep. He put a few stitches in the cut on your leg but apart from that you're absolutely fine.'

'Does Joanna know I'm safe?'

'I rang her myself,' Billy said. 'She slept by the telephone so I was able to speak to her in person. Don't look so panicked, my friend, she's absolutely not coming here to see you.'

'I need a bath and my uniform's ruined.'

'You're not kidding. I brought everything you need. What do you want to do first – bathe or eat?'

'Bath then food. My legs are like jelly. Give me a hand, please. I don't want to fall flat on my face again.'

An hour later, he was fed, correctly dressed and ready to leave. 'I want to phone home. Is there a public telephone anywhere here?'

'You can use the one in the matron's office. You're a hero and nothing's too good for you.'

'I bailed out of my kite and by some stroke of fortune was picked up and survived. That's hardly heroic. Did Chalky get back okay?'

'You shut down an ME 109 before you ditched. You completed your mission successfully in the most appalling conditions – of course, you're a bloody hero. Don't argue with your superior officer.' Billy grinned. 'And yes, Chalky is tickety-boo.'

John made a feeble attempt at a salute. 'Yes, sir. I've told you everything in detail – does that mean I can go home without being grilled by the spy?'

'Your trusty steed is here – I rode it myself. There's an erk hanging about outside waiting to drive me back to Hawkinge. If you're up to it, then you can go home to your wife. Don't come back until after the baby arrives.'

'What? That could be two weeks or more.'

'You've got a week's crash leave and then two weeks' actual leave. I've got a couple of new bods arriving tomorrow, so you won't be missed.'

'Give Chalky my regards. I'm glad he got back safely too.'

'I certainly will. Enjoy your R and R. Merry Christmas, John.'

They shook hands and then Billy strode across to the waiting vehicle and jumped into the passenger seat. The AC1, the erk, had been standing guard over the bike. Billy had got him a new helmet and goggles. His Irvin jacket had been dried somehow during his short stay at the hospital, as had his boots.

He kickstarted his bike and headed for home, thankful to be alive. He was halfway home when he realised he hadn't made the phone call. Joanna wouldn't know he was coming and he wasn't sure his sudden arrival would be good for her.

It was only a quick flip from Margate to Stodham so hardly worth stopping at a telephone box now he was on his way. He couldn't wait to see her face when he walked in.

Hopefully, the fact that he'd survived against all the odds would be some compensation for the loss of her beloved Elizabeth.

* * *

Joanna knew she should be sad but the fact that John was alive made Elizabeth's death seem more bearable. If he'd died, and it was a miracle that he hadn't, then her life would never have been the same. Even the baby couldn't have made up for John's loss.

The house was wonderfully warm, extravagantly so, but as long as they had the fuel, from now on she intended to have fires in every room and keep the boiler going so the radiators were also warm.

'Ma, when will John be home?'

'His squadron leader said John was recovering in hospital, exhaustion and exposure, but nothing worse. He'll be back as soon as he's well enough to collect his motorbike from Hawkinge.'

'I can't believe that he fell out of his Spitfire into the sea and was picked up several hours later still alive,' Joe said shaking his head.

'I prayed that he'd be safe and I'm sure that you did, too, and our prayers were answered. I think the Lord thought losing Elizabeth this week was enough for this family to deal with,' Joanna said, but even to her these words seemed false. Sometimes entire families were wiped out, leaving just one member alive – didn't they deserve to have God take care of them?

'I sing in the choir, I worked for the vicar and his wife looking after their children, but I'm not sure that I really believe there's a God watching over us,' Liza said. 'If there was, there wouldn't be a war, would there? Last time I went to a St John's meeting, they were saying that the most dreadful things are happening to Jewish people in Germany.'

'Let's not talk about that now, Liza, let's just be thankful that John's coming home to us and that Elizabeth believed she was going to a better place and died peacefully after a long life.'

'I meant to tell you, Ma, Miss Biggins has finished clearing out Grandma's room and is packing her own things. I think she intends to leave first thing tomorrow morning. She doesn't want to go to the funeral after all.'

'I've no idea if I still owe her any money. Joe, could you please ask Jean if there's anything in the drawer in the kitchen that I could give her by way of a bonus and thank you?'

'How much do you want?'

'Five pounds would be perfect. I'm trying to work out when John's likely to be back. If he's released from hospital today, he just has to return to Hawkinge and so should be able to come here tomorrow morning – weather permitting.'

As she finished speaking, the distinctive sound of a motorbike could be heard thundering up the drive. He was here. She recognised the sound of his powerful bike.

# 25

John was feeling decidedly seedy by the time he coasted to a standstill in the barn of Goodwill House. He dropped both boots to the ground and sat for a moment, hoping his head would stop spinning. He didn't want to worry Joanna by passing out as soon as he got in.

The ancient doctor who'd taken care of him had wanted him to remain in hospital for another couple of days, but John had insisted he was well. He'd much rather recuperate at home than in Margate. Now he was regretting his decision.

The house was in mourning for Elizabeth and the last thing anyone needed was an invalid on their hands. Too late to change his mind, as the boot room door opened and Lazzy burst out.

John hastily swung his leg over the saddle, heaved the machine onto its stand, and moved away from his precious motorbike. 'No, Lazzy, you'll knock me down if you jump up,' he said to the overexcited dog.

'Lazzy, no. Come here at once.' Joe snapped the command and to John's astonishment the dog stopped and slunk back to sit, tail brushing the ground, looking up at the boy.

'Thanks, not too steady on my pins. He'd have had me over.'

'Fair enough. Joanna's desperate to see you. Glad you got home safely,

John.' The lad hesitated and then rushed forward and flung his arms around him. 'We thought you'd died. We thought you'd gone for a Burton.'

John rubbed his back, touched the boy was so moved as he hadn't realised he meant so much to him. 'I'm fine, just tired. Being in the drink for several hours does that to a bloke. Sorry about your grandma. She was a grand old bird.'

Joe sniffed and stepped away. 'She was. We'll all miss her.' He managed a watery grin. 'Having you back makes it seem a bit less sad.'

'It's cold out here, shall we go in? I don't need anything from the panniers, I've got civvies here. I'm going to wear those indoors.'

It was a major effort to remain upright but John was determined not to show how unwell he felt. If he could maintain this façade for a couple of hours then he could crawl off to bed without causing comment.

'Shocking news about the Japs' bombing of Pearl Harbour last night, wasn't it?' Joe said as he closed the boot room door behind them.

'We'll be overrun with Yanks in the New Year, but nobody was surprised. It's been brewing for weeks. Maybe this place can go to them instead of to the RAF – at least we'd be certain we'd get it back eventually.'

There was no time for further conversation with his stepson. He was desperate to see Joanna. 'Where is she?'

'In the grand hall. That's where we sit at the moment as Ma doesn't want to use the sitting room.'

'I'm not surprised, too many memories.'

John paused for a moment, took a deep breath, and surged forward as if full of energy when the reverse was true. Arriving at the double should convince her he was suffering no ill effects.

In two strides, he had his arms around her. They had to stand side by side and embrace, but that didn't matter. 'Darling, I can't tell you how happy I am to see you and how sorry I am about Elizabeth.'

Joanna rested her head on his shoulder. 'You gave us a dreadful scare, my love, and having you back for three weeks makes even her death seem less painful. I'm going to miss her dreadfully, but if anything had happened to you…'

'We're going to win this bloody war now America's involved. Let's not talk about it, sweetheart, let's pretend we're a normal family in normal times gathering for the funeral of a loved relative.'

'Sarah and Angus are coming and three of the land girls that became particular friends of ours will also be there. I want it to be a celebration of her life, not a sad occasion.'

'Let's sit down, it'll be better for both of us.'

'We didn't expect you until tomorrow so it's a lovely surprise to have you here today.'

He sat first, taking the end of the chaise longue with the fancy rolled back and then she sat next to him and put her feet up. This meant they were comfortable and as close to each other as they could be. He had his hands resting on her distended belly and the baby moved beneath his fingers.

'Doesn't that hurt?'

'No, I love it as that means everything is tickety-boo in there. If we have a girl then I'd like to call her Elizabeth.'

'I was going to suggest that myself. It seems right somehow that as one life goes another one's about to arrive. Let's hope our child remains in situ until after the funeral at least.'

'I was a bit late with Sarah and I've still got almost two weeks left until my due date. The midwife said the head's not fully engaged so I won't go into labour until that happens.'

He'd no idea what this meant and wasn't sure he wanted to know. Joe came in carrying his panniers.

'Don't know what you've got in this one, John, but it weighs a tonne.'

'I didn't pack them, my orderly did, at least I think it was him. Hand it over and I'll have a dekko.' John flipped open the buckles and pulled back the canvas top. He laughed when he saw the contents. 'Look at these, you two.'

He dipped into the bag and held up a couple of beautifully carved wooden animals. 'I reckon there are twenty or more in here and if they're all as good as these the kiddies will be delighted.'

Liza and Jean joined them and they examined each of the lovingly whittled animals, cars, planes as well as three wooden whistles that actually worked.

'How kind of your squadron to send these. Did you do any of them?' Joanna asked.

'No, my whittling skills proved inadequate. Almost cut my thumb off trying.'

'Come and see what we've got ready,' Liza said.

'Not now, sweetheart, I'm too comfortable. We've got another two weeks before they have to be delivered, so plenty of time.'

She wasn't to be deterred. 'You stay there, John, Joe and I will bring you a selection.'

The two of them dashed off to the study. 'Damn, they could have taken the pannier with them.'

Joanna was still rummaging in it and triumphantly held up a bulging brown paper bag. 'This is full of sweets. We've got a hundred stockings made and I think there's enough here for one each at least.'

'I think they must have come from the NAAFI. We must make sure that the parents of the children are aware that Hawkinge contributed to their Christmas surprise.'

An enjoyable hour later, the toys were returned to the study and Jean called them in for supper. Joanna leaned heavily on his shoulder in order to get to her feet. The last thing he wanted was to spend more time being sociable.

'Stay where you are, my love, I'll get Liza to bring you a tray. Then go to bed before you're unable to get up the stairs unaided.'

'Sorry, would you mind if I went up without eating? I'll be fine tomorrow. It's lovely to be home, even in these circumstances.' His head was swimming and there were spots dancing in front of his eyes.

'Joe, Tony, can you come here please?' The fact that she raised her voice demonstrated how worried she was.

Between the two of them, they managed to manhandle him up the staircase and down the long passageway to the bedroom.

'I'll use the bog first. I can manage from here, thank you. Don't tell Joanna, but I should have stayed in hospital for at least another day. I wanted to come home.'

'We'll wait here. Don't be long, our supper's getting cold,' Tony said firmly, and John was grateful they'd ignored his suggestion.

He sat on the edge of the bed, raising and lowering his limbs as instructed, and fell beneath the covers in his underwear. He was aware when Joanna joined him later but didn't wake up fully.

'I love you, John, you can rest for as long as you need. Please don't feel you've got to pretend to be all right when you're obviously not.'

* * *

Joanna lay beside her beloved husband, listening to him breathe, and couldn't quite believe he was there. She dreaded to think what might happen when he went back to join his squadron in the New Year but pushed those unhappy thoughts aside.

She had him here, safe and well, at least for the moment. There would be thousands of families spending Christmas without the man of the house, without their sons, and her heart went out to them.

It wasn't comfortable lying on her back and lying on her front was impossible, so she slept on one side or the other and was relatively comfy this way. John was on his side. She wriggled so her back was pressed against his. Satisfied that she'd know if he needed assistance during the night, she fell asleep.

Joanna woke some hours later to discover that she'd wet the bed. She was lying in a puddle and so was he. It took a few moments to register that this wasn't an embarrassing accident, but her waters had broken.

'John, wake up. I'm so sorry but the bed's wet.' She thought it might not be sensible to wake him up by saying she was in labour. When he was alert would be time enough.

To her surprise, he was instantly awake. 'Don't worry, sweetheart, accidents happen. I'll soon get it nice and dry again.'

He reached out and switched on the bedside light. 'No, I've not peed in the bed, my waters have broken. I don't understand it as I've not had a single contraction, not even any backache.'

'Bloody hell – what do I do next? Call the midwife? The doctor? Jean?'

'Get dressed first and then help me to get into a dry nightdress. There's no rush, the baby can't come until I get contractions. Then, whilst I sit and watch, would you be so kind as to change the bed sheets? There's a maternity pack in the bottom drawer of the chest. I'm afraid you won't be allowed back in. The bed in the adjoining room's been made up for you.'

She watched him get into his uniform with commendable speed – he was obviously feeling a lot better as he'd scarcely been able to walk last night. She glanced at the overmantel clock and saw it was just before three.

He then tenderly lifted off her soiled nightie and dropped a clean one over her head. 'It's warm in here, sweetheart, so you'll be fine as you are. I'm going to ring the midwife before I change the bed. I won't be long.'

He reached the door before he turned with a lopsided grin. 'I neither know her name nor her number.'

Joanna gave him both; she listened to see if he was going to pound down the corridor and wake everybody. She smiled. He wasn't panicking because she didn't hear anything at all.

There was a soft tap on the door and Jean put her head around. 'John woke me on the way past. He's going to get the range going whilst I sort things out in here. I doubt that he'd know how to arrange your bed.'

'I don't want to wake up the twins. It might be hours before the baby's here.'

Jean had already stripped the bed. 'Good thing you suggested we put the rubber sheet on last time I changed it. Would have been a shame to spoil the mattress.'

By the time John came back carrying a welcome tray of tea, the bed was ready. She had on her dressing gown and was wandering about the room as she was strangely restless.

'I got no answer from the midwife so she must be out on a call. I'm sorry, but I rang Dr Willoughby and he's on his way.'

'I'm not sure that's entirely necessary as I don't have any contractions, but as my waters have broken, I suppose that was sensible.'

Dr Willoughby – James – sent Jean and John from the room so he could examine her properly. 'Are you sure you've not had any contractions? You're already two inches dilated.'

'A few twinges, but I wouldn't call them contractions. I'd like to have a bath – would that be permissible?'

'Perfect. But not on your own. Have John in there with you, as you might have to get out in a hurry.'

This was quite ridiculous – she'd had one baby and had spent a very unpleasant twenty-four hours producing her. She didn't believe that this time it was going to be so different.

The bath was exactly what she wanted as she'd felt rather grubby after the mishap earlier. Giving birth was a messy business but it was better to start nice and clean.

'James said you weren't to stay in here too long, darling.'

'All right, but I'm going to need your help to stand up.'

John put his arm around her waist, she gripped his shoulder and he pulled her to her feet with no difficulty at all. The benefit of having a young, very fit, very strong husband even if he'd just been rescued from the sea.

He dried her and, as he was replacing the clean nightdress, she got her first real contraction. 'Oh my, that was strong,' she gasped and smiled reassuringly. 'I'd better get back. Good thing you fetched James because I think this baby is going to be here in a rush.'

She wasn't wrong. An hour later, Joanna was holding a beautiful baby girl in her arms. Jean had stepped in and acted as assistant, although James had delivered the baby splendidly.

'Can John come in now? I want to show him our lovely daughter. Thank you so much, James, I couldn't have done it without you.'

He chuckled. 'I don't think you'd have had any choice. That little girl was determined to come. You're lucky that not even a stitch was needed.'

'Before he comes in, I need to tell you that I'm going to the funeral and I know he'll say that I shouldn't. The baby will be five days old – I'm sure that millions of women all over the world are back at work the next day.'

'I'm sure they are, Joanna, but in Britain we do things differently. However, I'm happy for you to go the funeral but don't take the baby. Are you feeding her yourself?'

Joanna raised an eyebrow. 'As I don't have a wet nurse waiting in the wings, then obviously I am.'

'Excellent – nothing like a mother's milk to help an infant thrive. National Dried is a good substitute and nutritious, but not quite the same in my opinion.'

He finished putting his instruments away and was ready to go. 'I'll make sure the midwife knows you've delivered. She'll call in sometime tomorrow. Don't hesitate to ask me to come back if you're worried about anything.'

'Elizabeth weighs exactly eight pounds – goodness knows how big she'd have been if I'd gone full-term.'

'John, come in now. Everything's tidy and your daughter and wife are waiting to see you.' James waved goodbye and stood aside to let the proud father rush in.

'See, my love, she looks just like you.'

'God, I hope not, I wanted a daughter to look like you.' He perched on the side of the bed and she handed him the precious parcel.

'She's got a mass of black hair like yours. Her eyes are grey now but those could change as she gets older.'

John cradled their daughter and stared down as if he couldn't believe his eyes. In that instant, Joanna knew the bond between them was forged. With one finger he pulled aside the crocheted shawl and gently stroked the baby's face.

'She's exquisite, I've never seen anything quite so wonderful in my life.' He looked up and his eyes glittered. 'Thank you, my darling, for giving me this gift. I've never held a baby before and never thought to hold one of my own.'

'Do you think she's even more beautiful than your beloved Spitfire?'

He grinned and pretended to think about it. 'Well, she comes in a close second, I suppose.'

'I love you, and you're going to make a wonderful father.'

'I hope so. I'm the happiest man in England. I can't understand how I've come to be married to you and now have a beautiful daughter.'

'I'm the lucky one. I'm the envy of the WI, being married to such handsome fighter pilot.'

He leaned down and kissed her and she wished this feeling could last for ever. He raised his head and his eyes blazed for a second, reminding her that in a few weeks they could be lovers again. Then he straightened, took a last fond look at their child and changed the subject.

'I've spoken to Sarah. I managed to contact her through her landlady and she says she can't wait to meet her baby sister.'

'Golly, you shouldn't have woken her up in the middle of the night. The news could have waited until a sensible time.'

'I thought she'd want to know. I've also told the twins and they're waiting outside to meet their new sibling. I'm going to send a telegram tomorrow – no – it's today already, isn't it? Do we have a middle name for our daughter?'

'What's your mother's name?'

'Lily – do you think we might use that?'

'Yes, Elizabeth Lily Sergeant – that sounds absolutely right. It's five o'clock so we could still catch a couple of hours' sleep. Elizabeth won't need feeding again for a while.'

'I don't want to leave you both so I'll sleep on the chair.'

'No, you could lie on top of the bed and put the eiderdown over you. Would you put her in the crib and make sure she's snugly tucked in?'

The baby didn't murmur when she was put down, which was a good sign. Was it possible that not only was the baby beautiful but she was also going to be a good sleeper?

The twins crept in and admired the sleeping infant, kissed Joanna, hugged John, and then returned to bed. Jean had already done the same. Only Tony was unaware of the unexpected arrival and he'd be told first thing tomorrow.

As she and John settled down to catch some much-needed sleep, Joanna couldn't stop smiling. The baby was sleeping peacefully in the crib beside the bed, John was safe, and in a few days all the family would be together to celebrate the life of her baby daughter's namesake. If only Elizabeth could have been here too.

# 26

John wasn't happy about Joanna being up and about so soon after the birth of their daughter. 'I know what James said, sweetheart, but it's too soon for you to be going out of the house.'

'Stop fussing, darling, as it won't make any difference. We both know that I'm going whatever you say. I'm absolutely fine, the baby's fine, the twins are fine, the only person in the family who isn't is you. Anyway, Sarah's almost a doctor and James is one and they will both be there.'

He smiled and shrugged, knowing when he should admit defeat. 'Sarah and Angus come today – I'll reserve judgement until I know that they are both absolutely fine with you going too.'

'I love you, and despite the fact that today's the day we bury the last Lady Harcourt, I'm bursting with happiness.' Joanna leaned over the crib and smoothed the coverlet.

They no longer referred to the old lady by her first name, as the only Elizabeth, as far as they were concerned, was their beautiful daughter. Associating death with the baby was unthinkable.

For the past two days, he'd been carrying the crib down to the grand hall every morning and taking it back when he and Joanna retired. There was no shortage of willing adult helpers for the baby and everyone was besotted with the new Elizabeth.

Mind you, that wasn't surprising, as she was the most beautiful baby ever. He loved to see Joanna feeding her, had helped with bath time but drew the line at changing nappies. Jean, Liza and Joanna were more than enough to take care of that. His parents and two older sisters were thrilled with the arrival and his entire family – brothers-in-law, three nieces and a nephew as well as his parents – would be arriving two days before Christmas. The baptism would be held in the local church the day after everyone arrived.

Having Goodwill House filled with children at Christmas seemed appropriate. The fact that they were his daughter's cousins made it even better. He had to report for duty on 4 January and they were moving two days before that, so he would have two days sleeping in their new home with his family around him before facing whatever was coming.

He and Joanna didn't discuss the war. They both knew it was unlikely his squadron would remain as it was. With the Yanks due to arrive in droves, the experienced fighters on his squadron wouldn't remain where they were. He pushed these unwelcome thoughts aside and concentrated on the here and now.

'John, you're daydreaming. I'd like you to be awake when I speak to you. Surely by now you know that every word I utter is a pearl of wisdom.'

'I know that I'm a henpecked husband. Now, dearest wife, what do you wish me to do?'

'Nothing at all but pay attention to me. I really don't like wearing black but it's expected and Lady Harcourt deserves to be honoured in a way that she'd have wanted.'

'I think we should have held the baptism immediately after the funeral as that way all the family would have been there.'

'Not yours, and they're part of Elizabeth's family. I'm glad that she has at least one set of grandparents.'

'Let's hope that Sarah and Angus can get away a second time as they should be there too,' John said.

'I've been thinking about that. What if you lend Angus your motorbike? They can get from London and back and attend the ceremony easily in a day if they have that and don't have to rely on the trains.'

'As long as I have it back by the 4th, as I can't get to Hawkinge without it.'

'It's time to go, Tony has the Bentley outside. It's kind of Jean to remain behind and take care of the baby and let the rest of us attend the funeral. I know she loved Lady Harcourt as much as we did.'

There was more than enough room in the luxurious car for the four of them but it would be a tight squeeze for six on the return journey. Sarah and Angus were making their own way to the church but would come back with them in the car.

The church was packed, the service interminable, but the old lady had told the vicar exactly what she wanted as if she'd known she was going to die soon. It was strange being congratulated on the arrival of the baby as well as commiserated with for the loss of their family member.

The interment in the Harcourt plot at the back of the churchyard meant more as it was just for family. When the last handful of dirt had been thrown onto the coffin, they made their way solemnly to the waiting car.

There would be about forty coming to the house for the wake and the majority of those would be walking or catching the bus. There weren't many private cars still on the roads. The Bentley would be put on blocks for the duration once they moved to Stodham.

'I'll sit in the front with Tony,' Joe volunteered.

Angus took one of the fold-down seats and John took the other, leaving the leather seat for the three ladies.

There was scarcely time for a proper conversation as the journey was over in a few minutes. Thankfully it wasn't foggy, raining or snowing, but it was bloody cold. He didn't envy those having to walk the two miles from the church.

'I can't wait to hold my baby sister,' Sarah said. 'We don't want children until the end of the war but will definitely have them after that.'

'We intend to have another fairly soon as I don't want Elizabeth to grow up on her own as you had to,' Joanna told them.

This announcement silenced the car. John filled the awkwardness. 'Of course, it all depends on if I'm around. I could well be posted overseas. In which case you could both be having babies at the same time. Elizabeth would then be an auntie as well as a sister, wouldn't she?'

Angus shook his head and laughed. 'She would but if Sarah and I have a baby before you have your second one, then your second one would be an aunt or uncle and younger than their niece or nephew.'

'I'll be grandfather to your children, Sarah, which is even stranger,' John added.

They were all smiling when they hurried from the car into the house. Today they were using the front door. Joanna looked at him lovingly.

'I'm going to feed the baby. If I'm not done in time, will you greet our guests?'

The crib was no longer in the hall as John had moved it just before they left. There was plenty of time for the local populace to meet the baby at her baptism. Today was to celebrate the long and happy life of the other Elizabeth.

There were no long faces, everybody was smiling and talking, sharing anecdotes about the dear departed. Joanna had been delighted to catch up with Sal, Daphne and Charlie, the three land girls who'd become almost part of the family when they'd stayed here.

John stood to one side in his uniform, feeling a bit out of place as he was the only one not in black. How had he come to be part of this world when it was so far away from his expectations and beliefs? He was a socialist and disliked everything that hereditary power and money stood for.

Then Joanna turned and smiled at him. All his doubts vanished. It didn't matter how different they were, what mattered was that they loved each other. He was where he was meant to be and couldn't be happier.

# ACKNOWLEDGMENTS

Once again, I want to thank the wonderful team at Boldwood and especially my fabulous editor Emily Ruston, who has loved this series as much as my readers have.

# BIBLIOGRAPHY

*Chronicle of the Second World War* edited by Jacques Legrand and Derrik Mercer
*A to Z Atlas and Guide to London*, 1939 edition
*Oxford Dictionary of Slang* by John Ayto
*Wartime Britain* by Juliet Gardiner
*How We Lived Then* by Norman Longmate
*The Wartime Scrapbook* by Robert Opie
BBC Archives: WW2
*Call the Midwife* by Jennifer Worth
*First Light* by Geoffrey Wellum
*Ginger Lacy, Fighter Pilot* by Richard Townshend Bickers
*Christmas at War* by Caroline Taggart
*Christmas on the Home Front* by Mike Brown
*Wartime Christmas* by Anthony Richards
*Spitfire* by Brian Lane
*Into the Silk* by Ian Mackersey
*The Blue Arena* by Bob Spurdle
*Hornchurch Eagles* by Richard C. Smith
*Hornchurch Offensive* by Richard C. Smith
*British Airfields of the Second World War* by Stuart Hadaway

# ABOUT THE AUTHOR

**Fenella J. Miller** is a bestselling writer of historical sagas. She also has a passion for Regency romantic adventures and has published over fifty to great acclaim.

Sign up to Fenella J. Miller's mailing list for news, competitions and updates on future books.

Visit Fenella's website: www.fenellajmiller.co.uk

Follow Fenella on social media here:

facebook.com/fenella.miller
twitter.com/fenellawriter

# ALSO BY FENELLA J. MILLER

**Goodwill House Series**

The War Girls of Goodwill House

New Recruits at Goodwill House

Duty Calls at Goodwill House

The Land Girls of Goodwill House

A Wartime Reunion at Goodwill House

Wedding Bells at Goodwill House

A Christmas Baby at Goodwill House

**Standalones**

The Land Girl's Secret

www.ingramcontent.com/pod-product-compliance
Ingram Content Group UK Ltd.
Pitfield, Milton Keynes, MK11 3LW, UK
UKHW042004020325
455730UK00002B/6

9 781801 628839